TWINFINITY

HANGING CHADS BOOK V

EVAN CLOUSE

COVER IMAGE ILLUSTRATED BY
ARPIT MEHTA

Contents

This book is dedicated to every person who cares about our personal freedom. To every person who cares about our democracy. To every person who shuns the politics of hate and division. To every person who accepts and embraces others for who they are. Thank you for your voices. Thank you for your caring. Thank you for your kind hearts. I love you all.

Acknowledgments

I would like to thank every person who has supported me and understands just how important this work is to me. Thank you for reading. Thank you for your input. Thank you for caring. You know who you are.

PROLOGUE

It was always the first thing that she noticed. The faint scent of iron as the sticky thick molasses gently dribbled off her claws and onto her awaiting tongue. She felt a slight sense of satisfaction as her furry ears positioned themselves to intensely listen to the faint exhalation of air passing through her latest victim's mouth which was now permanently formed into a silent scream. Then, the sound of the blood droplets hitting the floor. Slowly at first, like an annoying leaky faucet. *Drop....drop....drop....*then faster as the taught skin surrounding his jugular gave way completely to unleash a crimson waterfall which hit the hard wood floor as though someone had poured an entire gallon of milk upon it. She pulled her claws completely from his throat while loosening her fangs' grip from his hair. Then the familiar thud as the lifeless body succumbed to gravity completing the merciless fait accompli.

A mischievous smile forced the upward curling of the right side of her mauve lips and whiskers. *This was successful. This was liberating. This was justified,* she thought to herself as she positioned herself on the man's chest and began eagerly lapping up the blood that was gushing out of his slashed throat. She looked down upon the mess that he had created as the pool of newly released blood expanded outward like a growing hurricane churning above warm water. She heard two sets of familiar footsteps approaching. The door opened and she looked up innocently at the two pairs of frantic eyes that were staring down at her.

"Oh, *there* you are sweetie!" a relieved Jessie exclaimed as her shoes sploshed across the hardwood floor to her cherished pet. "We have been so *worried!*"

"Yup, there she is," Jules dryly stated. "And *here's* the asshole that tried to escape. Nice job, cat. You kinda made a mess, though."

"Not as much of a mess as *we're* making downstairs," Jessie playfully replied. "Oh my God! Can you believe how *loud* these pricks can scream? I mean, I thought all the *previous* fascist fuckers were loud, but this *new* batch has them beat. By a mile. And man, do they piss their pants! At least LucyFur's…um… *friend* didn't last long enough to piss everywhere. This won't be *nearly* as big of a clean-up job as ours."

The two friends could not help but let out an amused giggle as they watched LucyFur's blood-soaked face mew up at them, then return to her evening's meal. She began purring loudly as she continued her ravenous feeding.

The women's giggles turned into unbridled, full-throated laughter as they watched this blood-soaked furball's euphoric feeding. "Well," Jules observed. "At least we won't have to feed her tonight."

"What are you talking about?" Jessie shot back. She bent over her beloved pet and picked her up. A new coat of fresh blood was squeezed out of LucyFur's matted hair and saturated Jessie's designer top as she hugged the enraptured cat. "Oh, my sweetie *always* needs her nummy-num-nums, now, *don't* you?"

LucyFur's purring continued as she lovingly rubbed her drenched face against that of her "owner." The giggling and purring of the pair continued until Jessie said, "And once dinner time is over, I think I know a certain little *someone* who is going to need a B-A-T-H."

Upon hearing the ominous four letters being uttered, LucyFur shrieked with intense fear and began thrashing her paws violently into the air until Jessie was forced to let her go. The shoes of Jules and Jessie were splattered with blood as LucyFur's plump body cannonballed into the crimson pool. LucyFur looked up at Jessie with disdain, turned her back and returned to her morbid meal.

"Yeah, *that* shit's not happening," Jules replied. "And she *really* should have been named 'Maddy,' because that's one blood-lustful little bitch."

"Yeah," Jessie agreed before concluding with, "or Josie."

CHAPTER 93

TIME MACHINE

The four perpetual ten-year-olds were giggling uncontrollably as they began their journey to the year 1958. They were surrounded by the multi-colored flashing strobes of the universe and a kaleidoscopic mist that encased their tiny bodies. Each was wearing all-white cowboy and cowgirl outfits, complete with fringe on their respective vests, boots, skirts, chaps, and cowboy hats that covered their wispy-white shoulder-length locks. The boys had their hair parted down the middle. The girls parted their hair on the right side of their scalp. They each had light caramel skin with the faint outline of a lightning bolt embedded into each of their tender faces. Each also had one eye that was a rich brown and one that was electric blue.

On their hips, they wore double holsters. But instead of guns, which the children found distasteful and unsportsman-like, they contained knives, hatchets, and other toys that the children found amusing and useful. They rode upon the backs of their best friends and protectors. Fifteen evenings prior, these four were ushered into the world during a violent battle to save the soul of humanity both on Earth and in Enlightenment. Standing steadfast astride their respective birthmothers during the mayhem were four protective Shetland ponies. The four ponies that the children now rode into their destiny.

The first twin girl of Rachel and Adam, Sigourney, rode her pure white pony that she had named 'Snowball.' Her twin sister, Euna, rode a black pony that she had named 'Blackjack.'

Their cousins, and soulmates, were the sons of Kayla and Aaron. Kane rode a red horse that he had named 'Flame.' His twin brother, Thanatos, rode a pale green Shetland that he named…

"Snot?" Sigourney yelled out to her cousin. "What kind of name is '*Snot*'? *We* all named *our* friends something cool. Your horse's name is…um…well…it isn't very *dignified*, now, is it?"

"Hey!" Thanatos shot back. "I know we all share the same soul and when we speak to others, we usually speak as one. But we each have our *own* personalities. We each have our own *preferences*. And this is *my* horse, and *my* preference is to call him 'Snot!' Because he kinda looks like that and it's easy for me to say and it's kinda funny! Plus, he always has a runny nose. So, you name your horse how *you* want, and I'll name my horse the way that *I* want!"

"Knock it off you two! We don't have time for this silly bickering." Euna interjected. "I think that we're almost there."

"Yes, it would appear so," Kane agreed. "Look at how the mist is dissipating, and the beautiful lights are slowing down. And look there! I believe that I can see the outline of buildings and streetlights and, oh my, old cars."

"Hey! Get out of the road you crazy kids!" and enraged man yelled out his driver's side window as he swerved to miss the four riders who had suddenly emerged from the evening fog.

"We're sorry!" The Junior Quad yelled back in unison as they gallantly strode down the middle of the street of Lincoln, Nebraska on March 1, 1958. The Shetland's hoofs made uniform 'clopping' sounds upon the frigid asphalt road as the

JQ turned the corner as elegantly as a well-disciplined marching band.

"We're close," Kane observed. "I can feel him. The presence of his soul is strengthening."

"Yes," Euna agreed. "I can feel him too. The first of many that Vetis will try to corrupt. The first of many that he will try to indoctrinate into his evil plans. The first of many that we must vanquish. But first, stop!"

"What? What is it?" Sigourney yelled out as the four Shetlands came to an abrupt halt in the middle of the street and three of the four rushed toward the window of a local department store.

"Oh, just look in this window, sister!" Euna excitedly shouted out. "Just look at those wonderful saddle shoes and poodle skirts!"

"Wow!" Kane added. "And look at those new records! And baseball cards! This store is awesome!"

"Do they have any chewing gum"? Thanatos inquired. "I just *love* chewing gum."

Euna squinted her eyes to block out the glare of the reflected streetlights and scanned the store before yelling out, "Yes! Yes, they do! And one of them is called 'Black Jack!' How perfect! Oh sister, can't we *please* stop and do a little shopping? They have such *wonderful* treasures here."

Sigourney slapped her forehead in frustration and said through her gritted, newly acquired permanent teeth, "No, we do *not* have time for shopping right now. Although we know *who* Vetis will target somewhere in time, we do not know exactly *when* he will arrive. All that we know is that we are somehow connected to his intentions and once he decides on his latest conquest, *we* must get to them before *he* does. Otherwise, he will have corrupted another soul that will lead a parallel fascist movement to overtake the Earth. A parallel movement to the one that our parents just helped to defeat.

So, we do not have time for skirts. Or baseball cards. Or gum. Or records."

"Oh, *come on* Sigourney," Kane whined. "There's *always* time for new records! There's *always* time to discover great new music! Pleeeeease?"

"Kane, I totally understand what you are saying," Sigourney answered while attempting to remain calm. "But our *mission* is the most important thing right now. Maybe….and I do mean *maybe*…if we are successful tonight, we can go into that shop and pick up a few things. But we only have so much room in the saddlebags, so don't be greedy. Now, can we get to work?"

"Yes, of course you're right, sister," Euna conceded. "And there will be *plenty* of time to go shopping after our successful mission. And we *will* be successful. We have seen it. So, come on boys. Let's ride."

"Cool," Thanatos responded. "As long as I get some chewing gum. And some tissues. Snot's nose is really runny tonight."

The foursome approached a disheveled one-bedroom house a few blocks from the department store. With a light tug upon their reins, the ponies and their accompanying 'clopping,' stopped. "This is going to be fun. Kinda like that mailman yesterday," Sigourney whispered to her twisted little associates.

"So, what's the plan?" Thanatos inquired. "Are we just gonna go up to the door and knock?"

"Yup," Sigourney answered as her innocent face turned red and twisted into a joyfully sadistic expression.

"We gotta *do* somethin' to stop this fuckin' government," the man inside the dilapidated home said to himself as he paced around a beaten coffee table that was littered with pamphlets from the John Birch Society. "Look at what my country's become. Ever since women got the vote forty years ago, it's all gone to shit. And now even the (derogatory term omitted) *Blacks* are gettin' all uppity and demanding to have the same rights as us! The *real* Americans! They want to send their kids to *our* schools! Drink out of *our* water fountains! Go to *our* stores! No, we gotta *do* somethin' and these John Birch folks may have the right answer. If I could join them, then convince my friends and family to join them, and so on, we'd have enough people to take this country back from the skirts and the (derogatory term omitted) gays, and the (derogatory term omitted) Jews and the (derogatory terms omitted) minorities. What the fuck was Ike thinkin'? Why the hell did we defeat the Nazis, anyway? Oh sure, I get bombing the fuck out of the (derogatory term omitted) Japanese. They don't look like us, don't pray like us, don't eat like us and don't have any place on this Earth. But Hitler had the right idea. Cleanse this planet of all the vermin, so we true White Christians can live together in peace without worryin' about them takin' our money and spreading their diseases. And now Ike's the fuckin' President! He took down one of the greatest men to ever live and now he's the one pushin' to let these…these…fuckin' *rats* mingle with us! With *our* kids! Hell, *our* kids are already gettin' indoctrinated by that Goddam (derogatory term omitted) *Black* music! All those white kids gyrating around listening to the Devil's music! Hell, it won't be long before our White daughters are havin' little (derogatory term omitted) Black kids! It just makes me sick. We gotta do somethin' and we gotta do somethin' *now*, before we lose this entire generation. Before we lose our country. We gotta…now who the *hell* would be knockin' on my door at this time-a-night?"

The tall, skinny twenty-year-old man grabbed his double-barrel shotgun and yelled out, "Hey! Cantcha read? No soliciting! Now get the fuck off-a my property!"

There was a momentary silence then another light rap on the withered wooden door. "Okay, motherfucker!" the man yelled out. "You asked for it!" He threw open the door and pointed his shotgun outward. Seeing nothing as he squinted through his sight, he looked down and found four giggling, tan-skinned children looking up at him.

"What the fuck do you (derogatory term omitted) kids want? You're on the wrong side-a town. You'd better get back home to your kind…um…whatever *that* might be. I can't tell if you're a (derogatory term omitted) or a (derogatory term omitted) or a (derogatory term omitted). But it don't matter none! You don't belong here! Now get your vermin little assess off-a my porch before I blow big fuckin' holes in ya!"

"No, we belong here," the four children said in unison with sweet voices. "We were sent here to play with you. We're here to have fun with you."

Euna took a lasso from her belt and threw it around the man's neck. She pulled firmly and the confused man fell upon his face, causing his nose to shatter on the hardwood floor. "W-what the fuck?" the man screamed out as Kane took his lasso, rapidly wrapped it around the man's ankles and wrists and hog-tied him within seconds.

Euna kicked the fallen gun to the side, grabbed her end of the rope and dragged the man to the center of the living room, leaving a streak of blood and teeth on the floor. Sigourney smiled innocently, slammed the door, and approached the bound, quivering man while Thanatos retrieved a knife from his holster.

"Okay, you little bastards!" the hysterical man began shouting. "You're gonna be in big trouble! I'm gonna ki… AAAAAAAAAH!"

The man's threats were interrupted as Thanatos straddled the man's back, pulled his head upward and placed his petite, tan hand into the man's open mouth. The man's screams continued as Thanatos pulled the man's tongue out and began sawing it off with his knife. The man was shedding tears and blood of pure agony as Thanatos inquisitively looked at the severed tongue, placed it into his own mouth and began chewing.

"*BLECH!*" Thanatos exclaimed as he spit the bloody tongue across the room. "*That* doesn't taste like chewing gum."

Thanatos took his place alongside his laughing soulmates. They looked down and watched as the thrashing man was frantically trying to free himself from his bindings. They then said in their childish voices, "We understand this is confusing for you. You must be wondering what it is that you have done for us to have been summoned to play with you. And since you no longer have a tongue, you will be unable to ask your question. But we will answer it anyway. The answer to your question is that we are not here because of what you have done. We are here to prevent you from doing things that you have been *chosen* to do in the future. We are here to *prevent* you from creating another fascist movement that would be a threat to humanity. *And* we are here to have fun."

Sigourney nodded at Kane, who dutifully went in the kitchen. A few moments later, he returned with a dented electric toaster. He placed the man's bound hands into the slots of the toaster and squeezed the metal casing tightly around them. He plugged the toaster into a cracked outlet. The children looked on with delight as the man's exposed wrists began glowing orange and smoke began pouring out of the toaster.

"'Op it! Pwease 'op it!" the tortured man was screaming as he felt his hands being incinerated by the intense coils. The amused children giggled, and Euna sat astride the man's back. She took a scalpel from her holster and split the man's dirty, white T-shirt open. She then used the scalpel to carefully cut and peel off a sheet of flesh from the entirety of his back. "Oh look!" she exclaimed excitedly. "A new canvas for Auntie Alexa!"

The sweet face of Thanatos then emerged from the billowing smoke. He held his small, tan hand out which was holding a small porcelain container. He tipped his hand and began shaking salt onto the skinless back of the writhing man. His screams intensified as the salt ate into his tender flesh while his hands were turning black from being scorched by the toaster.

"I was wrong," Sigourney admitted. "This is even *more* fun than the mailman!" She then took a long piece of barbed wire and began wrapping it around the hysterical man's face. She kept pulling until the tightening wire was lodged firmly in the man's cheeks, chin, nose, ears, and eyes. Blood and puss trickled out from the edges of the barbed wire as the giggling children went skipping out of the home to their dutiful steeds. They retrieved baseball bats from each of their saddlebags and went skipping back into the house where they proceeded to mercilessly beat the man with the bats while skipping around him and whistling. The man finally let out his final breath. The four blood-soaked children held hands and looked down at their work. His body was covered with contusions and his head had been beaten into a gelatinous putty. They smiled down at him, then at each other. Their smiles then faded into looks of deep concern.

From the darkened hallway, a hulking figure appeared. The children cautiously looked up at the imposing figure that had begun lurching towards them. For the first time in their short lives the members of the Junior Quad felt confusion and fear.

"I don't know who this is," Sigourney whispered to her sister. "All I know is that he isn't supposed to be here, and we aren't supposed to play with him."

The children's anxiety immediately dissipated when the large man let out a loud belly laugh before saying, "Well, you kids sure are a part of the family alright. Very creative. And messy. Alright, now kids. Playtime's over. Let's get you four home and into your jammies. Your parents are worried sick about you. But *first*, I wonder if there are any all-night diners where we could get some ice cream?"

CHAPTER 94

———

I PUT A SPELL ON YOU

"I was so fuckin' close," the demon Vetis said solemnly to his unwillingly loyal servant, Gobbo. Gobbo was picking scabs off his spindly, pale arms. His lanky, arched frame followed Vetis down the corridor of the recently arrived screaming dark souls. His black, sunken eyes looked down his hooked nose and into those of the justifiably tortured who were hanging from chains. Vetis used his long fingernails on his four hands to slice open the screaming souls' abdomens as he sauntered by them in full contemplation.

"So fucking close!" Vetis roared. "I thought it was perfect. I thought that I had chosen the right souls to convert into darkness who then, in turn, converted millions of others into our supremacist cause. So many died at their hands. So much innocent blood ran in the streets of the Earth. But then, they all went to Enlightenment, which did nothing but strengthen their numbers there. Another miscalculation. It was almost perfect. Almost. That…that…*woman* tipped the scales. The offspring of the Pastor and the Copperhead. *She* was to be the one to fight at her parents' side and usher me into domination of the Earth and Enlightenment! *She* was the key. And she turned out to be a failure. She twisted her natural tenacity and bloodlust into killing *us*! She had a special gift that inspired loyalty to those around her. And that loyalty drove them to fight even *harder* against our movement. First on Earth, then in Enlightenment. And then there was *her* daughter. And her fucking half-sister. No, the Pastor was a failure. The Copperhead was a failure. My dullard, bulbous, orange, personal cocksucker was a failure. They allowed her to tip the scales against us. So now, we must tip the scales back.

"We must find a way to overload them. They just *barely* succeeded in defeating us. But if we had just a *few more*. A *few more* willfully ignorant human assholes that we can convert. It might just be enough. So, here's the plan, Gobbo…Gobbo! Are you listening to me?"

"Of course, Master," Gobbo reverentially answered with his bald, white head bowed. "I am *always* listening to you. Please continue, Master."

"Very well, then," Vetis replied as he turned and continued his long strides down the blood-soaked cavernous hallway. "Here's the plan. We go back in time. We find *other* souls who we can convert and then, in turn, can convert others. But here's the trick. We want to convert humans who are destined to die before the great wars of the Twenty-First Century are engaged. Humans who were not available to us at that time. We will find one such human, then guide him to find others who are destined to die and convert them. We will keep them safe from harm. We will keep them away from their preordained deaths and keep them alive. We'll have them find cabins in the woods or some shit to just sit and wait and train and prepare. And breed. We'll keep them in the dark so that the only information that they have is *my* information. The only facts that they will have will be *my* facts. After several decades of sitting there and being immersed in my indoctrination, they will be *completely* insane. And ready to do *anything* that I order them to do. Then, once our original battle has commenced and is flourishing into its full-scale war, we will unleash *these* tens of thousands of converts. They will then be engaged in the battle and our adversaries will be taken off-guard. They will be surprised. And they will be overwhelmed. And there's *nothing* that that red-headed bitch will be able to do about it, heh, heh, heh. Yeah, I'm really looking forward to taking over Enlightenment and fucking that bitch up…for eternity."

———

"Where's all my fuckin' ice cream?" Maddy roared as her ass was sticking out of her freezer. She pulled her chilled copper-haired head out and swung around to look at the sheepish expression of her beloved husband, Erick.

"Um…well…" Erick began tentatively. "You see, um, well, Herbert, Jason, Clyde, Joe, Charlie, and Howard came over last night to play some cards and, um…"

"Whoooooa!" Maddy exclaimed. "*Howard?* You had *that* perverted motherfucker into our house? While I was sleeping upstairs? No, no, no, no. I don't give a fuck *how* useful he was in protecting Enlightenment! You want to have a little boys' night? Fine! But you are *not* going to have *that* twisted little fucker over and give him the opportunity to do some of his twisted little shit to my dainty spiritual ass! No fuckin' way!"

"Maddy, come on," Erick replied defensively. "I think you're overreacting just a bit, don'tcha think? Howard's really trying to fit in. I mean, he doesn't even *suggest* that we all watch porn and engage in a circle jerk anymore. That's progress, right?"

"Well, *that's* a low fuckin' bar to hit now *isn't it?*," Maddy shot back. "Oh good. I don't have to worry about stepping in cum in the morning. Gee, thanks for that. And the fact that he ever suggested that in the first place is…is…just fuckin' gross! So, do *not* invite him over *ever again*, got it?"

"Yeah, okay," Erick conceded. "So, what do you want to do today? We have all of Enlightenment to explore. I think Woody Guthrie is doing a show at the pub later. Wanna go?"

"Oh, no," Maddy countered as her five-foot-four-and-a-half-inch-frame marched toward the couch and plopped onto Erick's lap. Her intense green eyes stared into his as she continued. "You're not getting off the hook *that* easily. Now tell me. What the *fuck* happened to my ice cream?"

Erick's spiritual form began sweating as he attempted to avert his gaze from that of his eternal wife. She grabbed his chin and forced him to look at her before he began explaining. "Well, as I said, some of the fellas came over and we wanted a snack and so…um…well, what's the big fuckin' deal *anyway?* We're in Enlightenment! You can just conjure some *more* up!"

"I will *tell* you what the big fuckin' deal is!" Maddy yelled back. "Numero-Uno: That was *my* fuckin' ice cream! Numero-Two-O: If it's *so easy* to conjure this shit, then conjure up your *own!* Numero-Three-O: Now that I know that *Howard* was over here, there's no telling *what* fucked up shit he did with *my* ice cream! And Numero-Four-O: Yeah, I can conjure up some more, but that shit takes *time* and I want my ice cream *now!* So, from now on, when you see something in the fridge or the freezer or the cabinets that is *mine* keep your *fuckin' mits* off of it! And, just in case you don't know what is *mine*, here's a little clue. I've written M-A-D-D-Y on *all* of my favorite conjured foods! Got it?"

"Yeah, fine," Erick begrudgingly agreed. "It's just that you're *really good* at conjuring up food. I mean, you really *sucked* as a cook on Earth, but you can *really* conjure up some fuckin' ice cream! I just can't seem to get the knack of it. I mean, the shit that *I* conjure up is okay, but its just never *nearly* as good as yours. So, in a way, my eating your ice cream and other snacks is *really* a *compliment* to you and your incredible gift."

Erick smiled to himself as he saw his wife's green eyes turn from intense frustration to haughty arrogance. He could always put a spell on her by playing to her oversized ego and he knew that he had bested her once again. Now, he wanted to push the envelope.

"So, how about if you conjure up some of your special ice cream and we can share it?" he asked in a child-like tone.

"Oh, okay," Maddy chuckled. "I guess I can't blame you. I *do* conjure the best fuckin' ice cream in Enlightenment. I mean, how could you resist, right? And…wait…what the fuck? Yeah, this is Lil' Red. Over and out. Come in Soul Sister. Over and out. Wazzup? Over and out."

———

Gobbo sat nervously at the feet of Vetis as he trimmed the demon's jagged toenails. "Oh, Gobbo. Perhaps I've been a bit off lately. I believe that I will give you a chance. A chance to prove your loyalty and worthiness to me. Yes, I believe I will give you the opportunity to select the one that I shall tempt into my unholy vision of world domination. Peer through time. Find someone who is destined to die before 2016. Someone who is susceptible to my manipulations. Someone that I can pervert their religion or sense of patriotism into an inhumane anti-democratic crusade. Someone who has the charisma to influence others. But someone easy! I'm not feeling up for a challenge right now. I'm going to lay down for my nap. I expect you to have found someone by the time I awaken."

"Why, yes, Master!" Gobbo enthusiastically replied. "And thank you Master! Thank you for this grand opportunity! I will *not* disappoint you!"

"Yeah, whatever," Vetis answered through a loud yawn. "I'm tired. Just fuckin' do it. And stop kissing my ass. It's kinda creepy."

"Of course, Master," Gobbo replied before adjourning to

his ice-cold corner of the universe. His tired spiritual bones let out a loud crack as he sat cross-legged on the frigid stone. He placed his boney elbows on his extended knees, shut his black eyes and concentrated. His mind began flipping the calendar and scanning all the souls that lived upon Earth in the previous nine decades. He knew that he could not go too far back into time, otherwise the chosen one would perish from old age before the great war had begun. Perhaps as early as 1950 or so, he thought to himself. Someone young enough to still be alive and relatively healthy in the year 2016. There were so many options that flashed through his brain. "No, too old," he would say to himself as he began narrowing his selections. "No charisma." "Too sensitive." "Too ugly. Vetis will want him to look the part." "Too tall." "Too fat." "Too… completely the wrong race." "Too…completely the wrong gender. Vetis has had it with trying to convert women. He says they are too headstrong. But I know that many of them are simply too empathetic and intelligent to fall for his bullshit."

What would be hours on Earth went by as Gobbo's tiring mind continued to absorb thousands of prospects from the past. "Once again, too sensitive." "Too…um…well *that* one is a maybe." "Too gallant." "Too…wait. Yes, this might be the one. Only twenty years old at this time. That would make him fifty-eight in 2016. Tall. Rugged. Already beginning to indoctrinate himself in extremist ideology. Yes. He would be an easy convert. And easy on the eyes. He would prove useful with less evolved women as well. Yes, I believe that I will go wake up…

"Master! Please wake up, my Liege! I have done it! I have found the one to hide and lead the parallel movement!"

"What the fuck?" Vetis asked drowsily as he rolled over and swung one of his four arms to knock Gobbo into the far wall. "Why are you awakening me? I still have…let's see what time is it? Yes, I still have four years to nap. What's so fuckin' important?"

"I am so sorry to disturb you, Master," Gobbo began as he picked his broken bones off the floor and approached his overlord. "But I believe that I have found him!"

"Found who?" Vetis roared back.

"Him, my Lord," a trembling Gobbo answered. "The one for you to tempt and manipulate into your parallel movement so that you can reign over both Earth and Enlightenment."

"Oh…him," Vetis answered as he wiped the sleep from his flaming red eyes. "Oh yeah, cool. So, who is it?"

"Well, Master," Gobbo began with more confidence. "I am sorry to awaken you, but I felt as though you would be quite excited to see my selection. And time is of the essence. Once you have made your selection you must go back into time and convert them before…um…before…well…before *they* get there."

"I don't wanna talk about those little bastards," Vetis replied dismissively. "Now, where and when are we going?"

"Well, Master," Gobbo answered as he stood as upright as his curved spine would allow. "We are going to Lincoln, Nebraska. Midnight, March 2, 1958."

"Those little motherfuckers," was all that Vetis could mutter as he looked down at the carnage that was to have been his latest demonic convert. The man was hog-tied, and smoke was billowing out of the toaster that was scorching his hands. The flesh from his back had been removed and was encased in salt. The man's head had been beaten to a pulp and was lying on the floor like hardened, pinkish-red play dough. "How? How the *fuck* did they get here before us?"

"Well, Master," Gobbo began nervously. "They are connected to you. The moment that you have made your decision on who to convert, they are summoned. They travel back through time, find your latest project, and dispose of them before we can arrive. They are the prophecy, Master. Perhaps you should abandon your plans and live out your hellish existence in the plane that you already dominate."

"Fuck the prophecy!" Vetis yelled out as he slapped Gobbo across the room. "No! those little fuckers will *not* best me! I will try. And try *again*. And try *again*! For all of *eternity* if I have to! Go back to their own time. 2042. And find someone to take the fuckers out."

"B-b-but Master," Gobbo stammered. "It is quite *impossible* to kill them. We failed at our chance. They had to be murdered in their mother's womb. Now that they are born and fully developed, they are simply too *powerful*. You *know* who they are, Master. You *know* the souls that their bodies possess. I am pleading with you Master. *Please* do not fight them. For if you do, the prophecy will come true, and they will destroy all of us."

"Well, Gobbo," Vetis replied calmly as one of his four hands stroked his massive chin. "You make some good points. Yes, I know the souls that inhabit their child-like bodies. And I know that those four souls have converged into one and that they are acting in concert. And I am *very well aware* of what has been prophesized. But prophesies can be...altered. Now, what *you* do not know is just how *badly* I wish to rule over the Earth and Enlightenment, so...find someone in 2042 to kill these little pricks! And their little ponies too!"

Chapter 95

Searchin'

"Oh fuck, oh fuck, oh fuck, what are we going to do?" a sweaty Josie was stammering to herself as she nervously paced in the living room of the estate in Upper State New York. Arima, Jessie, and Rosa could only look on as Josie frantically continued. "Jesus! What is *wrong* with me? I'm the head of an international assassin freedom fighting syndicate, and I can't even keep track of four fuckin' *kids*? And what are we going to tell their *parents*? What are we going to *say* to them when they get ho…ooooooh, hey guys! You're *back* already! Sooooo, how was your evening out?"

"I don't want to talk about it!" Kayla angrily answered as she and her sister stormed into the room.

"Y'know," Rachel added, "It would be *really nice* if just *once* we could go out, have a few drinks, have a few laughs, and not *murder* someone!"

"We're sorry, ladies," a forlorn Adam stated followed, as always, by his twin brother Aaron. "Yes, we are very sorry. But that man was hurting that woman. We could not just stand by and watch that happen. And it has been days since we have been able to play our games."

"Yeah?" Rachel roared back. "But didja have to make such a *mess* of him? You *could* have just snapped his *neck* or something, but *nooooooo!* *You* two maniacs had to pull out your knives and carve him up like a roast beef! And now, now, my dress looks like *this!*"

Rachel opened her overcoat to reveal her sequined party dress splattered in the abusive man's blood. Kayla followed suit, revealing her own ruined dress, and the glaring pair stood in front of their husbands with their arms folded while they angrily tapped their feet.

"Oh my," Adam stated, followed immediately by his brother's, "Yes. That is quite a mess. But we told you that you were standing too close. We told you that you were in the splash zone. Nevertheless, we are sorry about your pretty dresses and will buy you new ones. Plus, we were able to get the skin from the man's back. Alexa will be so pleased with her new canvas."

"Yeah, great," Kayla replied as she rolled her eyes. "Our dresses are ruined, but your sister gets a new canvas for her art show that she's planning. What the hell is she calling her exhibition again?"

Rachel replicated her sister's eye roll and said sarcastically, "*Hanging Chads: The Lineage of our Ascension.* Whatever the hell *that's* supposed to mean. Sounds stupid. Whatevs. The night's ruined. Let's just read the kids a story and put them to bed. And while we're doing *that, you two* are going to get *rid* of that prick's body and clean the trunk of the car! Okay, where are our children? Sigourney! Euna!"

Kayla then began calling for her twin sons. "Kane! Thanatos! Come on out! Mommies are home! Do you want to hear a story before bed?"

Josie, Arima, Jessie, and Rosa just watched in awkward silence as the frustrated mothers continued calling for their children. Rosa nudged Jessie and silently mouthed, "Say something." Jessie shook her head and nudged Arima, who said in her mellow voice, "So, hey, Niece Josie. You wanna maybe tell them about the kids?"

"What *about* the kids?" Rachel and Kayla said in unison as they swung around to look into four pairs of sheepish eyes."

"Riiiiiiight," Josie began through a forced chuckle. "The *kids*. Well, it's *really* kind of a funny story if you *think* about it. You see, we had ordered some pizza, and I was cleaning up their bedroom, and...oh...I found the body of the creepy mailman under one of the bunk beds, by the way. So, good news! We don't have to worry about *that* fucker anymore. Anywhoooo, as I was saying..."

Kayla and Rachel went up to Josie and stared into her green eyes and said tersely, "Josie. *Where* are our children?"

"Yep, I was just getting to that," Josie replied as she ran her hand through her sweaty, curly copper mop on the top of her head. "So, it *seems* as though *your* little guys, who are absolutely *adorable* by the way! Have I *told* you that? They are the *cutest* little children. And smart. Oh *my*, are they smart. And spirited! Yes, they have such *wonderful* spirits! Yep, you four *definitely* have just the most *wonderful* children. And *cute*! Did I mention how *cute* they..."

Kayla and Rachel took one more step towards the stammering Josie until they were inches away from her befreckled nose. They smiled innocently and said in unison, "Josie. Please stop stalling for time and tell us..." Their soft voices exploded into a shout as they concluded with, "Where the *fuck* are our children!"

"Um, 1958," Jessie's meek voice interjected.

Kayla and Rachel swung their caramel bodies to face the couch, looked down into Jessie's brilliant blue eyes and said with a forced calm through gritted teeth, "*What* did you just say?"

"Um," Jessie answered while avoiding eye contact with the twin mothers. "They're *kind* of in...um...1958. March 1, 1958, to be exact. In Lincoln, Nebraska."

Adam and Aaron watched in shocked silence as their wives approached Jessie. Kayla yelled out, "What the fuck do you *mean* they're in Lincoln, Nebraska in 1958? How the hell does *that* make any sense? Listen, I don't even know why you and Rosa are here. We left Josie and Arima in charge. And Arima and Josie are going to find our children right fucking *now!*"

"Yeah, we were just talking about how we were going to do that," Arima lazily replied as she finished the last bite of the last slice of pizza. "You see, apparently your children can travel through time, so it appears that they got on their ponies and…well…traveled through time. We're not sure why they went there and we're not quite sure how to bring them back. But one thing that we're *sure* of is that you guys are out of 'tato chips. We kinda ate them all. Sorry about that."

"*We?*" Josie yelled out. "*We* ate all the 'tato chips? Oh no. *You*, my dear auntie ate all the fucking 'tato chips. And all the *pizza*! All you had to do was watch the kids while I tidied up upstairs. But no! You had to satisfy your fucking cravings!"

"Oh my, oh my, oh my," Adam and Aaron began muttering in unison as they began nervously pacing around the living room. "Oh my, our children are missing, brother," Adam stated. Aaron replied with the same anxious cadence, "Yes. They are missing. And although they appear to be much more mature than their age, they are still children. We have not had the time to teach them how to play many of our games. Oh brother, what if our children get into trouble? What if something has happened to them?"

"Okay! Everybody just shut up and calm down!" Rosa uncharacteristically shouted out. "Listen, this isn't anybody's fault. Josie and Arima. Nobody cares about the goddam 'tato chips and pizza right now. And Adam and Aaron. Just calm down. I can feel your energy rising and I don't want to know what happens when you hit maximum capacity, so just chill the fuck out. And Rachel and Kayla. We know that your children are fine…um…at the moment. Everybody. Please just sit down and we'll explain. Then, we'll figure out how to get them back, okay?"

Kayla and Rachel threw themselves onto the couch on either side of Jessie, who gulped hard and looked down at the grey striped furball that was contently purring on her lap. LucyFur's eyes dilated, and she stared up at Rosa, as though she was enjoying the spectacle that was unfolding in front of her.

Once everybody was seated, Rosa wiped the trail of sweat from her tan forehead and began. "Okay, thanks. The only way that we're going to get through this is if we all just remain calm, think about this logically, and work together. Okay, here's what we know. The kids were in the back yard playing with cadavers when the pizza arrived. Josie was upstairs doing some housekeeping. Arima got…um…distracted by the pizza. The next thing Josie and Arima knew, the kids and their ponies had just disappeared. They looked all over the house and all over the estate for them. When they didn't turn up, they called Jessie and me to come over to help them. I tapped into Jessie's energy and enhanced it to strengthen her ability to Behold and locate their souls. We thought that it would be easy. The ponies are fast, but not *that* fast and if they were anywhere close, Jessie should have been able to locate them quickly. But she couldn't. I kept increasing her energy and Jessie began searching for their souls throughout the entire country. And, although the sensation wasn't strong enough to be their souls, Jessie would feel *something* every time she searched around Lincoln, Nebraska. She focused on that area, and I kept increasing her energy. She was *convinced* that the children were there, somewhere, but the sensation simply wasn't strong enough. So, she focused her Beholding ability on the year *before* in that same geographical location. And the sensation got slightly stronger. Then back another year, and it was stronger yet. She kept going back until she could fully Behold their souls in Lincoln, Nebraska. March 1, 1958.

"And that is where we're at. We know *when* they are, and we know *where* they are. What we *don't* know is why they went there. Nor do we have any idea on how to bring them back. I mean, *maybe* they can find their way back themselves, but we don't know that. And they are children. Rather…um… *precocious* children who could get themselves into trouble, so we need to figure this out. Any ideas?"

"Well," Kayla began. "My *first* thought is that we *really* need to find new babysitters."

"Kayla…Rachel," Josie began pleading. "I'm *so* sorry. We had no *idea*. I *swear*, we'll find a way to bring them back. I *swear* it."

"Uh, huh," Rachel replied. "Well, you had *better*. It's *one* thing for you to have lost my pink sweater a few weeks ago. This is quite something *else*, don'tcha *think?*"

"Yes, yes, of course," Josie answered in a beleaguered tone. "I am *so sorry* that I lost your children. And I'm sorry about your sweater too, but…well, that isn't important right now. I've been racking my brain trying to think of a way to go back through time. I mean, I'm a genius, but not so much that I can just whip up a time machine! Maybe Rod could. No, he couldn't either. I mean, if we could have invented a *time machine*, we would have done it already. I have no idea. I feel so lost. I feel so sorry. I feel like a failure."

Josie put her head in her hands and began sobbing before Arima said, "Um, I might have a thought, Niece Josie."

"Y-y-yes?" Josie said as she lifted her head to peer hopefully at her aunt.

"Well, I seem to remember something that your mother told me one time. But I could have gotten it wrong. I was kinda baked. And there was so much stuff going on what with our protecting the estate here on Earth and the battle for Enlightenment and everything. And then there was the victory concert. Man, that was sweet. Remember how cool it was when we heard Prince start to play and all the blood that was pouring out of Enlightenment upon the Earth turned to a warm purple rain? Man, that was cool. And then…"

Arima was cut off by an interrupting Josie. "Aunt Arima. Could you *please* just tell us what you are thinking? You know, to find the *kids*?"

"Oh right, the kids," Arima replied casually as she reached for a half-smoked joint. "So, I think that your mom told me that there isn't anything like time in Enlightenment. All the souls that live there exist in a world that they conjure. They can make their world anything that they want it to be. And they can have their world be in any time because there *is* no time in Enlightenment as we know it here on Earth. It is a plane of existence. And they are immortal. So, there is no *use* for time.

"And we *also* know that the blessed souls of Enlightenment can return to Earth and help out with stuff, if it is for some sort of higher calling. If it is for a *pure* reason, like protection of innocents or defeating evil or shit like that. Not sure how babysitting ranks in that, though. Anyway, we saw Erick do it to battle the copperhead after Maddy's murder. And I saw Maddy's Uncle Joe do it when we defeated the Pastor on what was supposed to be me and Marcus's wedding day. And he wasn't just there is spiritual form, like Erick was. He somehow was able to conjure his body and physically intervene. I think. So, maybe they can do that for a specific period of time in order to complete a specific mission. So, I'm thinkin' that maybe Maddy could go back to 1958 and bring the kids home. Or not. I dunno. It's just something that I thought I heard her say. I wish I hadn't eaten all the 'tato chips. That sounds really good right now."

"Okay, let me get this straight," Rosa stated as the solemn Adam and Aaron wrapped their comforting arms around their despondent wives. "*If* there is no such thing as time in Enlightenment, *then* a blessed soul *may* be able to travel back to any time and any location here on Earth and they *may* be able to appear in their physical human form if it is for a right-eous cause. And *if* they can do *that, then* they can make contact with the JQ and bring them home. Did I get that straight?"

"Yeah, I guess so," Arima answered. "I dunno for sure. We'd have to ask Maddy. As you all know, our souls are connected so she can inhabit my soul here on Earth at any time and I can inhabit hers in Enlightenment. I just need to give her a ringy-dingy and we can find out. Want me to contact her?"

"Oh fuck," Josie muttered under her breath as she buried her head in her hands once again. She reluctantly lifted her head, let out a deep sigh, and asked, "By chance, Aunt Arima, is there anyone *else* that you can connect with in Enlightenment, like maybe my dad?"

Arima blew out pungent smoke rings before answering. "Um, nope. I'm not soul mates with your dad. Or anyone else. Just your mom. I have to contact *her* first. Why?"

"Well," Josie replied in a resigned tone. "It's not that impor-tant and I know that my mother loves me, but she's *never* going to let this go and she's gonna give me shit for all eternity, I bet. But I suppose there's no other way. Yeah, go ahead and call her. And have her say 'hi' to my dad for me. Fuck. This is gonna *suuuuck.*"

Chapter 96

Help!

Arima lazily slid her ass off the couch and stood in the middle of the room. She could feel the hopeful eyes of her friends and family watching as she focused on the soul of her departed half-sister. Her body floated three feet off the floor as she slipped into a trance and began trying to make contact.

"Lil' Red, this is Soul Sister. Please come in," Arima stated out loud so that the onlookers could hear. She felt her half-sister's opening soul welcoming her. As her soul floated out of her physical body toward the promise of Enlightenment, she saw wisps of colorful light swirling around her spiritual form. She smiled at the explosion of peaceful brilliance and warmth that she was being encased in. She then heard her half-sister's voice. The connection had been made. Arima's soul was now entwined with that of her half-sister, Maddy. They were once again two souls in one. They were reunited.

"Yeah, this is Lil' Red. Over and out. Come in Soul Sister. Over and out. Wazzup? Over and out."

"Yeah, hey Maddy," Arima coolly replied. "Sorry to bother you, but we have a little situation down here on Earth that we were hoping you could help us with. Oh, and you really don't have to say, 'over and out' after every sentence, okay?"

"Roger that! Over and out!" Maddy answered much more loudly than necessary. "And please use my cool code name in future correspondence! Over and out! So, what's the sitch? Over and out!" The onlookers snickered to themselves and rolled their eyes as they heard Maddy's reply coming out of Arima's floating body.

Arima let out a deep sigh of slight frustration before answering. "Well, you see, me and Josie were babysitting the JQ so the twins and the Twins could have a night out. They were outside playing with the leftover dead bodies with their ponies when the pizza arrived. It was a combo from a new place in town. It was *really* good. You *really* need to try it the next time you visit me. I got the works on it. There was pepperoni, sausage, onions…"

Arima's fond memory of the recently enjoyed pizza was interrupted by the stern voice of Josie. "Aunt Arima! Please! Tell her about the kids!"

"Oh yeah, the kids," Arima stated before Maddy interjected. "Oh, is that my darling daughter? Over and out! Hello, sweetie! Mommy loves you! Over and out! Erick! Come here! I've got Josie on the party line through Arima's soul. Apparently, we can hear what *she* hears. Here baby, come into my soul so that *you* can hear too."

"Hi sweetie!" Erick yelled out at the same unnecessarily loud volume as his wife. "How are you? We have missed you so much! How's Lionnel? Keeping his hands to himself? He had better be or else I'm gonna have to pay him a visit!"

"Dad!" Josie yelled out. "I'm *eighteen* now, and what I do in my relationship is *none* of your business. I love you, but just leave it alone. And that's *not* why we called. Aunt Arima, *please* tell them about the kids."

"Oh yeah, *that's* why we called. Sorry Niece Josie. So, about the kids…"

Arima was once again cut off by Maddy. "Hey! Before you tell us about the sitchie boll weevil, who *else* is there, hmmmm? Didja see how I was bein' all Snoop Dogg and shit there? Pretty funny, huh? Over and out!"

Arima let out another deep sigh and answered, "Jessie, Aaron, Adam, Rachel, Kayla, and Rosa. And Maddy, I mean, um, Lil' Red, dead white women really shouldn't try to imitate Snoop. That made no sense at all."

"Yeah, whatevs. People don't get my great impersonations, either. Anywhooo, *that's* quite the murderer's row! Over and out!" Maddy responded. "Hey everybody! Nice to talk to you! So how come you got *this* fuckin' rogues gallery together? Over and out!"

"Oh my God!" Rachel screamed. "Would you *please* just ask her if she can find our kids?"

"Wait, what? Over and out!" Maddy replied before bursting out in laughter. "Are you telling me that our *genius* daughter lost your children? Hey Erick! Did you hear that? Our *genius* daughter fucked up babysitting and lost the JQ! And who did she have to call for help? Nope. Not *Ghostbusters*. Lil' ol' me! Our *genius* daughter once again needs her Mommy to bail her out. Oh sweetie, I love you, but this is gold! Pure fuckin' gold! I'm gonna give you shit about this for eternity! Over and out!"

"Oh, goddamit. I knew this was a bad idea," a red-faced Josie muttered under her breath before a frantic Kayla interjected. "Maddy, this is Kayla. *Please*, can you *help* us? Apparently, the JQ and their ponies can travel through time. They just disappeared and Jessie beheld their souls and found them in Lincoln, Nebraska on March 1, 1958. We don't know why they went there or if they're alright or if they know how to get back home. So, since there isn't anything like time in Enlightenment, we thought that maybe you could go there, make contact with them, and send them home. Can you do that? Please, *help* us! We don't know what else to do!"

There was silence on the spiritual line as Maddy sat in

Enlightenment and pondered the request. She looked into the eyes of her beloved husband who smiled and nodded at her. She had heard the despair and urgency in Kayla and Rachel's voices. She understood that her response would need to be delicate and supportive. She understood that she could not fuck this up. Maddy fucked it up.

"Well," Maddy began in a contemplative tone. "I suppose I *could* go back to that date and find your kids. But I think we need to get permission or some shit before we intervene in Earthly affairs. So, I suppose I *could* ask and see if I can *do* that, but…" Maddy's voice trailed off for a moment before she roared, "But why the fuck *should* I? How is this *my* fuckin' problem? Do you know how much *paperwork* there is just to make a request like this? I'm busy! I was just about to conjure up some ice cream, which I *wouldn't* have to do if my husband and his perv friends hadn't eaten it all! Besides! I *told* you four that those fuckin' kids were going to be trouble! And *now* look who's right once again! Me! Only fifteen days after they were born and they're already running around unsupervised fucking up the space-time continuum or some shit! Nope. Not my fuckin' problem. You wanted to pump out those four little hellions, so *you* can figure out how to raise them. Otherwise, *I'm* going to be constantly interrupted every time those little fuckers get themselves into trouble. And I got shit to do! I have an eternity of lounging around with my husband and watching cool concerts from dead rock stars to do. I can't live peacefully while constantly wondering when I'm gonna get interrupted! Not fuckin' happening. Call somebody else. Over and out!"

A shocked Rachel and Kayla began angrily kicking their crossed legs before they heard another voice. It was a voice that they had not heard since the day of her death. The day that the Pastor had massacred her and many others on what was to have been Arima and Marcus's wedding day. It was the voice of an angel. It was the voice of their fallen sister, Gwen.

"Hello, Rachel. Hello, Kayla," Gwen greeted them affectionately.

"Wait, what the fuck? Over and out!" Maddy interjected. "What the fuck are *you* doing in here Gwen? I didn't invite you and there's only so much room in my soul, and it's getting fucking *crowded* in here! Over and out!"

"Maddy," Gwen began calmly as the Earthly onlookers listened in attentively. "I do not believe that you have *any* room to say *anything* right now. My sisters need help. They need *your* help. And not only have you refused to help them, but they had to listen to you lecture them. While in a time of need. Quite frankly Maddy, *you* are acting like a spoiled little bitch."

"Whoooooa, motherfucker!" Maddy shot back. "Who are you calling a bitch, *bitch*? Do you know *who the fuck* you're talking to? Do you know how many motherfuckers I've cut up in cold blood? Well, do you? Is it *my* fault that your sisters don't know how to keep track of their fuckin' kids? Erick! Are you gonna let this bitch talk to me like that? Over and out!"

"Yep, I sure am," an embarrassed Erick replied. "Because she isn't wrong. I've seen you be selfish before, but when it comes to refusing to help children just because you want some fucking *ice cream*, well, I'm sorry my love, but you are just fucking *wrong* right now. Everything that you have just said is fucking wrong. So, I would advise you to take a step back and think about what you have just said. And who you have just said it to. In all your wisdom, you have chosen this moment of great need to lecture our friends and loved ones. Those that we have battled alongside. Those that we have literally wept and bled with. And, most disappointingly to me, you have even refused to help our daughter. This is *not* a good look for you. So…whatcha gonna do there, Ace?""

There was once again dead silence. The Earthly onlookers could almost feel Maddy's seething as Arima's connected body began glowing red. After a few moments, Arima's skin returned to its natural caramel and everyone heard a repentant Maddy say, "Oh shit. Erick, please don't be disappointed in me. And Josie. And, um, everyone. I'm sorry you guys. I guess I *am* being a bitch. Its just that…well…I haven't been up here very long, and I haven't figured out how to do what you're asking of me. So, I guess I was just lashing out because I'm kinda embarrassed that I *can't* help you. I always get defensive and arrogant when my self-confidence gets threatened. All I can think of to do is fight back. I did it my whole life against those that tried to oppress me. And then I'd go and fuck up a 'Chad' or something and then I would feel better and get my self-confidence back. But I can't do that up here. There aren't any 'Chads' up here. Well, kinda Howard, but that's beside the point. And none of that is an excuse. There *is* no excuse for refusing to help you or for what I just said. All I can say is that I'm sorry and I hope you all can forgive me. And I'm sorry that I don't have the ability to help you right now. But I know someone who *can*. I'm pretty sure that Uncle Joe has done that before. Would you like me to call for him? Um…over and out."

"Yes, Maddy," Gwen answered sweetly. "Thank you. I would go myself, but I am tied to Enlightenment. I have been tasked to be the one to approve such Earthly missions. And I most certainly will be approving this one. Also, because of my enhanced soul tracking ability, I can guide those who *will* intervene on Earth to their destination. Yes. Your Uncle Joe would be perfect. Please call for him. I will guide him, and he will find them. Together, we will bring my precious nieces and nephews back to their parents. We will bring them back to my beloved sisters."

Rachel and Kayla stopped kicking their legs, looked at one another and yelled out, "Woooooooo!" "I don't miss *that* shit," Maddy whispered to her husband as she rolled her green eyes at him.

"Okay, bye Lil' Red. Thanks for, um, *something*," Arima

stated as her bare feet once again touched the hardwood flooring. Her half-sister responded with, "Okay! See ya Soul Sister! See ya everybody! We love you, Josie! Mommy and Daddy are proud of you! I'm *still* gonna give you shit though for fucking up babysitting! Maddy over and out!"

Thirty seconds later, there was a brilliant flash of light from outside the home and a joyful male voice that said, "Hey! Anyone missing some kids?"

The entire group ran out the door and looked upon the front lawn. Basking in the brilliant spiritual light of Uncle Joe were four giggling perpetual ten-year-old children on the backs of their Shetland ponies.

"Oh, thank God! Our babies are home!" Rachel and Kayla yelled out in unison. Adam ran down the stairs followed by his brother Aaron. They picked up and tightly hugged their respective children. Adam then said, "Oh my, we were so worried about you four." Aaron then contributed, "Yes. Please don't frighten us like that again children."

"We're sorry fathers, mothers," the quartet replied in unison. "But we had to go. We were called to play games with a bad man."

"Games, you say?" Adam asked followed by Aaron's, "Yes, games? Please tell us about your games, children."

Uncle Joe let out a gutteral laugh and said, "Well, if they were playing games, I sure as fuck know who lost. Man, what they did to *that* motherfuckin' douchebag. He was hogtied and his hands were roasting in a toaster. His back had been stripped of its skin and there was salt covering it. *That* must have been unpleasant for him. And his head was *completely,* and I do mean *completely* bashed in. Yep, that was a helluva game, kids. I haven't laughed that hard in a long time. It was so nice to see you all, but the mission's finished and Gwen is calling me home. Plus, Blair's conjuring up her famous fried chicken and mashed potatoes. I think Patty's conjuring up a half-eaten bag of chips or something. I love her, but she never could cook. Not even in Enlightenment. Oh, and I'm going to teach my niece how to do this shit. I hear she owes you one. And she'll make it right with you folks. My little buttacup always does, heh, heh, heh."

"Thank yooooooou!" came the unified response from the relieved Earthbound members of Murder, Inc. as they watched Joseph Argento's soul dissipate into the black night.

"Let's get you four inside and you can tell us all about your games," Kayla said as tears of joy ran down her brown face. Once inside the warm home, the four blood-covered children stood in front of the entire group and said in unison, "Once again, we are sorry to have worried you. We are sorry Aunt Arima and Aunt Josie. But we have no control over when we will be called. The war with Vetis is not over. We have been born upon the Earth to vanquish him. He is trying to go back in time to corrupt other souls who will lead a parallel demonic movement upon the Earth. A parallel movement to the one that you just defeated. He believes that the two movements working together will be enough to overwhelm you. Then, he will be dominant over the Earth and will once again use his dark souls to attack Enlightenment. We are here to stop that parallel movement from happening. We are connected to his intentions. The moment that he has chosen a person to corrupt, we can sense it. We know who it is, where they are, and when they are. We will then ride our ponies to that time and place and shall destroy that person before Vetis can get to them. It will happen many times. We have seen it. Just as we have seen the final battle. We're tired. May we go to bed now?"

"Yes," Rachel said as she and her sister took each of their children by their tender hands and began leading them toward the staircase. "But *what* did you get all over your beautiful white western outfits?" Kayla asked before answering her own question. "Is that chocolate ice cream? Do you know how hard it is to get that out of white clothes?"

"We're once again sorry," the members of the JQ answered.

"Yes, it is chocolate ice cream. Uncle Joe took us to an all-night diner after he found us, and it seems as though we may have spilled a bit. We are sorry. We will try to be more careful."

"Oh, its okay our darlings," Kayla answered. "We were going to have to clean the blood out of them anyway. Maybe these can be your every-day western outfits that you can play your games in, and we'll get you some new ones to keep clean for special occasions."

An exhausted Arima looked over at her equally fatigued niece and said, "You know what sounds kinda good right now?"

Thirty minutes later, Josie and Arima were basking in the calm silence of the home next to a roaring fire in the sitting room. Josie allowed her latest bite of melting chocolate ice cream to slide down her throat before earnestly saying, "I'm *never* fuckin' babysitting again. No fuckin' way. I can order hits. I can shoot people in the head with arrows. I can make battle plans to save both the Earth *and* Enlightenment. I can skin fuckers alive. But babysitting four ten-year-olds? Nope. Not my thing. Too much stress. Plus, I'm *never* calling my mother again for help. I love her and everything, but she can be *such* a pain the ass! I'm glad *I* didn't turn out like her."

A smirking Arima silently nodded and looked over at the sleeping Jessie and LucyFur on the adjacent couch. LucyFur opened her sleepy green eyes and stretched her furry grey and white round frame as far as she could. She looked at Arima, mewed politely, and jumped down onto the floor. As she made her way towards the pet door in the kitchen, she thought to herself, *Well, that was exciting. For stupid human shit. I'm hungry.*

Chapter 97

Vampire Girl

Lucyfur was cute and she knew it. She carried herself with the same conceited swagger that normal looking cats possessed. But LucyFur was *anything* but normal looking. Cute? Yes. But *far* from normal looking. She looked to be a mash-up of several unrelated animals in one body. Her coat was long and shaggy. It was grey and white with light streaks of rust. Her head was three times smaller than what would look normal on a nearly-completely round, rotund body which was supported by stumpy legs and enormous paws. The finishing touch on her odd appearance was a twelve-inch long full, bushy tail. She was indeed odd-looking. And cute in an odd-looking sort of way.

So, LucyFur knew that she was cute. And she knew that she was special. Her feline spiritual guide had told her so. She had been told from the time of her birth alongside her four sisters that she would be called to assist her human pets. She had been told that she would fight alongside special humans who would battle for the soul of humanity. The feline community, both on the Earth and Enlightenment, didn't particularly care about the plight of the humans on the planet.

What they cared about was what the humans were *doing* to their planet. They were concerned that the human's greedy and irresponsible use of the planet's natural resources posed an existential threat to every living being on the Earth, including themselves. So, armed with this knowledge, one of their most brave souls was placed into an oddly formed kitten. A kitten that was part obese, part runt. A kitten who was told to take multiple long naps throughout the day to save her energy for more important endeavors. A kitten who took full advantage of that directive. A kitten who would be loyal to a select few humans on the planet and would assist them however she could.

First, it was Arima who had adopted her following the passing of LucyFur's first human pet. Then, LucyFur set her sights on Jessie. LucyFur did not care for Jessie much at first, so she put her through many trials and tribulations before deciding to pledge her loyalty to her. Jessie was arrogant, but also had a deep loving and caring side to her. Plus, LucyFur thoroughly enjoyed watching Jessie manipulate and dominate her husband, Cliff. LucyFur found this spectacle amusing. But the human that LucyFur *most* cared for was a woman who held the same 'who gives a fuck' attitude as every cat on the planet. This woman gave her love sparingly to others and to only those that she deemed worthy. Everyone else was a mere annoyance to navigate around. Or go through. Human emotions were not important to this woman. Loyalty was. And the promise of getting laid or fed. That was it. And this woman possessed the ability to communicate with other cats. LucyFur had found ways to communicate with Arima and Jessie. And she most *definitely* had found a way to communicate her disdain for Arima's red-headed half-sister. But she could communicate *directly* with this other woman. They could read each other's thoughts. This woman had become somewhat of a mother-figure to LucyFur. And for the first time in her short life,

LucyFur experienced true love and affection for one of her pets.

LucyFur went out the kitchen pet door and made her way across the lawn and through the tall, dead brush of the estate. She stopped briefly to look at the apiary before ducking under a wooden fence and making her way through the dense woods. She crawled over leaves, twigs, branches, and the decomposing severed arms, legs, heads, and torsos of fallen marauders from just fifteen-days prior. This scene made her chuckle to herself. The trek continued for nearly four miles. She saw the lights of the small town that was near the estate. One light, in particular, drew her attention. She made her way through the nearly vacant streets and jumped upon a windowsill in front of a neon beer sign. She adjusted her focus through the bright glare and saw what she had been searching for. She saw the person that she had sensed, sitting at a run-down round wooden table alongside her wheelchair bound friend and her friend's brawny husband. She let out an innocent mew. The woman looked up to the window.

"Aw fuck, cat," Jules slurred. "What the fuck are *you* doing here?" Jules reluctantly got up from the table and opened the front door. LucyFur strutted in then stopped suddenly when the elderly female bartender yelled out, "Hey! No cats in here!"

Jules and LucyFur glared into the eyes of the barkeep until she relented and said, "Well, just this once. And if she pisses on the floor, you're cleaning it up!"

"No, I won't," Jules dryly replied as Sam and Henri burst out in a drunken laughter. Although fifty-four years old, and with one of them being in a wheelchair, it was widely known throughout the area that these two best friends were not to be trifled with. Their exploits with Murder, Inc. were spoken about in hushed tones as was their involvement with the other saviors of Enlightenment. Sam and Jules were both revered and feared in the small community. And that was exactly how they liked it.

Sam's husband, Henri, on the other hand, was simply revered. He was ten-years the junior of his beautiful wife and looked much more imposing than the women. He was tall, dark skinned, and muscular. But he also possessed a smile that could melt hearts and a boisterous laugh to accent his off-beat sense of humor.

LucyFur jumped on the round table and mewed a polite greeting to the friends before curling up on the napkins and listening intently.

"It's always so nice to come up here and get away from the city for a while," Henri stated through his thick Cameroonian accent. "The people are always so nice, and the beer is so cheap. I can get drunk on twenty dollars here, then stagger across the street to the little motel if I'm unable to make the drive back to the estate. It's perfect."

"Yeah," Sam contributed. "But I have to say those bedsprings in the motel are awfully loud. Everyone in the entire town can probably hear what we're up to and that makes me feel a bit...cheap."

"Oh, embrace your cheap side you old fuckin' prude," Jules admonished. "Ever since college, you've had a stick up your ass. And now that you're getting a steady cock up it, you're bitching? You're married to the guy. There's nothing cheap about it. Just let him spread your paralyzed legs and enjoy the ride."

"Jules," Sam retorted in her condescending tone. "Must you use such tawdry language? And just where is *your* husband tonight? Where is Jerry?"

"Oh, he decided to stay at home," Jules answered. "I like to be respectful of his being on the wagon, so I don't drink at home. But once in awhile I wanna get my fuckin' drink on. Hey! Barkeep! Didja hear that? I'm here to get my fuckin' drink on! How about another pitcher!"

"Comin' right up," the barkeep begrudgingly replied.

"And it was nice to see the twins and Twins out tonight,"

Henri continued. "Although they didn't stay long. I wonder why they only had one drink and left? And Kayla and Rachel did not look pleased."

"Probably not," Sam answered as she put a cigarette out on the squealing head of Pogo II who was chained under the table. "It's a rough crowd in here tonight and I saw the Twins follow that guy that was yelling at that woman at the end of the bar. My guess? There's probably a hell of a mess outside."

"Either that," Jules interjected. "Or Josie and Arima fucked up babysitting somehow. But how hard could it be to watch over four ten-year-olds? The worst thing that could happen is Arima eating all the pizza. I'm sure nothing happened and everything's fine. It's probably that first thing. I think I'll go out back and see what happened."

LucyFur internally chuckled as she thought about the hysterics from earlier in the evening. She jumped off the table and began following Jules. Once the pair reached the jukebox, LucyFur lightly swiped at Jules's ankle, then pounced on top of the jukebox.

"Yeah, alright," Jules stated as she reached into her pocket for a dollar bill. "We'll play your song." Jules inserted the crumpled dollar into the jukebox, pressed the appropriate buttons for the desired selection and went past the restrooms and out the back door.

LucyFur stood on top of the jukebox. Her fur was being illuminated by the dancing lights as "Stray Cat Strut" began booming out of the speakers. The other patrons in the bar looked over at the scene, shook their heads in drunken disbelief, and retreated back to their warming drinks.

Jules took out a flashlight and lit up the cracked concrete of the parking lot. The lot was empty with the exception of a semi with out-of-state license plates. Jules squinted her eyes to try to see the driver of the semi who was sitting silently behind the steering wheel. "Ah fuck, I hate aging," she muttered to herself as she reached into her purse and retrieved a pair of cat-eyed, black rimmed glasses. She put the glasses on in disgust and focused on the form. She saw a white man staring at her with a slight smile on his stubbled face. She flipped him off and returned to her inspection of the pavement.

Her attention was captured by something glinting on the ground. She picked it up and discovered that it was a tooth. The beam of light continued deeper into the parking lot to reveal another tooth. Then another. Then an ear. "Yep, here it is," Jules said to herself as the flashlight revealed a huge pool of drying blood surrounding a pile of extracted intestines. The bright white beam then followed a long crimson streak that abruptly ended right in front of the parked semi.

"This must have been where they were parked. Probably put him in the trunk to harvest his skin for Alexa's artwork. Wow. Those boys had *fun* with their games tonight. Good for them. They needed to get out. They were getting pretty high-strung from the pressures of fatherhood. Parents need an outlet, I guess. Now, I see the four fingers, but I wonder what they did with the thumbs?"

Jules did not have long to ponder her question as she was suddenly grabbed from behind and lifted off the ground. "Awwww, goddamit," Jules stated as she felt the man squeezing her thin frame. Her arms were pinned against her body, and she began kicking her legs as the man said, "Well, hellllloooooo there, sweetheart! Yeah, I knew these little towns would provide me with some fun! Just wait outside one of the local watering holes and wait for my entertainment to come staggering right up to me. Now, just calm down there, sweet-heart. I ain't gonna hurt you none. Well, *maybe*, heh, heh, heh. You play nice with *me*, and I'll play nice with *you*. So just keep your fuckin' yap shut and let's get you outta those black jeans. Then, I'm gonna take you to the *real* party."

"Dude, you have *no idea* who you're fucking with," Jules angrily stated before the man put her on the ground, spun her around, and violently slapped her in the face. Jules wiped a slight trail of blood from her split lip and looked up intensely at her attacker. She then heard a light 'mew' from the hood of the semi. Both the would-be rapist and Jules looked at the hood and saw a small, somewhat freakish-looking cat sitting there cleaning her fur. Jules began laughing and the man slapped her again before turning his attention to the cat. "What the fuck are *you* starin' at, cat? You're not the kind of pussy that I'm lookin' for, so just get going."

LucyFur glared directly into the man's eyes as Jules continued laughing. Jules was laughing because she knew one other thing about this cat. From the moment that she was born, this kitten had an insatiable appetite for human blood.

LucyFur let out one more innocent mew. Her eyes then dilated fully. Her twitching, twelve-inch bushy tail extended like it had just been shot full of static. She let out a low growl. She then pounced upon the man's face. The man let out a pained shriek as he felt the cat's claws deeply slicing his face into ribbons. LucyFur opened her jaws, reached around the man's head, and chewed his right ear off as her razor-sharp claws continued their brutal onslaught on his face. The man fell to the ground and LucyFur immediately repositioned herself with her head over his neck. Her back claws began thrashing at his sliced-open eyes as she sunk her fangs into the man's gurgling jugular. She began purring as the man's body ended its flailing and she serenely sucked the blood from the gashed neck.

"Thanks, cat," Jules said. "I coulda taken care of it myself, but at least *one* of us gets a meal out of him. Just stay there. I think it's time to leave."

Jules went back into the bar and approached her friends. "Hey guys, I think we need to go. Anybody sober enough to get us back to the estate? LucyFur's made a bit of a mess out back. And I think I found my own ride. I'll just follow you."

"Well, I really shouldn't be driving," Henri slurred. "But I suppose if I have to. It's all backroads and I'll just pull over if there's any traffic. Let me settle the bill and I'll be right out."

Sam yanked on the heavy chain that she was holding and said, "C'mon Pogo. Get your worthless stumps out here, or else I'll drag you behind my chair…again."

The bar patrons breathed a sigh of relief as they watched this mid-fifties ebony beauty depart their bar with her grotesquely scarred pet limping behind her on his stumps.

Henri followed his beloved wife out the front door and to their awaiting sedan. He delicately lifted her from her chair, gave her a tender kiss and smile, and placed her in the passenger's seat. He carefully folded up her weaponized wheelchair and placed it in the trunk. He then picked Pogo II up, and haphazardly threw him onto the backseat before sitting behind the wheel and began patiently waiting for Jules.

Jules picked her assailant up and dragged him to the back of the trailer. She then took out her walkie-talkie. "Hey Josie, this is Jules. Pick up."

Jules only had to wait a few moments before she heard a response. "Yeah, this is Josie. Wazzup Jules?"

"Yeah, well, we're in town," Jules began. "We ran into a bit of trouble. Some guy tried to rape me, and LucyFur, um, well, LucyFur's been fed tonight. Anyway, could we use a semi and trailer? I've got one that I want to drive back to the estate. I need to get rid of this guy's body and I *really* don't want to sit next to Pogo in the back seat of the sedan. He always gets blood and snot and shit all over me. So, can we drive it up and crash there for tonight?"

"Um, sure," Josie answered. "Who all is coming?"

"It's just three of us," Jules replied. "Well, three and a *half* if you count Pogo. But we can chain him to a tree outside. Otherwise, its me, Sam, and Henri."

"Yeah, okay," Josie agreed. "Stellan and Paciano are in Atlantic City with Kaneko, so you guys can use their quarters. Hey, is there anything good in the trailer?"

"I dunno. Haven't looked," Jules responded. "Hold on a sec."

Josie could hear the creaking of the trailer's metal doors being opened through the walkie-talkie before Jules said, "Ooooooh fuck. Hey, why don't you make sure the twins and the Twins are sleeping with the JQ before we get there. I think this is something that we shouldn't bother them with right now."

The eight battered women were carefully led out of the trailer and into the welcoming warmth of the estate. Rosa and Jessie delicately washed and tended to their bruised bodies. They were put into fresh, loose clothing and invited to join the other representatives of Murder, Inc. downstairs.

The group struggled to hold back their tears as they listened to each woman recount their own harrowing story of abduction and abuse. Their anger increased as they were told that they had overheard the driver say that they were being taken to an address in Brooklyn. They were being taken there to be abused once again. Repeatedly. Until they died. For some sadistic bastard's amusement. Sam's mind kept flashing back to her own torture that she had endured. She would frequently turn to her husband and say coldly, "Kick him again." Henri would dutifully lift her paralyzed leg and thrust her six-inch stiletto into Pogo II's punished face. Sam felt little relief as she was mournfully transfixed by these women's horrific stories and shattered psyches.

Arima wept quietly and held Josie's hand. Josie said nothing. She just stared intensely with her glowering green eyes as the women told them their tales of brutality. She said nothing and just stared intensely as the sobbing women were led back upstairs to lay their sore bodies and broken minds down peacefully for the night. She said nothing and just stared intensely into the cold morbidity of the room.

Sam turned to Jules and whispered, "Do you remember in college when someone was talking to Maddy about their, um, *troubles?*"

"Yeah," Jules replied.

"Do you remember the look on her face as she listened?" Sam inquired further.

"Yeah," Jules once again replied.

"Look at Josie's face," Sam continued. "*That's* the look. She looks *just like* her mother at that age. She looks *just like* her mother as she was plotting her revenge. She looks *just like* her mother before she went out."

"Yep," Jules agreed. "Because Josie has *become* her mother. And may God help anyone who ever gets in her way."

Josie finally got up from the couch. She quietly picked up the ice cream bowls and spoons, took them to the sink, and washed them. There was a slight 'clack' as the bowls were placed in the dish drainer. Sam, Jules, Rosa, Jessie, Arima, and Henri looked on in grim silence. They knew what was about to happen. And they both welcomed it and dreaded it simultaneously.

Josie turned around from the sink and calmly walked into the living room. She lifted her head upwards. Chills ran down the group's spines as they saw a pair of intense green eyes glowing from under a mop of curly copper strands. Josie's mauve lips curled upwards into a sinister smirk as she said in a deep, devilish voice, "Ladies. Gentleman. I do believe that it's time to hold another 'Slashdance.'

CHAPTER 98

DANGEROUS TYPE

A solitary tear fell from Lionnel's eye and landed upon the framed photograph that he was placing into his suitcase as he listened to raucous laughter from across the hall. He solemnly stared at the picture of himself hugging his dearest friend and love on the opening night of Josie's teenage-oriented hang-out and restaurant, LOHAD. Although only four years had passed since this image was captured, to Lionnel it felt like a lifetime ago. He gazed into the brilliant emerald eyes of this hopeful young woman. She had just turned fourteen on the day the picture was taken. He was three years older than her, and although he knew her overprotective father would be disapproving, he could not help but fall in love with her.

The pair had been connected since Josie's birth. His beloved mother, Abana, had been mercilessly decapitated while babysitting himself, Josie, Adam, Aaron, Vai, and Alexa. His father, Henri, had joined the ranks of Murder, Incorporated following this tragedy and his family was immediately intertwined with that of Josie's. He had held her as she sobbed on his shoulder following her father's murder. He had performed that same sorrowful obligation following the assassination of her mother. He had stood dutifully by her side and proudly watched her ascension to the highest throne of the deadliest freedom-fighting hit-man syndicate in the world. He had shed tears with her. He had shed blood with her. He had also shared laughter.

Despite the constant violence and tragic loss that they both experienced over the past four years, there had also been plenty of tender moments between the two of them. Slow dancing while holding each other tightly. Hysterically laughing at each other as they gorged themselves on popcorn and ice cream while they watched a movie. Secretly making goofy faces at one another while she presided over assassination meetings. Picnics at the estate. Making love. He chuckled to himself as his mind recaptured the image of his love rustling under all the weaponry in her flower-adorned, 1976 yellow VW Bus to retrieve a wicker basket filled with fried chicken, ham sandwiches, and potato salad. His tears flowed more freely as he recalled the vivid image of his bare-footed, floral dress adorned lover sauntering toward the blanket that had been laid in the lush green grass. He remembered looking up at her. He remembered the feeling of his heart swelling at that moment. The brilliant sun had been shining directly behind her and her curly, copper locks glowed as though they were encased within a halo of love and tranquility. She looked like an angel. And she was. She was *his* angel.

He had fallen in love with a girl that became a young lady who was the embodiment of peace. She was free-spirited. She was intelligent. She was beautiful. She had the most wonderful sense of humor. She considered herself to be the protector of any soul that had fur. Or scales. Or wings. She spoke properly, usually, and never said harsh words toward others. She believed in human kindness. She believed in protecting the innocent. The vulnerable. The abused. The downtrodden. Despite her lofty position, she did not consider herself to be above anyone else. Everyone that Josie met loved and adored her. They instinctively knew that they were safe with her. There was no judgement from Josie. There was only caring, kindness, and genuine friendship that accompanied a beaming smile and twinkling green eyes. It had always been said about Josie that she did not belong to anyone, including her parents. It was said that Josephine Patricia Sommers Parker belonged to the world. But her *heart* belonged to *him*. And *his* heart belonged to *her*.

Lionnel lightly kissed the tips of his fingers and placed them upon the picture. He was frozen for a moment. He did not want to let go. A final tear fell upon the image as Lionnel righted himself. There was a 'click' as he closed and fastened the suitcase. He slid the bag off the bed that he and his love had shared in the Sommers-Parker home for the past two years. He prepared himself, opened the bedroom door, and trudged across the hallway. The girlish laughter and banter became louder with each step he took toward his dreaded future. There was a crack in the door. Lionnel peered in and his heart sunk even further.

"Ow! Fuck Vai!" Josie was yelling out. "Do ya have to tie the ribbon so fucking *tight*?"

"Do you *really* want your pigtails coming out halfway through the massacre?" the thirty-year-old Vai calmly asked. "I *really* don't have much time to mess with this, my dearest. I still need to dye my hair black and put my silver streak in it before I put on my dress."

"Well, um, no, I *don't* want my hair to look a mess while we're slashing these fuckers up," Josie answered. "But *fuck* man, I don't wanna be fuckin' *scalped* either! Which reminds me. Alexa! Didja want us to start keeping some scalps from the 'Chads'? It's not a big deal if you want 'em. We're *already* hanging onto large portions of their skin for you to use as your canvas. I thought maybe you'd want the scalps too. It might be cool to paint with brushes made from the human hair of these motherfuckin' douchebags. You want 'em?"

The twenty-four-year-old petite blonde beauty squealed in delight and said, "Oh my god, *yes*! I hadn't thought of that! That will *really* get me in the mood to work on my art. Oh, I just can't *wait* for everyone to see the pieces I'm working on! I think you're *really* going to love them. And I just can't *believe* that you got me a show at that gallery! It's going to be *such* a magical evening!"

"Yeah, well, I've got, um, *connections*, heh, heh, heh." Josie replied in a mischievous tone. "I made the fucker who owns the joint an offer he couldn't refuse. I mean, he isn't really a bad guy, but he's got his secrets. And I've got a flock of little birdies who just *love* to chirp!"

"I don't think your mother would approve of that, Josie," Sam mentioned as she was dolling up her fifty-four-year-old best friend, Jules, to look as close to sixteen as possible. At least in dim lighting. "Your mother only went after men who truly deserved it. This man, from what I understand, simply has a few, um, personality quirks."

"My *mother*," Josie answered with a chuckle. "God, how I love her, but I *really* don't want to talk about my *mother* right now. She was good at what she did, but she never took *full advantage* of the power that she wielded. Listen, I'm not saying we should just go around randomly harassing or killing people. All I'm saying is that the world is transactional, and we should take *full advantage* of that. I have something that *this* asshole wants, and he has something that *I* want. So, we struck a deal. No biggie. Besides! Is it *my* fault that this prick can't keep it in his pants? Is it *my* fault that he's running around cheating on his husband? No! So, *he* gets to keep his little secrets and *Alexa* gets to throw a kick-ass art show. No muss, no fuss. Everybody's happy. Hey Vai. Hand me that lipstick wouldja?"

Jules looked at herself in a hand-held mirror and said softly, "Jesus. I look ridiculous. I mean, she's had some crazy fuckin' ideas, but *this* is just twisted."

"Yeah," Sam quietly replied. "And I think that we were wrong the other night. She hasn't *become* her mother. She has *surpassed* her mother. Saving the Earth and Enlightenment has really gone to her head. She was close to snapping two years ago when Maddy was killed. She became someone different on the day of her funeral. But she was able to hold it together. She was still Josie. Just, with a bit more tenacity. And foul language. Now I think that all the tragedy and loss throughout the years combined with her newfound realization of just how much power she possesses has sent her down a dark path. She needs a wake-up call. Maybe I'll talk to Arima and Rosa about it. See if they can't talk to her. But not tonight. She's hellbent on violence tonight. And once she has violence in her mind, there's no stopping her. Just like her mother."

"Hey! What are *you two* bitches whispering about over there? Whatevs. Keep your fuckin' secrets. It's too bad Kayla and Rachel couldn't join us tonight," Josie's excited rambling continued. "If it's one thing those two hate, it's human sex traffickers. But, hey, that's what you get when you have kids. You have to be tied down constantly. Man, I'm *never* having fuckin' kids. Nope, I'm *never* going to be tied down spending my day doing laundry and picking up after some snot-nosed, screaming asshole. Then, bringing Lionnel his pipe and slippers when he gets home from work. Can you imagine? Fuck that! Naw, that's not for me. I need to be foot-loose and fancy-free to do whatever the *fuck* I want, *whenever* the fuck I want. Which reminds me. I'm kinda pissed off that Rosa and Jessie aren't here tonight. They're spending the evening trying to hone their ability to track those little hellions through time the next time that they pull that shit. Kids. What a pain in the ass. Oh, hey Jules! Can I borrow that rouge?"

Lionnel lightly rapped on the door and said, "Hey. Can I come in?"

"Oh, hey baby!" Josie screamed out. "What do ya think? Don't we look cute?"

Lionnel felt ill as he looked upon Josie, Alexa, Vai, and Jules. They were all fully dressed, except for Vai who was still wearing a robe. The others all wore short, pink, Lolita dresses complete with pigtails and white stockings. Their faces were made up in a garish combination of colors. To Lionnel, they did not look cute. They looked…

"Disgusting. No, I don't think you look cute. I think that you look like you're all five-years-old. I think that this is sick, Josie."

"Oh, my fucking *God*, Lionnel!" Josie yelled back. "Of *course*, its sick! That's the whole fuckin' *point*! These twisted fuckers get off on abusing women and children, right? So, we show up and give them a moment to live out their perv fantasy and then…and then…just look at what we have buried in these ruffles!"

Josie began excitedly digging into pockets that were hidden within the outlandish ruffles of the dresses. She began extracting knives and hatchets and throwing stars. She pressed a button on her bracelet and spikes emerged. She tapped the back of the heels on her pure white vinyl buckled shoes and blades ejected from the front of the soles.

"See?" Josie exclaimed as she bounced up and down while clapping and laughing. "These motherfuckers are not going to know *what* hit them! Just picture it! We come in all chained up looking scared and innocent and shit. Then, I hit the button on the portable CD player and…oh Lionnel! I've picked out the *perfect* fucking song to play while we're cutting these fuckers up! Anywhooo, I push play on the CD player and then…well…Slaaaaaashdaaaaance motherfuckers!"

Josie strode over to her beloved boyfriend and embraced his rigid frame. "Jesus, you're uptight," she whispered to him before saying playfully, "Y'know, if ya play your cards right, we *might* be able to use this dress for some *other* type of fun. Whatdoyasay, hmmmmmmm?"

Lionnel wiped a tear from his eye, grasped Josie's petite

hands and dislodged her grip from him. He took two steps back from her and said with as much force as he could muster, "No Josie. I'm not into making love to women who look like little girls. That's sick. Josie, I'm leaving."

"Whatevs, you fuckin' prude," Josie replied dismissively as she began walking back toward her makeup table. "But I'm tellin' ya. You're missing out. I'm gonna be all *sorts* of ready when we get done with these fuckers. Oh well. I'll see ya when I get home. Have fun doin' whatever you're doin' tonight."

"No, Josie," Lionnel tried to explain. "You don't understand. I'm leaving. I'm leaving this house. I'm leaving this relationship. I'm leaving *you*."

Josie had heard the words that her beloved boyfriend had just spoken. She realized that she needed to respond delicately. Josie knew that she could not fuck this up. Josie fucked it up as she immediately bent over and clutched her ribs to protect them from her sudden onslaught of violent laughter. "Leaving me? Okay, you guys. Who put him up to this? It's not really funny, but the thought of Lionnel leaving me? C'mon. You'd *never* leave me. You *love* me. Knock this shit off. I'll see ya when I get home."

"Josie," Lionnel began again with a cold determination. "You are right. I *do* love you. So much that it hurts. Or at least I love the person that you *were*. I loved *you*, Josie. The girl who built a pet shelter and adoption agency at the age of four. The girl who smiled constantly. The girl who immediately saw the bright side of taking out the wireless internet. The girl who didn't walk but *skipped* through life. The girl that *always* had a positive outlook no matter what tragedy had befallen her. The girl who turned the site of a massacre into a safe space for teenagers of all walks of life. The girl who *everybody* loved and adored and respected. The girl that made my heart beat rapidly every time I looked into her eyes. Josie, please listen to me. My heart doesn't beat like that for you anymore. Because I am no longer looking into *your* eyes. I am looking into the eyes of your *mother.*"

"Oh….you….*motherfucker*!" Josie roared. "How fucking *dare* you! I love my mother but she's all *sorts* of fucked up! I am *nothing* like her! And how *daaaare* you say that I am! You wanna leave? Then get the fuck *out* of here! What the fuck do *I* care? I can get *any* guy in this city! Hell, I can get any guy in this entire fucking *world*! Do you know how many guys would love to be the boyfriend of the girl who saved the world? Here's a hint. Fucking *all* of them! What makes *you* so fucking special, huh? Who the fuck are *you* to tell me who I should be. I'm going to be whoever the fuck I *want* to be or my name's not Josie *fucking* Parker! And *that's* my name, so *that's* how it's going to be! Now get the fuck out!"

Stunned silence fell over the room. Lionnel looked hurtfully at each of the cartoonishly painted women standing before him. He gave each of them a slight nod and dejected smile, picked up his suitcase and turned toward the door.

Lionnel!" Josie called after him. "I'm *sorry*, okay? I didn't *mean* any of that! Just come back and let's talk, okay? I *love* you! I'm just amped up for tonight, that's all! Lionnel, c'mon! Let's talk! Lionnel! Get your fucking ass back in here! That's an order!"

From down the hallway, Josie heard Lionnel respond with, "Josie, I am not one of your servants. I am your boyfriend. Well, at least I *used* to be. Good-bye Josie."

Chapter 99

Kerosene

No one in the room dared to speak. They just stood silently watching Josie. They studied her and were transfixed as Josie's face turned bright red. She then shed a single tear from her emerald eye and her bottom lip began to quiver. Within moments, her face exhibited an eerie serenity. The final transformation came, and she projected an evil little smile before saying, "Fuck him. He'll be back. He can't live without me. Let's get this show on the road. Vai, get into your dress. Don't worry about your hair. It's black enough. And where the hell is Marcus, Gregory, and Henri?"

Sam grabbed the walkie-talkie from the arm of her wheelchair and called her husband. "Hey Henri, where are you guys? We're just about ready to go."

There was static on the line, then Henri's soothing voice. "Marcus and I will be there in about five minutes. We had to stop by and pick up our special guest. And we just received a report from Rod who is overseeing our surveillance team. We're not expecting any surprises. We have hit men, um, I mean execution specialists, or whatever we're calling them, positioned outside the warehouse. The moment we go through the gate, the guards will be taken out. We'll drive into a loading dock. There are eight men inside. The men are the heads of the most prominent human traffickers operating on the Eastern seaboard. They like to sample their, um, they like to, um, well they do stuff to their victims before shipping the orders. Um, I guess. I'm sorry. I don't know how to say this, it's just so disgusting. Sam and our special guest will wait in the van and be on standby in the event we need them. Marcus and I will lead the four of you ladies inside. You will be hand-cuffed and leashed. The handcuffs are breakaway, and the leashes are made of razor wire just in case you ladies want another toy to play with."

Josie walked over to Sam and grabbed the walkie-talkie from her. "Hey, Henri. Josie here. That sounds great, but where the fuck is Gregory? He's supposed to be in on this."

"No, Josie," Henri replied through the static. "He wouldn't come. He said that he is only responsible for the diplomatic end of our operations and does not want to be involved in our more violent escapades. That was the deal that he made with your mother from the start."

"Yeah?" Josie screamed back. "Well, that's fucking *insubordination*! There's nothing that I can do about it right *now*, but as soon as this shit is done, Gregory and I are going to have a little *chat* about who's in *charge* here! And it *isn't* my fucking *mother*! And if you speak to him, you *might* want to remind him that I know that his first name is 'Chad!' *That* should make the point. Just get your asses over here. We're ready to fuck some shit up."

"What the hell is wrong with *you*?" Henri yelled back. "Josie, you have *no right* to…"

"Hey, baby," Sam interrupted after she caught the walkie-talkie that Josie had flung at her. "Hold the line for a sec. Josie, I've got to use the restroom."

"Whatevs," Josie answered as her frustrated hands tight-ened the ribbons on her copper pigtails. "Just hurry it up."

Once inside the privacy of the restroom, Sam said, "Hey, listen. There's been a bit of drama tonight. I don't want to get into it right now. I'm sure you'll find out about it when we get home. Let's just say that I think Lionnel will be staying with us for a while. And don't tell Gregory what Josie said. She's just a bit out of sorts tonight. We'll do this job, then get Rosa and Arima on it. See you soon."

"Yeah, alright," Henri replied. "You know how much I love and respect that girl but I'm not going to take any shit from her. I told her mother that when I joined up and I am not afraid to tell the girlfriend of my son that, either. We'll be there soon."

As the black passenger van pulled around the corner and began entering the driveway of the abandoned Brooklyn warehouse, Sam looked at Henri and said, "My lord. You look so creepy with that white man's face."

Henri chuckled and said, "Yeah, I know. And I had to paint my neck and hands white to match it. But Lionnel did a wonderful job cutting the semi-driver's face off his skull. It fits me perfectly. He will be such a talented surgeon someday. I'm so proud of my boy. Hey, Josie! Do you and my son have any plans for later tonight? Sam and I are going to an all-night diner to get some burgers and shakes. You and Lionnel are more than welcome to join us if you would like."

His invitation was greeted by chilled silence. Henri looked into the rearview mirror and saw Josie's glaring green eyes staring straight ahead. Her arms were folded, and he could feel her foot violently kicking the back of his seat. He looked over to the passenger seat at Sam who looked back and silently shook her head. "Okaaaay, then," Henri said to change the subject. "It looks like we're here! Marcus, are you ready?"

"Yeah, man, I'm good to go," Marcus replied. "But, hey. If you don't mind, I think that Arima and I would love to join you guys for dinner tonight."

"Yeah, that's cool man," Henri answered. "Okay. Everybody be cool. We're coming up to the gate."

The black-clad guard checked the driver's credentials which Rod had created. The van was waived through. There was a loud 'clang' as the gate was shut behind them. The passengers in the van were completely silent as they drove toward the loading dock. The only sound that could be heard was the van's running engine and several light 'popping' sounds from behind them. The passengers looked out the rearview mirror and saw twelve guards lying on the cold concrete in pools of their own blood.

They backed into the loading dock where eight men in expensive designer suits were seated, smoking cigars, and laughing. One of the men stood up and shouted out, "The party has arrived, gentlemen!"

Sam gave her beloved husband a light kiss before she and their special guest crouched down in their respective seats so as not to be seen. The party exited the van to jubilant applause. Marcus was carrying a CD boombox and holding the leashes of the "bound" Alexa and Jules. Henri was leading Vai and Josie. "Now, *this* is gonna be a party!" One of the men exclaimed. "But, hey! There were supposed to be *eight* of these bitches. Where's the other *four*? And who is *this* guy that's with you? And what the hell happened to your *face*? You look weird."

Henri responded while trying to sound as redneck as possible. "Well, uh, sorry about that, sir. This here's my friend Marcus. You see, these bitches got a bit unruly, so I brought Marcus along to help keep 'em calm. And you can see what they did to my face. Anyway, four of 'em just couldn't be handled so we had to, um, well, let's just say they were damaged goods. But we got these 'uns all dolled up fer ya. Wanna meet 'em?"

The men's attention was immediately distracted away from Marcus and Henri as they gazed lustfully at the four women standing in front of them wearing pink Lolita dresses, white stockings, pig tails, and bright, glittered make-up. If it weren't for their height, Josie and Alexa could have passed for ten-year-olds. Vai perhaps could have been mistaken to be in her mid-teens. And fifty-four-year-old Jules could have passed for…

"That one's cute and everything, but just how old *is* she? Like, *fifty-two*? Ah well, she'll still be fun for one of our buyers. Might have to reduce the price a bit though." All eight men began laughing. Marcus and Henri also forced themselves into an overly dramatic laugh while the women stood there and "trembled." Except for Jules. She internally seethed as she detected a familiar presence.

One of the men walked up to Josie. She recoiled at the foul smell of his breath as he said to her "sweetly," "Well, aren't *you* just a precious little thing. We'll have to take *turns* with *you*. No need to have a war over a cute little piece of ass, now *is* there? What do you say, sweetheart? You ready to play some *games* with us? All *eight* of us? While your little *girlfriends* watch? Yeah, that'll be nice, *right* honey? Have your little *girlfriends* watch what's gonna happen to them *next*. Then, it'll be off to your new *masters*. And *believe* me, sweetheart. What happens to you here tonight is *nothing* compared to what your masters will do to you. I sure hope you like knives."

Josie looked up at him and smiled innocently. There was a glimmer in her emerald eyes as she said in a childish voice, "I sure do, mister. But do you know what I like more than knives?"

The man chuckled and turned around to look at his guffawing companions. "Naw. What is it that you like *more* than knives, there honey?"

Josie smiled once again and answered. "Well, I *really* like lollipops. Do any of you men have a big *lollipop* that I can suck on?"

The men's laughter exploded before the vile man replied,

"Yeah sweetheart. I think we can arrange that. Why don't we see if you like *my* lollipop?"

"Okay, but can I just ask one question first before I suck on your lollipop?" Josie inquired sweetly. "I was just *wondering* if any of you are named 'Lionnel.' I *really* like that name."

The laughing men looked at each other with amused expressions. "Hey! We got a Lionnel in the house?" the man yelled out. "Lionnel! Come on out! You got a visitor!"

"No, but my names Larry!" a tall, skinny man in the back of the group shouted out gleefully.

"Close fuckin' enough!" Josie roared. "*That* fucker's *mine*! Play the fuckin' song!"

Marcus pushed 'play' on the CD player and the child-like harmonies of The Chordettes' "Lollipop" came blaring through the speakers. Before the men could react, Josie snapped her handcuffs, pressed a button on her bracelet and used the protruding metal spikes to slash the man's throat open. He began gurgling and fell to his knees as he clutched his throat to slow the flow of blood that was gushing out. Josie took the leash from around her neck, wrapped it around that of the wounded man, and began sawing back and forth with the razor wire until the head flopped backward. Josie stared into the dead eyes that were looking up at her as the blood from the severed head sprayed on her made-up face. She smiled sweetly once again, leaned down and gave the corpse a delicate kiss.

"SlaaaaaaaashDaaaaaaaaaance!" Alexa squealed as she pulled a meat cleaver from one of the ruffles in her dress, pounced on the nearest man, and began ferociously hacking at his face.

The van began rocking back and forth and there was a loud rumble before the doors swung open. "W-w-what the fuck is *that*?" One of the terrified men yelled out. Lumbering toward them was the six-foot-seven-inch *Dragenstein*. She was wearing her customary Monroe-esque white dress. She approached one man and gave him a playful spin. The circulating air caused the hem of the dress to lift above her waist revealing an eighteen-inch rock-hard phallus. She paused for a moment and said in her breathy, high-pitched voice. "Sorry to be such a *drag, tee, hee*." She then grabbed the man's shoulders and pushed him to his knees. She forced his mouth open and thrust her granite-like member into it. She moaned ecstatically as she forcefully pulled the man's head backwards and forwards, backwards and forwards, backwards and forwards until her throbbing member shot through the back of the man's skull. A stream of blood, bone, brain, and cum shot out of the dead man's head, hitting Jules on her half-exposed breasts.

"Oh, fuckin' gross," Jules lamented. "I've heard of hard enough to cut through glass, and I've heard of skull fucking, but *that* shit's ridiculous, bitch."

Dragenstein blew her a kiss, twirled, and said," Anyone got a cigarette? *Tee, hee*" before grabbing another man by the scruff of his neck and throwing him toward Vai. Vai looked down at the man with a cool intensity and pulled two sewing needles from inside her ruffles. "My mentor, Aunt Blair, showed me how to use these. Only it *wasn't* for knitting." She then thrust the needles into the screaming man's eyes. Vai began laughing uncontrollably as she watched the blind man desperately crawling on the floor as he tried to find any type of exit from this torturous hell. Vai tapped the back heels of her shoes, causing blades to shoot out of the front of the soles. She then began to violently kick the man repeatedly in the groin until he collapsed in a pool of his own blood and vomit.

The four remaining histrionic men began running toward the back exit. Jules smirked, closed her eyes, and concentrated. From out of nowhere, thirty-eight feral cats descended upon the men from metal shelving. The men began flailing helplessly as the felines ripped at their faces.

"Hey! *Dragenstein!*" Josie yelled out. "Grab that skinny fucker and hold him down! I want him alive!"

Dragenstein pranced over to the skinny man and cautiously made her way through the misty cloud of blood and fur. "Excuse me, pussy. Excuse me, pussy. Excuse me, pussy," she said in her breathy voice until she reached her target, threw him on the ground and sat on him.

Alexa's brilliant blue eyes seemed to be glowing as she approached the bloody form of the largest of the men. "Ooooooh yeah," Alexa snarled. "I know *exactly* what I'm going to paint on *you*. And a full head of hair *too*. Perfect."

Alexa took her cleaver and buried it in the man's forehead. She pulled on his shirt, and he tumbled face first. There was a loud 'snap' as his nose was crushed against the concrete floor. Alexa giggled and sat astride on the twitching man's back. She retrieved a scalpel from her dress and used it to cut his coat and shirt open, exposing the large frame of his back.

"P-please, S-s-stop," the man pleaded before Alexa screamed out. "Hey! Shut up! And stop trembling! This is delicate work!" She carefully cut the perimeter of his back and pulled the skin from his body. She began squealing in delight and yelled out, "Oh my god! Look everybody! This is my largest canvas yet! Oh, thank you sir!"

She then took the scalpel and cut around the quivering man's hairline. She pulled on his thick, black hair and his entire scalp came free. "Oh my God! I can make so many *brushes* out of this! Oh, you *really* have been just *too kind* sir! Thaaaaaank yooooou!" Alexa concluded before playfully skipping away with her treasure.

"Okay cats, get off of them and thanks," Jules stated to her feline friends. They mewed politely up at her, licked the blood from their whiskers and retreated into the shadows of the warehouse. The two dying men laid on the concrete whimpering as blood flowed out of the myriad of deep gashes on their faces.

"So, what should we do with *these* two? Just let them bleed out?" Sam inquired as she wheeled herself towards her friends. "And, what about that skinny one?"

"Well, first things first," Josie answered in a devilish voice as her eyes were attracted to a rusty, metal can in the corner of the warehouse. She went over and picked up the five-gallon cannister and held it over the dying men. "I'm going to do to *them* what should be done to *all* of these sadistic fuckers. I want these men to suffer! I want them to *suffer* just like they make us *women* suffer! They make us suffer with their fists and their harsh words! With their tiny little pricks! And *then* do you know what they do? Oh, I'll *tell* you! They tell you that they love you and they buy you nice gifts and hold you while watching movies and make love to you and smile at you and say nice things to you and buy you flowers and shit, and then…and then…they *break up* with you! Fuckin' misogynistic, sadistic *bastards*!"

She unfastened the cap, tossed it aside and began pouring the pungent liquid contents on the pair of sex-traffickers. She giggled as she said, "Hey, Marcus. Toss me your lighter." Marcus reached into his pocket, took out his lighter and tossed it toward Josie. The lighter hit Josie directly in the hands, then bounced off and landed on the floor.

Jules leaned down to Sam and whispered, "She sure as hell can shoot arrows, but she kinda catches like a girl."

"Hey! I heard that!" Josie yelled as she picked the lighter up along with a piece of discarded paper. The flame of the lighter reflected in her emerald eyes as she gleefully lit the paper on fire and dropped it onto the two men who were saturated in kerosene. The men screamed in agonized torture and began flailing as the wicked flames consumed their bodies.

"Now, for *this* one," Josie nonchalantly continued as she sauntered over to the skinny man that *Dragenstein* was sitting on. "Sooooo, Dragalicious. Do you think you could…," Josie began to inquire before bending down and whispering into her ear.

Dragenstein giggled and said with breathy anticipation, "But *of course*, my dear." *Dragenstein* lifted the left leg of the tortured man and yanked the knee joint forward. There was a loud 'crack' as the left knee snapped in two. She continued to pull the leg back and forth, back and forth, back and forth, until the leg was ripped from the body at the joint. Blood began pouring out of the fresh wound as Josie and *Dragenstein* shared the same amused expression. The man shrieked in tormented agony as the right leg was removed in the same gruesome manner. Then the left arm at the elbow. Then the right.

"That was so fuckin' *cool*!" Josie gushed. "Now, hold his limbs over the fire to cauterize the wounds. I want to keep him alive. Sam has her Pogo and I've got my Lion…I mean, my *Larry*! Fuck *you*, Larry! Oh, but goddammit!"

"What's wrong, dear," Vai asked tenderly as the man screamed for mercy while the flames licked at his mutilated appendages.

"Well, it's just that I wish I had some hot dogs. And some ketchup," Josie regretfully answered.

"Um, Josie?" Marcus asked. "Do you think I could have my lighter back? I kinda wanna smoke this joint. Oh, and ketchup on hot dogs is doing it wrong."

CHAPTER 100

───────────

BEAT'S SO LONELY

Arima and Rosa cautiously ascended the staircase that led to the third-floor party room and converted art studio of the Sommers-Parker home. They approached the metal door and heard a succession of 'Thump!' 'Aaaaaaaaaw!' 'Thump!' 'Aaaaaaaaaw!' 'Thump!' Aaaaaaaaaw!'

"What the hell is she *doing* in there?" Rosa asked before Arima carefully opened the door. "Um, hey Niece Josie?" Arima inquired carefully. "Um, whatcha doin?'

Josie was standing in the middle of the dance floor in her pink floral pajamas. In one hand she held a tumbler of bourbon. In the other, she was holding...

"Just playing darts with Larry," Josie answered in a slightly drunken slur. She pulled her right arm back and slung the dart toward the far wall. There was a loud 'Thump!' followed by a man wailing out 'Aaaaaaaaaaw!'

Rosa and Arima looked over at the far wall and saw the quadriplegic Larry. He had hooks under his armpits that held his beaten body to the wall. He was naked except for a diaper that was leaking pungent urine and feces. His torso was dripping trails of blood from around the multiple darts that were penetrating his beaten, dark purple flesh.

"Hey everybody!" Alexa squealed as she pulled back the curtain and popped her blonde head out from her half of the third-floor space that she was using as her art studio. "I painted the dartboard on his chest! Pretty cool, huh?"

"Uh, yeah, it looks really great, Alexa," Rosa responded before turning back to Josie. "Hey Josie, could we maybe have a little chat with you?"

"Sure," Josie answered in a depressed tone. "Why not? What's the point of doing this? What's the point of doing anything? Life is just a series of heartbreaks. I may as well listen to whatever bad news *you two* are going to give me. I just have one dart left anyway. Hey. See that little hole in his left ear where he used to have an earring? Watch this shit." Josie pulled her right arm back once again and launched her final dart. It slammed perfectly into the hole in his ear, lodging it into the wall. The man screamed out, "Aaaaaaaaaw!" and Josie allowed herself a moment of quiet satisfaction before sitting on a red vinyl love seat. "Even drunk, I'm pretty good. Maybe next time Larry and I play this, I'll use my arrows. Okay. I'm here. What do *you* two want?"

"Um, Niece Josie?" Arima began sheepishly. "Well, it's just that we're a little bit worried about you. We understand that you're heartbroken over Lionnel, but…"

Arima was cut off by a belligerent Josie. "Who? Who the fuck is this *Lionnel* that you speak of? I've never *heard* of the motherfucker. Nope. The only Lionnel that *I* ever knew is fucking *dead to me* and I don't want to hear his fucking *name* ever again! Got it? Is that all? Can I get back to playing with Larry now?"

"No, you may not," Rosa answered in a stern maternal tone.

"Whoooooooa! Rosa's gonna get all *medieval* on her ass," Maddy exclaimed from her perch in Enlightenment. "Erick!

Come here! I've connected with Arima's soul so that I can listen in. I can see and hear everything that *she* does. But I can't interact, because I kinda snuck into her soul and she doesn't know I'm there. Hold my hand so you can listen in too!"

"What the hell is going on *now*?" Erick replied in a disinterested tone.

"Hey! Don't use that fuckin' tone with me!" Maddy shot back. "Just hold my hand. Lionnel broke up with Josie and…"

"What?" Erick roared. "That little bastard broke my little girl's heart? I'm going to go talk to Gwen and see if she'll give me permission to haunt his ass!"

"Yeah! He totally did!" Maddy answered. "And do you know *why*? It's for the *dumbest* fuckin' reason! He said that she was becoming too much like *me*! He should *be* so fuckin' lucky to be with a girl just like me! I'm like perfect and shit!"

"Yeah, well," Erick quietly replied as he avoided his beloved wife's glowing green eyes. "You *are* kind of an acquired taste, so I *kinda* get where he's coming fr…"

"What are you babbling about?" Maddy interrupted. "Get over here and hold my hand and shut the fuck up! I wanna hear what Rosa is going to say."

"Listen, Josie," Rosa began. "We understand the pressure you've been under. I mean, my God, you've just turned eighteen and look at all the things you've had to deal with. You're the leader of an international freedom-fighting hit-man syndicate. You've just helped coordinate the salvation of both Earth and Enlightenment. You have lost so many friends and loved ones in your short life. Your parents have died, then were reborn, then left you again. The pain that you have experienced is unimaginable. We understand. But Josie, you are going down a dark path. You are becoming something that doesn't come naturally to you. You are naturally a very sweet girl who cares deeply about others. And who cares deeply about ridding the world of pure evil. And those two contradictions are battling each other. The innocent side that wants to cherish life and the dark side that must order others to commit very violent acts. Both come from the same place. Both sides want to protect the innocent. The downtrodden. But Josie, your dark side is taking over. You are becoming something that we no longer recognize. You are becoming the very thing that you have fought against. You are not becoming your mother. She always was able to keep a check on her dark side. It would come out when it was needed, then she was able to bottle it back up again. That isn't true with you. You are becoming something *more* than your mother. You are becoming your *grandmother*. You are becoming sadistic just for the sake of being sadistic. You are beginning to thrive on seeing others suffer. You are turning our syndicate into a cult of personality. A cult that is beholden only to *you*. You are losing the sweet side of yourself. You are losing that little girl who would dance around the house in a hippie dress with a flower in her hair. You are going too far. And that is why Lionnel broke up with you. And it is why you are at risk of losing the loyalty of others as well. This is your wake-up call. Come back to us Josie. Please. Do you understand?"

Josie sat silently for a moment. Her green eyes began tearing up. The tears immediately dried and her eyes began to shimmer. "Huh," Josie said. Rosa and Arima smiled at one another. They felt that the wall had been penetrated and that the true Josie was present once again.

"Well," Josie began calmly before screaming out, "Isn't *this* just a crock of shit? Yeah! I've got a lot on my plate! And I don't need *you* two bitches or *anyone else* for that matter to tell me how to live or who I should be! Do you know who saved the Earth and Enlightenment? Me, *that's* who! This world would be consumed in the fucking flames of *Vetis* if it wasn't for me! So, yeah! Maybe people *should* bow down and kiss my fuckin' feet! And you come in here and dare *criticize* me? You fucking traitorous bitches! You want to leave me too? Then fucking *do* it! What the fuck do *I* care? Everybody that I've cared about has left me! Why should *you* two be any different? I don't *need* you! I don't *need* L-L-Lionnel..."

Josie broke down and held her tearful face in her hands as she screamed out, "Oh my fucking God, I miss him so much! Why did he *leave* me? I *need* him! Oh, goddammit, *now* what?"

The trio looked up at the door and saw Jessie rushing into the room. "Hey everybody," a breathless Jessie began. "Sorry to interrupt whatever *this* is, but I was about to go pick Jamie up from the hospital. She's being discharged after her successful sex change surgery, and I got a call on that stupid land-line phone. Anyway, it's happened again. The JQ is missing, and the twins and the Twins are besides themselves. Aaron and Adam are starting to sharpen their toys, and that's *never* good. Rosa, Arima, we need to get up to the estate and try to find those kids. Then Arima, we need you to get in touch with Maddy and see if someone can go bring them home."

Josie shook the tears from her face and the heartbreak from her soul before yelling, "Do you *see* all the shit that I have to deal with? Now, I've gotta coordinate *this* shit! Now *I'm* ultimately responsible for a bunch of little time-traveling *bastards*! And, *now* what?"

Josie was interrupted once again as Rod entered the room. "I-I'm very sorry Josie, but I have that report that you were wanting."

"Jesus Fucking Christ Rod, can't you see that I'm *busy* here?" Josie roared at him. "Fine. Give it to me. What do you have."

Josie stood up and approached the quivering Rod. His pop-bottle lenses were steaming up from all the sweat that was pouring down his face. He looked Josie squarely on her chest and began stammering. "U-um, well Josie, I have found where the reconstituted Underground Autocratic Movement is. Vetis has given them the word to stand by. He has told them that there will soon be reinforcements coming. Reinforcements that he is recruiting from the past. The new UAM is congregating now and waiting for their orders. I do not yet know who the top leaders are. They apparently have been held back in the shadows this entire time. But I will find out who they are as soon as possible. What do you want to do?"

Josie stood silently and pondered her options. Her intoxicated genius brain was clicking through the various scenarios. She then came up with her plan.

"Okay, here's what we do. Rosa and Arima. Go to the estate with Jessie and get those fuckin' kids back. Rod, give this report to Gregory and have him, Marcus, and Cliff get a meeting at the United Nations. We can't make a move without their approval. That was the deal. Then, have Sam and Jules get a group of assassination technicians together and be prepared to attack these motherfuckers. Alexa, go pick up Jamie. Larry, you just hang from the wall and bleed, you fuckin' douchebag. We'll reconvene tomorrow morning. Got it? What the fuck are you all *waiting* for? Chop, chop, motherfuckers!"

"Um, yes Josie," the stammering Rod replied as his magnified pupils stared at her chest. "R-right away."

"And, hey Rod!" Josie yelled out. "Why the fuck are you staring at my chest? You've *never* done that with me!"

"I-I'm very sorry Josie," Rod replied as he lifted his gaze from her chest to the ceiling. "It's just that I have difficulty maintaining eye contact with people I'm intimidated by."

"Yeah?" Josie countered. "I fucking *know* that. So why are you doing this to *me* now?"

"Because I am intimidated by you Josie," Rod answered in his nasal staccato. "You were always the one person in this entire world that did not intimidate me. You never judged me. From the time that you were an infant, I knew that you were special. I knew that you were somebody that I could trust. Somebody that I could be myself around. Somebody who would love me for who I was. You never judged my awkward appearance or my speech. You never judged my awkwardness. You were sweet. You were my sweet Josie. You were the *world's* sweet Josie. You aren't that person anymore. You are judgmental and becoming cruel. You never raised your voice to me or anyone. Before tonight. You yelled at me Josie. You treated me like a servant. You used to think that we were all equals. You don't believe that anymore. Power has gone to your head. And that power is corrupting you. You are now the opposite of what you have always been. You are cruel now, Josie. And I am afraid of you."

"Oh fuck," Erick whispered to his wife. "He's right. My little girl has changed. All the loss and heartbreak has corrupted her. It has corrupted her soul. If she continues on this path, she won't be allowed into Enlightenment when it is her time. The one thing that has kept me from going crazy is the thought that someday I will be able to spend eternity with my family. My *entire* family, including my little girl. But what if she isn't allowed here Maddy? What will I do? What *can* I do? I feel so powerless."

Maddy leaned over and gave her husband a light kiss on his spiritual lips. She then whispered, "You *aren't* powerless. You know *exactly* what to do. She loves you more than *anyone*. You two have a special connection. A special bond. You will know *exactly* how to reach her. Now, let's be quiet. And when Arima calls out to me, pretend that we haven't been in her this entire time. Just be cool, okay? I don't want her to rescind her invitation to use her soul as my Earthly B & B whenever I want."

The room fell into a chilled silence. Even Larry had stopped his annoying whining. Josie's face turned bright red, then softened. Her cheeks returned to their normal light pink as she said in a controlled cadence, "Thank you for your observations, Rod. Now, would you all please complete your assignments? I feel the need to be alone at the moment. Thank you. Thank you for your time tonight. I will see you all in the morning. And Arima? Please say 'Hi' to my mother for me. That will be all."

The entire group left the room in silence. Josie watched them depart. The moment the metal door was shut, she fell to her knees and began sobbing. "Oh, my lord, what have I *become*? How could I *treat* them like that? I have always been a person that attracted others to me. Now I'm the person that is driving them away. They can't stand to be around me. And I can't blame them. They are right. I've become a total bitch. And Lionnel…oh my God how I miss you. You were my rock. And I drove you away. I stopped listening to you. I ignored you. I belittled you. I took your love for me for granted. I thought that you'd always be by my side. And now you're not. Because you couldn't put up with my shit any longer and I can't blame you for that. I have to prove myself to you. I have to get you back. But to do that, I have to find *my* way back. Back to the person that I was. But *how*? Is it too late? Am I *already* too corrupted? Dad, if you can hear me, can you help? I'm so lost, and I miss you so much. I think losing you again was the final straw. You were the one who was always able to show me the way. And now you're gone. And now, I'm lost. I feel so powerless. I just wish you could hear me. I need my father right now."

The lights in the party room suddenly shut off. Josie immediately wiped the tears from her eyes and looked around in the darkness. She tightened her muscles and prepared herself for battle. She stood up in the middle of the dance floor and waited for the impending attack.

The dance lights began flickering above her curly, copper mop. The speakers began to buzz. Josie listened intently then began to laugh and twirl. She began to laugh and twirl to the song that her father used to play for her as a child. She remembered squealing with joy as her father would lift her up and spin her around the dance floor. She remembered her flowered dress floating in the breeze as she giggled in her loving father's arms. She remembered the feeling of pure joy and peace as they danced to The Fifth Dimension's, "Aquarius."

Josie began swaying to her father's music. She then felt fur rubbing around her ankles. Her cats that she had brought home from the estate, Mika, Mike, Peter, and Bill were purring and mewing up at her. Josie fell to the floor and allowed herself to be bombarded by their feline love. She rolled on the floor with her kitty friends and laughed. And squealed. And cried tears of pure joy. The fever had been broken. Josie was with her father. Josie was with her pussy-cats. Josie had found her way back home. And Josie's heart was once again at peace.

Chapter 101

Roadrunner

"Oh, Master! I have exciting news!" Gobbo announced joyfully as his frail, bent body sprung into Vetis's inner chamber. Vetis was sitting on his throne, twiddling his four thumbs while watching one of his remaining screaming dark souls melt away into a vat of acid. "Yes, what is it Gobbo?" He asked in a bored tone.

"I believe that I have done it, Master!" Gobbo answered with delight. "I believe that I have found a pair of assassins on 2042 Earth that can eliminate your young interlopers. They are quite skilled. They are preparing for the assassination now. They have just received a shipment from the *ACME* company and are assembling the parts as we speak!"

Vetis lifted his dark red horned head up and looked at Gobbo with hopeful eyes. "*Really?* And you think that these two can pull it off? Oh, how *wonderful* that would be. I'm so bored just waiting around for my chance to go back into time and corrupt another soul so that we can have two parallel movements to conquer the Earth and Enlightenment. I really haven't been myself since our last failure. Even the screams of these boiling souls don't cheer me up anymore.

"Yes, I could really use some good news to lift me out of this funk. I wish that I could go there myself and take care of those little bastards. I wish that I could stand my nine-foot frame in front of them and take each of them into one of my hands and squeeze them until their little fucking heads pop off! Then, I would suck their blood and absorb their souls. Oh, how I *wish* that I could do that. But I can't. I can't expose my true physical form on Earth. I would then be vulnerable to an attack from all those fucking goodie-goodies on Earth. They would all converge upon me and rip me apart and destroy me. And wouldn't they all just enjoy *that*? Destroying *me* so that *they* can live in peace throughout eternity. Those pussy fuckers. They're no fun.

"No, all I can do is whisper into the souls of mortals. I can whisper to them and turn their souls black. Then, I can direct them to do my bidding. It was wise of me to not expose all my Earthly followers during this last battle. It was wise to leave them lurking in the shadows to await my next orders. And it was wise of me to install many of them as diplomats at the United Nations. Now, we will at least know what the mortals know and what they are planning.

"But those kids…those fucking kids. Somehow, they know what my plans are. Somehow, they know who I am going to corrupt and when on the timeline that I will arrive. Then, they simply arrive a little bit before me and take out my target. Who the fuck *are* they and where did they *come* from? Oh, I am quite aware of who they are. But *how*? Who *called* for them? I guess it doesn't matter. All that matters is that they are here disrupting my plans and that makes me sad. I hate those little fuckers. Come Gobbo! Let's watch your assassins at work. If I can't destroy the little fuckers myself, I at least can get some pleasure out of watching their cute little bodies blow up. Then, it will be time to corrupt our next soul. And then, my loyal Gobbo, let the fucking fireworks start."

"I *told* you I felt something!" Sigourney declared arrogantly to her twin sister and twin cousins who were watching from their perch on a high ravine. A pair of men were working beneath them. One man was connecting wires to a detonator behind a large boulder. The other was digging a hole in the middle of the gravel road. "And *once again*, I was right. But we have to travel down this road to get to the time portal. And those men seem to be burying a bomb in the middle of the road. I bet they're going to blow us up when we cross that spot. What shall we do?"

"I haf a iea!" Thanatos blurted out.

"What?" Euna asked. "Would you *please* take that giant wad of gum out of your mouth so that we can understand what you're saying?"

Thanatos reached into his mouth and pulled out a giant saliva covered ball of gum. "Here, Snot. You chew on this awhile," he said as he placed the gum into the awaiting mouth of his light green colored Shetland. "I said, I have an idea! Come on! Let's go back to the house. This shouldn't take long. Then, when we return, here's what we'll do."

Kane and Euna began giggling as they listened to the plan. "Oh! that sounds like fun!" Euna declared. "Oh yes! What a fun game we shall play with them! And that will be quite easy for me to build! But we had better be careful not to soil our new white western outfits. Our parents will be cross with us," Kane contributed before the Junior Quad turned their respective ponies around and trotted back to the stables.

"Hello sirs," Euna and Sigourney innocently said as they sat astride their Shetland ponies in front of the pair of sweaty, rugged-looking men who had just completed their work. "What are you doing? Can we be of assistance to you?" The pair of twin sisters smiled sweetly and awaited the desired response.

"Huh, there's two of them now," one of the men said to the other out of the side of his mouth. "This might be easier than we thought. Let's take out these two right now, then we'll find the boys."

The other man smiled and nodded before looking up into the brown and blue eyes of the children and saying, "Well, hello there children. Yes, you *can* help us. How about you two just get down off your ponies and come over here. We got some *candy* for you."

Euna watched as the man attempted to stealthily retrieve a hunting knife from his leather bag. She then turned to her sister and quietly said, "Hmmmph. *That* isn't candy. They aren't very honest. Good thing Thanatos isn't here. He'd probably fall for that."

Sigourney nodded at her sister before turning her attention back to the grinning pair of men. "Oh, that sounds fun! We love candy! But first, let's play a game. Now, what should we play? Oh! I know! Let's play tag! You're it!"

Sigourney and Euna lightly tapped their heels into the ribs of Snowball and Blackjack and the Shetlands dutifully burst into a sprint.

"Goddammit! They're getting away!" One of the men shouted. "You chase one with the jeep! I'll chase the other on the motorcycle! We'll divide and conquer these two little bitches!"

Euna and Sigourney heard the roar of approaching engines from behind them. They gave one another a knowing nod and smile and split off from one another. Dust was flying from underneath Snowball's hooves and the tires of the motorcycle. Sigourney was laughing with glee as she would allow the motorcycle to nearly catch up to her, then would abruptly turn in another direction. She laughed louder as she would hear her pursuer yelling foul names at her and shake his fist before turning his machine around and re-engaging in the chase. Sigourney, Snowball, and the motorcycle snaked their way across a vast field of dead brush. The motorcycle inched closer to Snowball's pounding hoofs. The man flashed an evil smile and accelerated one final time to ram the galloping pony. The motorcycle was three inches from the Shetland and its giggling, white-fringed rider when Snowball suddenly turned left.

The motorcycle drove off a steep cliff. It hung suspended in the air for a moment. The man looked directly into the eyes of the reader and sorrowfully waved good-bye before plummeting to his death. There was an incredible fireball that exploded from the bottom of the ravine and the giggling twin sisters sat astride their ponies looking down at the carnage.

"Nice job," Euna said. "I hid in the woods and mine got bored and gave up just like we planned. C'mon. Let's meet up with the boys and get to the time portal. We have more games to play."

"Where the fuck is he?" the man muttered to himself as he crouched on a wooden crate that he was using as a make-shift stool. "Maybe that other one hid too and he's still looking for her." The man got up and peered around the large boulder. "Well, looks like he's gonna miss out on the fun," he said as he smiled at the four approaching riders. The man tiptoed, for some unexplained reason, around the boulder and sat back down on his crate. His sweaty hands clutched the plunger of the detonator. His heart pounded with anticipation as he heard the 'clopping' of the approaching hooves. The sound became increasingly louder. He smiled to himself and pushed down on the plunger with all his force. He heard a light clicking sound coming from under his posterior. He then heard one of the passing boys say, "Oh, I put it under his wooden crate." The man's long, beleaguered face stared blankly ahead just before the bomb that he was sitting on exploded.

The children screamed with glee as they were showered with blood, internal organs, bone, and limbs. "Oh Kane, that was great! And what a great idea Thanatos!" Sigourney exclaimed.

"Oh, it was easy, "Kane replied as Flame trotted along. "It was a really easy bomb to build. I found the instructions in one of Aunt Lucy's trunks. So, while you two were distracting them, Thanatos and I just disconnected the bomb that they had planted in the ground and connected it to the one that I put under the crate. That was fun! But not as fun as this is going to be! Look everyone! Here come the beautiful swirling colors!"

———

"Nice job, dipshit!" Vetis roared as he backhanded Gobbo into a wall of flames. The screaming Gobbo got up and began furiously beating out the fire that had consumed him. Smoke billowed from off his ashen skin as he looked toward the floor and said regretfully, "I'm sorry master. I was so sure. But perhaps it is not too late to corrupt our targeted soul. And he will be so easy. He has already been corrupted by one of your previous minions. And he is scheduled to die long before our battle is to commence. He will be the perfect addition to your movement. Please, Master. Don't be glum. Let's go corrupt this soul."

"Oh, I suppose," a disappointed Vetis replied. "Where and when is he?"

———

"Lil' Red, this is Soul Sister. Please come in, Lil' Red." Arima was stating as her ebony frame hovered in the living room of the estate.

"Shhhhhhhh, give it a moment," Maddy whispered to her husband who was silently hiding with her in Arima's soul. "We don't want her know that we're already here or that we already know what's going on."

"Lil' Red, this is Soul Sister. We have another JQ situation. Please come in," Arima stated again as the frantic eyes of Adam, Aaron, Kayla, and Rachel looked on. Their children had explained to them that they would be going away on missions. The distraught parents knew that these missions would take their children into the past. But that knowledge did little to assuage their deep worry. Their children were gifted and formidable. But to them, they were still just children who were capable of being harmed. Kayla and Rachel sobbed on the white-coated shoulders of their respective husbands as they anxiously awaited Maddy's response.

"And *this* t-t-time, s-s-she had b-better not be a b-*bitch* about it," Kayla stammered as tears flowed from her mahogany eyes.

"What the *fuck*, man?" Maddy whispered to her husband. "*I'm* the one that's their connection in Enlightenment. *I'm* the one who sent Uncle Joe to go *get* their little brats. And *this* is the thanks I get? Fuck this."

Erick gave his wife a look. It was a look that she was familiar with. It was the look that her beloved husband would give her when he was unable to say, *Maddy, I love you. But calm the fuck down. You are once again overreacting. Get your emotions under control and listen to the situation. And don't be overly judgmental. These people have come to you for your help. And you will give it to them. And you will be gracious about it. Got it?*

All of that was said by just one brief look, so Maddy replied, "Yeah, yeah, yeah, I got it. Okay. Let's go. Hey there Soul Sister! This is Lil' Red at your service! Over and out! Wazzup? Over and out!"

There was a sigh of relief from the group in the living room as they heard Maddy's voice emitting through Arima. "Uh, yeah, hi Madd...um...I mean Lil' Red. So, the JQ's kinda missing again and we were wondering if Uncle Joe had taught you how to go back in time and get them yet? Or if there's someone else that could go? I understand that after something like that, that you spirits are really drained, so Uncle Joe probably isn't available. But could maybe you or Erick or somebody go pick them up and bring them home? Oh, and again, you don't have to yell or say, 'over and out' after every sentence, okay?"

"Roger that! Over and out!" Maddy yelled back as her husband silently shook his head in bewilderment. "Hey everybody! Nice to talk to ya again! Over and out! I'm gonna get Erick so he can hear too, okay? Over and out! Erick, come here and listen to this!"

"Oh, hey everybody," Erick greeted awkwardly. "I just got here. I haven't been listening in at *all*. What's going *on*? *I* don't have a *clue*."

Maddy looked at her husband and mouthed, *what the fuck are you doing?* Erick could only shrug back in response.

"Hey, Erick, nice to talk to you," Arima replied. "So, as I was just telling Maddy, um, I mean Lil' Red, the JQ has gone back in time again on one of their missions and the twins and the Twins are really upset. Rosa and Jessie have found them. So, do you guys think someone could go back in time and get them?"

There was silence. Erick looked at his wife. They both knew that their response would have to be delicate. They both knew that Maddy could not fuck this up. Erick took no chances and replied before his wife. "Um, hey, we still haven't been trained on that, so we won't be of any help. And Joe's still pretty tuckered out from the last time, so..."

Erick was cut off by his wife. "Uncle Joe is *what*? *Tuckered out*? Who the fuck talks like that, man?" She then said with a contrived sweetness, "Oh, your little *darlings* are *missing* again? Well, *of course* we would be *delighted* to help you. We know just how *precious* those little *miracles* are and we will do *everything* we can to bring them back home safely, *won't* we baby?"

"Maddy, let me handle this, please," a frustrated Erick replied. "As I was saying, we don't know how to do that yet and would probably do more harm than good. And Joe isn't an option because he's *tuckered out*. But I think that Blair and Patty could do it. I'll do all the paperwork and submit it to Gwen then go talk to them. I'm sure that they will be happy to help, okay?"

"Yes, thank you Erick," Adam stated followed by Aaron's, "Yes, thank you. You are much more civil with us than Aunt Maddy. Thank you."

"Yeah, fuckin' whatevs," Maddy replied in disgust. "We'll go find someone to help your fuckin' brats. Let's go Erick. Over and out!"

CHAPTER 102

PRECIOUS LITTLE MIRACLES

"What the *fuck* do you want?" Patty yelled out. "I've got my face buried in my wife's snatch! Then we're going to conjure up some old *Warner Brothers* cartoons and eat potato chips! Come back in an hour, or whatever the fuck an hour is up here! Now, go away! Damn. Angel pussy tastes good…like cotton candy…mmmmmmmmm."

"Patty, my dear sister," Blair answered calmly from outside the door of the conjured bedroom. "I am truly sorry to disturb you dear, but we are needed on Earth for a bit. So please wipe your mouth, get dressed, and come out."

Blair heard Patty's wife, Jacklyn, say, "It's okay, lover. We have an eternity together. Just go see what your sister wants." Blair then heard a grunt of disgust followed by her sister's booming, irritated voice. "Fine! But this had better be fuckin' important!"

Jacklyn covered her naked frame with conjured blankets as Patty threw open the bedroom door. "Alright Blair," Patty stated as she stood in the doorway wearing a sheer black robe. "You got me. What's so fuckin' important?"

"Well," the raven-haired Blair began in her customary cool

tone. "It seems as though the JQ have once again traveled through time to assassinate one of Vetis's targets for manipulation. And we have been tasked with finding them and bringing them back to their distraught parents. So please, Patty, put on something more appropriate. I don't think that you want the children to see you dressed like this."

"Alright Blair," Patty responded. "But I have a few questions first before I leave my little revved-up piece. First, why the fuck can't *Joe* go get them?"

"Because, my dear," Blair began to calmly explain, "these little adventures are quite taxing on us. Joseph just completed a mission, and he is too fatigued at the moment."

"Oh yeah?" Patty retorted. "Well, what about Maddy or her pussy husband? Why can't *they* go do it?"

"Because," Blair once again began explaining, "Maddy and Erick have not been in Enlightenment long enough. They do not yet possess the knowledge or spiritual energy required for this."

"Well, if the little fuckers can travel through time," Patty resisted, "Why can't they just find their way back when they're done doing whatever fucked up shit that they're doing? Why does *anyone* have to go get them?"

"That *is* a good question," Blair answered. "They *can* find their way back. They can travel to their destination, take care of their business, and find their way back home. But they are children. And children can become distracted or find other forms of trouble that they may not be prepared for. They are quite powerful, but we do not yet know just *how* powerful or what they might be vulnerable to. Plus, their parents are quite worried about them, just as any parent would be. They just want to know that their children are safe. Do you remember when Maddy disappeared in the year 2000 when she was twelve?"

"Yeah, I remember that," Patty answered sentimentally. "Man, was she pissed about that election. All she could talk about was having to do something about those fucking hanging chads on the Floria ballots. She just kept asking how something as insignificant as a little piece of paper could cause such significant damage. Her little mind was blown by it. She was *obsessed* by that shit."

"Yes, she was," Blair replied. "She stewed on that for hours that night, then she just disappeared. And although we knew your niece and our spiritual daughter was quite formidable, even at *that* age, we still worried about her whereabouts, didn't we?"

"Yeah," Patty conceded. "I don't think I've *ever* been so worried about someone. You called me up and said that you and Joe couldn't find her anywhere. I rushed over and we searched the entire house again. Then the neighborhood. Hell, we even called Detective Simmons to put an APB out on her. Yeah, I remember how frantic we were that night. I guess I can understand what the twins and the Twins are feeling. Alright Blair. Let's go get the little bastards. But I'm sure they're fine. Just like Maddy was. We finally found her in the one place that we had forgotten to look. In the crawlspace behind her bedroom wall. All curled up and sleeping with her blue baby blanket."

"Yes," Blair added. "And a butcher knife. If that wasn't foreshadowing, I don't know what is. She was desperately clinging to the innocence of her youth while embracing what would be her quite violent future. That moment was her crossroads and she looked so sweet and dangerous at the same time. She, Patty, was our precious little miracle. Just as the JQ are precious little miracles. Now, let's summon Gwen so that she can track them and lead us to their exact location."

"Yeah, let's go see what kind of carnage these *precious little miracles* have caused," Patty replied before asking, "just where and when are we going anyway?"

Blair looked into the blue eyes of her sister and said, "We

are going to the outskirts of Phoenix, Arizona. March 29, 1972."

———

There was a brilliant flash of light followed by a dense, red fog in the middle of the Arizona desert. The skyline of downtown Phoenix was barely visible on the vast horizon. Four tan-skinned children wearing all-white western costumes emerged from the dense crimson mist riding their respective Shetland ponies.

"There's a new sheriff in town, heh, heh, heh," Sigourney stated before being interrupted by her sister, Euna. "No, like this! There's a *new* sheriff in town, heh, heh, heh."

"Neither one of you two are doing it right!" Kane yelled out to his identical twin cousins. "We have to get this right. Just think about how Aunt Maddy told us *she* said it after their battle on Highway 61. Just think about that night that Aunt Maddy came into our dreams and told us that bedtime story. It was like this. There's a new *sheriff* in town, heh, heh, heh. See? Then it'll be funny!"

"I don't think *that's* quite right either," a contemplating Sigourney replied. "Thanatos, what do *you* think? Thanatos? Hey, where the hell is he? Oh, dammit."

The trio stopped and looked behind them. Twenty yards to their rear was Thanatos. He was excitedly rushing from cactus to cactus and placing them in his mouth before yelling out, "Ow! That one doesn't taste good *either*! Ow! Nope, not *that* one. How about *this* one? Ow!"

"Thanatos!" Sigourney yelled out. "Stop putting stuff in your mouth and get back here. We're rehearsing what we're going to say to this guy when he opens the door. We must rehearse so that it'll be really funny! And we're almost up to his shack!"

"Okay," Thanatos replied as he reluctantly climbed onto

the back of Snot and rejoined his male twin sibling and twin female cousins. "I don't know why you girls are rehearsing anyway. Only Kane and I can say that. Girls can't be a sheriff."

"What?" Sigourney and Euna roared back in unison. "What the hell are you *talking* about? Girls can do just *as much*, if not *more*, than boys!"

"No, you can't," Kane replied. "Girls can't be cow*boys* now, can you? You can only be cow*girls*. And cow*girls* are supposed to do stuff for the cow*boys*. You know, like do our laundry and cook for us and clean our bedroom. Stuff like that. And a cow*girl* certainly cannot be a sheriff. That is what we have learned."

Sigourney and Euna seethed before Euna bellowed out, "Just where in the hell did you learn *that*? It's 2042! Girls can do *anything* that boys can do! Anything! Including sheriff! And not only *that*, but the two of *you* can do *our* laundry and cook for *us* and clean *our* bedroom! Just like Uncle Lionnel does for Aunt Josie!

"Nope," Thanatos added. "That's not how it works. We've been watching old cow*boy* movies. And *those* things are true! And the cow*boy* is *always* the sheriff, and the cow*girl* is *always* doing the cleaning and getting the cow*boy* drinks. That's a fact!"

Euna's blue and brown eyes began glowing with rage. She shook her white, shoulder-length locks, composed herself and said, "We'll deal with this later. We're coming up to this guy's shack. Let's get off our ponies here and walk up and look in the windows. I want to see the layout before we knock on the door."

The Junior Quad were quietly giggling as they stealthily climbed onto the front porch and peered through the dusty windowpane. They held their hands over their delighted little mouths to stifle their laughter as they watched the man inside the run-down hovel.

"I *told* you, you were a fuckin' idiot Charlie!" the scruffy, skinny man was yelling at a small black and white television set with bent rabbit ears. "I *knew* I was right to get away from your fuckin' cult when I did! Murdering Hollywood stars ain't *no way* to start this race war! You gotta be more *subtle* about it. And that's just what I'm gonna do! I'm gonna get my *own* followers! Then we'll infiltrate the police. Have them plant shit on the Black Panthers. Have them go around and murder ordinary White families and pin it on the Panthers. In small town after small town, we'll get the sheriffs there on our side. We'll elect like-minded people to the city councils. Then, we'll just take out a few families, blame the Panthers, and White folks all over the country will rise up against those fuckin' (derogatory term omitted). It'll start in the small towns, then move to the big cities. There's gonna be Black blood running in the streets. Then, we'll come for the (derogatory term omitted) and the (derogatory term omitted) and the (derogatory term omitted). All I need to get started is for somebody to show me the way. Whisper in my ear. I've heard of a demon named Vetis. I'm gonna pray to him. Pray that he can show me the way. Then, I'll begin building my army. My army of cops and crooked politicians and egotistical media types. Then, my army of ordinary White folks who will be so brainwashed that they'll take to the streets and start killin' every (derogatory term omitted) that they see!

"Yep, that's how I'm gonna do it. Then, I'll be powerful. I'll have the money I deserve and the hippie pussy that I deserve. And I won't be sittin' on death row like *you've* just been sentenced to! Yep, you're gonna fry Charlie boy. Not because your ideas were bad. But because you were stupid. So, here's to you Charlie! Here's to giving me the right idea! And here's to you for teaching me the wrong way to go about it!"

The man held up a bottle of whiskey and took a big swig just before he heard a light rapping on his rotting wooden door.

"Now who the fuck can *that* be?" he asked himself as he

stomped toward the door. He pulled it open and looked around. He saw nothing until he heard giggling coming from below him. He looked down and saw a quartet of snickering tan children dressed in outlandish white, fringed cowboy and cowgirl outfits. He stood confused as he listened to the children bicker amongst themselves.

"*I* want to say it!" Sigourney cried out before being interrupted by Kane. "No, we already *told* you. Cow*girls can't* say it! *I'm* gonna say it!" Thanatos pulled a cactus from the side of the porch and put it in his mouth. He then said. "Ow! No, *I'm* gonna say it with my brother! Only cow*boys* can say it!"

"What the hell are you freaky kids talkin' about?" the man said in disgust. "Say *what*? And what the fuck are you doin' here? Get back to your reservation or wherever you belong and leave me alone!"

The four children stopped their arguing, looked up at the man and said in unison with their innocent voices, "There's a new sheriff in town, heh, heh, heh."

"That wasn't right," Sigourney lamented. "That wasn't *nearly* as funny as when Aunt Maddy said it. Who is a *girl* by the way!"

"Aunt Maddy was probably just confused," Kane stated bluntly. "And it wasn't right because *you two* said it! And cow*girls* don't know how to say it because cow*girls* can't be a sheriff!"

"Oh, just stop your bickering and let's do this," Euna said as she pulled a knife from her holster and split the man's abdomen open. The man let out a tortured scream as he fell to his knees and felt his intestines begin to tumble out of his body, sploshing onto the wooden porch. Thanatos took the cactus he was holding and shoved it into the man's open mouth. Kane then took a rope and tied it firmly around the man's head and chin to secure the spiked cactus in place.

Sigourney looked at the slimy intestines laying upon the ground and said to her sister, "Hey. I think I've got an idea."

"Well, *this* is a fuckin' mess!" Patty bellowed out as her black leather-clad form appeared next to the shack.

"Yes," a bell-bottomed, T-shirt wearing Blair agreed. "I believe that we have found them. But what on God's green Earth are they doing?"

Blair and Patty walked to the front of the shack and saw a man attempting to scream out of his punctured, bloody mouth. He was lying on his back on the ground and his intestines had been pulled from his cavity. Blair and Patty's eyes followed the trail of slimy entrails until they fell upon a delightfully disgusting sight. Euna was on top of Kane who was laying on his belly and had been hog-tied by the grotesque, rancid smelling intestines. Sigourney was in the same position over the similarly situated Thanatos. The twin girls were yelling at their male cousins.

"Say it, Kane!" Euna was screaming as her sister echoed, "Yes! Say it Thanatos!"

"No, we *won't* say it! It isn't *true!*" Kane and Thanatos responded.

"Then we're going to tighten these intestines until you say it!" Euna threatened. "And it's going to hurt!"

"We *won't* say it!" Kane yelled back. "And we're going to tell our parents! You're going to be in trouble!"

"We don't care!" Sigourney screamed. "Just say it so we can go home!"

"So, what is all this then, dears?" Blair asked.

"Hi Aunt Blair! Hi Aunt Patty!" the foursome replied in their sweet voices before Sigourney began explaining. "You see, Aunties, Kane and Thanatos said that cowgirls can't be sheriffs just because we're girls. So, we tied them up with these intestines and are holding them down until they say that we *can* be sheriffs."

"Why, you sexist little pricks," Patty blurted out before Blair held up a single index finger to silence her sister. "Please Patty, let me handle this." Blair had to turn away for a moment to hide her chuckle from the children before beginning. "I see. Well, it seems to me that those are some very outdated ideas, boys. You see, girls are just as capable as boys are. Perhaps more so. There are no roles that are exclusively male or female. Men can be whatever they wish and so can women. And that goes for little girls as well. And that includes being a sheriff."

"No! That can't be true Aunt Blair!" the resistant Thanatos yelled out. "That's not what the cowboy movies taught us! Cowgirls can't be a sheriff so they can't say that they're the new sheriff in town! That's just how it is, and I won't say that they can!"

"Well, I suppose that we're in for a long wait then," Blair replied calmly. She then knelt in front of the struggling Thanatos and lifted his head until his obstinate eyes met hers. Blair lowered her voice and said coldly, "Because these two girls are going to sit on you and tighten those intestines until your little arms break. That is, unless you say that girls can be sheriff. And I believe that Patty and I may have a little chat with your parents once you are home."

Thanatos gulped hard and looked over to his twin brother. They nodded at one another then said meekly, "Girls can be sheriff."

Ten minutes (Earth time) later there was another brilliant flash of light and the demonic spirits of Vetis and Gobbo peered down at the horrific scene. Gobbo began trembling as he looked at the frozen fearful face of the fresh corpse that was being torn apart and eaten by ravenous vultures. A despondent Vetis sighed deeply and said, "Y'know. Those fuckin' kids are *really* starting to piss me off."

Following another joyful family reunion and parental consultation with Patty and Blair, Euna and Sigourney were sitting on the couch in their pajamas watching *Stan vs. Evil*. "See?" Sigourney shouted out to a long-faced Kane who was coming downstairs with a loaded laundry basket. "*This* show is on TV and *this* show has a *girl* sheriff. So there."

Euna then barked out, "Thanatos! Where are our grilled cheese sammiches?"

"Coming right up!" an apron wearing Thanatos answered. He entered the living room of the estate and presented his cousins with two plates containing jellybeans, popcorn, pretzels, and… two half-eaten grilled cheese sandwiches.

CHAPTER 103

POSITIVE BLEEDING

"How about this?' a pink-robed Jessie West excitedly asked her best friends Arima Azan and Jamie Johnson.

"Oh sweetie," Jamie responded while shaking her thick afro in disapproval. "That would be fine for a slutty New Year's party, but for the United Nations? I think you may want to tone it down a bit."

"Yeah, you're probably right," the bubbly influencer replied. "Okay, how about this?"

"Jess," Arima answered casually. "That looks just like the last one, but without the sequins. Here, let me look. I'll find you something."

Arima lazily rolled off the bed, strolled over to the closet and began digging around. "Here, try this one on."

Jessie and Jamie burst out laughing at the suggestion. "Oh, my lord!" Jamie yelled out through her chortles. "A jogging suit? For the United Nations? Ladies, please get out of my way. I know that I've only had my official lady parts for a few weeks, but whether I had a cock or a cooch, I've always known how to dress for success. Now, let's see here. What to wear to make a good impression at the United Nations.

Hmmmmm. Oh, yes. Come to Momma. I'm going to have to borrow this from you dear."

Jessie and Arima could only smile and nod in approval as they looked upon the grey, pinstriped business suit with a smart white shirt and wide, black tie. Jessie enthusiastically grabbed the outfit from her friend's grasp and skipped to the bathroom.

Cliff West's jaw dropped as he saw his beautiful blonde wife strut into the living room in her form-fitting suit and four-inch black pumps. Arima plopped onto the couch next to her husband, Marcus Jefferson. They giggled at each other and proceeded to rip open a bag of corn chips. "Good, we're all here," Chadwick Gregory Davenport III, who had been advised many years earlier to go by 'Gregory' within this group, began.

He got up from his seat next to his loving wife, Rosa Alavarez, and turned to face this motley crew of a delegation. "Okay folks. We knew this day would come. We knew that the forces of evil would rear their dark heads once again and that we would have to report what we know to the United Nations. I just didn't think that it would be this soon after our incredible victory over the demonic forces of Vetis both on Earth and in Enlightenment. Enlightenment seems to be at peace and unthreatened at the moment. That isn't true here on Earth. Vetis is not going to give up. His ego won't allow it. He can't stand losing and he can't just be happy lording over his own little slice of hell in the universe. His ego has been bruised, so he will keep trying. And every time he tries, there's definitely a chance that he will succeed.

"He is now going back through time, searching for a new Earthly messiah that he can groom. A new man who was destined to die before 2016 but will now stay alive to lead a parallel movement to the one that we just defeated. Yes, my friends, we may have defeated him in the present, but he has the power to go back into time and *alter* our present. And our future. Everything that we have accomplished may be undone if he is successful.

"The Junior Quad can somehow sense when he has selected such a person, and they can go back into time and kill his target before he gets there. But we do not know if they will be capable of doing this every time. Just one mistake made by these children, and all could be lost. And he can do this for eternity. Hundreds, thousands of times. Until he finally achieves his goal. The only solution is the destruction of Vetis himself and *that* we have no idea how to do. All we can do is hope that the JQ can continue to be successful against him while we take out the small pockets of the waiting, reconstituted United Autocratic Movement in our present time. All that we can do is fight battle after battle and tread water until we figure out a way to destroy Vetis.

"We are going to the United Nations today to give them our report. That was our deal with them. All the nations of the world will support us in our endeavors as best they can, but only if we are completely transparent with them. They want to know what we are doing and why we are doing it. We must give them this report today and ask for their support to continue the battle. But I sense there might be a problem."

"Yeah," Cliff chimed in. "We're getting a funny feeling about thi…"

Cliff was abruptly cut off by his wife. "Cliff! Don't interrupt Gregory. That was rude! Now go get me a glass of wine. I need to calm my nerves after the stress of picking out this outfit."

"Um, yeah, okay, okay," Cliff stammered as Jamie and Arima rolled their eyes and made vomiting faces at each other.

"Yeah, man," Marcus then stated partially to contribute to the conversation and partially to support his spineless friend. "You see, we have actually got a meeting with the entire United Nations. Like, everybody, man. But we have been told not to bring any security with us. And that makes us nervous.

So, that's why you ladies are here. Jess, you can Behold if there are any purely evil souls there. Then, Rosa, Arima, Jamie, and we dudes can do what we need to do. It's just a little strange that we can't take security and we want to be cautious."

"Correct," Cliff agreed as he handed his wife her wine. "Cliff! Now you're interrupting Marcus? When did you get to be so rude?" Jessie admonished.

"Um, sorry," the beaten-down Cliff responded as his head dipped to the floor.

Gregory looked at his emasculated friend, shook his head slightly and continued. "Yes, that is correct. So, Jessie, you will let me know if you sense pure evil and from whom in the chamber. I will then give the report that I feel is…um…appropriate for the moment. Then, we'll report back to Josie, and she can give us our orders from there. Got it?"

"Cool," Jessie replied. "It seems as though *I'm* the most important one in this little grou…"

Jessie was cut off by the ever-diplomatic Gregory. "And Cliff, you have the *most* important role of all today. You are to keep your lovely Beholder safe. *You* are the key to this mission's success. Okay folks. The car should be here at any moment. Let's get ready."

Gregory fronted his entourage of Arima, Marcus, Jamie, and Rosa, with Jessie and Cliff to his immediate left and right. They entered the vast United Nations auditorium and Jessie immediately buckled over and dropped the note cards that she was holding. "Oh, sweet Jesus," she whispered to her attending husband. "There is a *lot* of evil here."

"Just say it, Jess. Say it and make the pain go away," a concerned Cliff quietly responded.

As UN security personnel rapidly approached the pained Jessie, she whispered to herself, "Malum tuum dolorem facit. et dolor meus es fortitudo mea. (*Your evil causes pain. my pain is my strength*)."

"Is everything alright here, miss?" one of the security

personnel inquired as he was reaching for his gun. Jessie's blonde head popped up as she righted herself. Her brilliant blue eyes were glistening in the bright white light of the auditorium as she said, "Yes. Just fine. In fact..." her voice trailed off as she gave Gregory a knowing glance. "In fact, I've *never* felt stronger. I just...um...dropped my note cards. I've been instructed to um...take notes during the proceeding."

"Very well then," the security guard replied as he and the rest of the security contingent returned to their normal posts. Gregory was introduced by the Secretary of the United Nations. He cleared his throat and approached the podium. Jessie laid the notecards in front of the microphone. On them, she had written the twenty-three names of the traitorous diplomats who were in the chamber.

Gregory looked down at the cards briefly, gave Jessie a slight smile of approval and began his presentation. Just before he began speaking, he decided to present option B. "Hello esteemed dignitaries from around the world. Thank you so much for this opportunity to speak with the entire assembly. I promise not to take up too much of your valuable time, but it has been a little over a month since our glorious victory over the forces of the demonic Vetis, and we promised to keep this body updated as to the status of his threat against us. And I am very pleased to report that...everything is fine. We have not detected any threat from Vetis himself. As we all know, there will always be evil in the world. But our current assessment is that Vetis is not currently engaged in any interference here on Earth. There remain pockets of his followers, but they are currently small and pose no threat to the people or great nations of the world. Our newfound humanity and mutual cooperation are beginning to reap rewards. In every nation on the planet, we are seeing people's lives improving. This is due to our sharing of resources. The sharing of technology. Medicine. Intelligence. Agricultural techniques. Conservation of our natural resources. The list goes on and on. And this sharing is no longer dependent upon past bigoted views of those who are different from ourselves. We no longer hate one another in large numbers. We no longer harbor the desire to eliminate those that we fear. Because we no longer *fear* one another. Because the vast majority of the demonic forces that were sowing this fear, then hatred, then violence amongst us have been neutralized. Yes, my friends, it is truly a glorious time to live upon this Earth. So, I am most happy to report that all is well. We will, of course, keep this body updated and will notify you should we need to take any action. But no action is required at this time. Thank you for your time and to your selfless contributions to mankind."

Gregory could not help but notice that the first dignitaries to stand for the ovation were the twenty-three names that Jessie had written on the notecards. Gregory smiled and waved goodbye as he thought, *Good. The remaining servants of Vetis think that we're in the dark. The bad news? We're going to have to go this alone.*

The party entered the underground parking garage toward their awaiting car in silence. Cliff heard a light 'click' from behind a parked vehicle. The former high-school football star instinctively jumped in front of his unaware wife. Jessie's pin-striped business suit was covered in her husband's blood as a bullet ripped through his abdomen.

"Cliff!" Jessie cried out as five heavily armed, black-clad men emerged from behind numerous parked vehicles. Arima took a hit off her "killer weed" and began floating above the scene, awaiting the dark souls that would emerge from the soon-to-be-former-assassins. Rosa's eyes began glowing. She focused all her energy on two men who were pointing their weapons at her. Their guns exploded the moment that they depressed the trigger, sending shards of metal and bullets into their shocked faces.

Jessie kicked her high heels toward Jamie, who caught them, did a back flip, and planted the heels into the eyes of an assassin. "Eeeeewww!" Jamie exclaimed as she wiped eye pus from her recently enhanced bosom. An enraged Jessie then used her evil-enhanced strength to rush the final two assassins. She tackled them, stood above them, and began crushing their skulls with her bare feet. When she had finished, she looked down upon her perfectly pedicured toes standing in the chunky red, pink, and white remains.

Dark purple smog emanated from the five fallen bodies. Arima opened her soul and pulled them into her essence. She bound them within herself then floated out of the garage. Her journey ended over the glistening blue waters of the New York Harbor. "See ya, assholes," Arima said flatly as she hurled the dark souls into the serenity of Pastor Tim and Jeremy's watery home. The souls screamed in anguish and dissolved the moment they hit the calm waves.

"Cliff!" Jessie screamed out as she rushed to the side of her fallen husband. "He'll be okay!" Gregory yelled. "Marcus, get him in the car, then call Lionnel. I don't trust taking him to a hospital. Not now. We'll take him to the operating room under the bookstore. And we can't wait for Arima!"

"It's okay," Marcus replied as he lifted the body of his bleeding friend. "She can float back home. She's high as a kite right now. Literally."

"Soul Sister! This is Lil' Red! Come in, Soul Sister! Over and out!" Maddy yelled at her half-sister. "Oh, yeah, hey Madd…um…I mean Lil' Red. What's up?"

"Weeeellll," Maddy began. "I just saw that you took a hit off the killer weed *without* me and I'm feeling a little bit *left out*, that's all. I mean, I *know* I'm dead and everything but it's still nice to not be *forgotten*. But that's okay. I understand how *easy* it is to forget about me. Over and out."

"Oh yeah, sorry Lil' Red," Arima responded. "Here. I'll take another hit so you can have some too. Better?"

"Oooooooh yeah," Maddy cooly answered. "That's the stuff. Ooooover and oooout."

Jessie held the head of her bloodied husband and wept as their car sped toward the Brooklyn bookstore. She sat there in shocked disbelief and prayed. She prayed that they would make it to Lionnel on time. She prayed for Cliff to have a speedy and full recovery. And she vowed to the universe that if her prayers were answered that she would *never* take his love for her for granted ever again.

Josie was sitting behind the desk in her mother's eclectically designed office beneath the bookstore talking to Rod when Gregory entered the room.

"Oh, hey Gregory!" Josie enthusiastically stated. "How did the UN presentation go? Everybody cool with supporting us?"

"Well…" Gregory began. He then paused and noticed that as Rod was speaking with Josie, his eyes were firmly planted on…her eyes. Gregory felt slightly relieved as the pressure of knowing just which Josie he was speaking with dissipated. He then presented Josie and a relaxed Rod with the details, including the injury to Cliff.

"But I'm sure he'll be okay. Lionnel has him in the operating room next door. I think it'll be fine."

"Well, that's good news," Josie responded before saying, "Soooo, you say *Lionnel's* here? Cool. Cool. Yep. That's cool. I probably shouldn't bother him while he's operating. Just, y'know. If you *happen* to see him, *maybe* just tell him I said 'Hi.' Y'know. Or don't. It doesn't matter. It's all cool. Okay, so let's do *this*. Let's get Sam and Jules ready to take out that small group in Indiana. I know they're small, but I think we want to keep the pressure on these fuc…I mean these *people*. But let's do it quietly. Bloody, of course, but quietly. We don't want to tip the diplomats off that we're up to anything. Nope. Looks like we're going to have to go this alone. In the meantime, my brilliant friend Rod and I have been discussing some tests that we can run on the JQ. We think that if we hook some electrodes up to their little brains, and Rosa taps into their energy, we might be able to collect some information about just how much power they posses and whether they can destroy Vetis. Oh, and could one of you ask Alexa when she thinks her art show will be ready? I *might* just have an idea. Yup, sooooo that's the plan. So, you say *Lionnel's* here, huh? Well, *that* doesn't matter. He's so busy. Okay. I have some work to do with Larry, so thanks you two. I truly appreciate everything that you contribute."

Josie gave Rod a large hug followed by Gregory. As Josie was embracing him, Gregory whispered into her ear, "Glad to have you back, kid." Josie whispered back, "Thanks. I'm trying. It feels good to be myself again."

Josie watched her colleagues exit the room then turned her flowered dressed form towards Larry. His battered and lacerated body was sitting pathetically on his stumps with his neck chained to an anvil.

"Okay, Larry," Josie began. "I need to run my plan by somebody. Since you can't talk because we ripped out your tongue, just nod or shake your head if you think that this will work. Okay, here it goes. Man, I'm so nervous.

"JOSIE PARKER'S PLAN TO WIN LIONNEL BACK
BY JOSIE PARKER

Numero-Uno: Um, nope. Not gonna say that. My mother says that and since Lionnel thinks that I've become too much like my mother, I think I'll go in another direction. Let's start again.

"JOSIE PARKER'S PLAN TO WIN LIONNEL BACK
BY JOSIE PARKER

Step One: Heh, heh, heh. Yeah, that's better."

CHAPTER 104

CRUSH ON YOU

"Is it me, or does it seem as though Murder, Inc. is getting increasingly female-centric?" Henri inquired of Gregory and Marcus as they were putting on their all-black outfits for the evening's mission in the dense woods of central Indiana. "I mean, it's great that they're really powerful and independent and everything, but it's starting to make me feel a bit emasculated being no more than a chauffeur. I'm a trained sniper. I have more to offer than being a cab driver. And why do you need to even be there, Gregory? You don't like getting your hands dirty. They easily could have sent one of the hitmen... um... I mean *assassination technicians* to fill in while Cliff recuperates."

"Well," Gregory began explaining. "I have been called in because Josie likes to have her most trusted members of her inner circle to run point on these operations. And as far as this organization being female-centric...well...I guess that's just something that *all* of mankind, and I do mean *man*kind, is going to have to deal with. Females are evolving at a much more rapid pace. They are evolving to use a greater amount of their brain capacity than we are. And that, my friends, is giving women great powers. My Rosa's ability to manipulate and enhance energy is just one example. Lucy's ingenuity. Maddy's fierce tenacity and ability to cultivate loyalty despite her rather, um, *interesting* personality traits. Arima's entire family lineage. Jules's ability to communicate with felines. Josie's intellect. They are evolving and becoming much more powerful than us, my friends, and *that* is something that we may as well accept if any of us want to get laid ever again."

"I think it's cool, man," a grinning Marcus contributed. "It's like being married to a superhero. Y'know, dress up in cute blue shorts and a red corset. Then tie me up with a rope and make me tell the truth and shit."

"We really don't need to know about the role-plays that you do with your wife, Marcus," Henri scolded.

"Naw, man," a chuckling Marcus countered. "We don't do *that*. It *would* be fun, though. Naw, what *we* do usually is Arima has me dress up in a fast-food restaurant uniform. And the bed is like the fast-food counter. Then, she comes in wearing something sexy and pretends to be a customer and orders a *really big* cheeseburger with *special sauce*. Then I…"

Marcus was abruptly cut off by Gregory. "Yeah, okay. We get the picture. It's a picture that I definitely never wanted in my head, but there it is. For all eternity. Now that I know that I'll go to Enlightenment and exist forever, I can thank you for always having that image emblazoned in my mind."

"You're welcome!" Marcus yelled out as he gave Gregory a firm slap on his back. "You think the ladies are ready yet? Let's go knock on their hotel room door and see if they're ready to go.

The trio of friends opened their door and gasped. Standing in front of them were the all-white suited Adam and Aaron. "Uh, hey guys," a surprised Gregory stated. "What are *you* doing here?"

"Well," Adam began explaining. "Rachel and Kayla told us that it was rude to knock on a closed door when you know someone is dressing." "Yes," Aaron contributed. "Quite rude indeed. They said that someone may be playing 'Hide the Sausage' or something and that we should not disturb them. So, we have been waiting here in the hallway until someone emerged from their room."

"Okaaaay," Gregory replied as he attempted to find the right words. "So, you have just been standing out here in the hallway? For how long?"

"Oh, about two hours," Adam replied. "Yes," Aaron added, "We have been standing here for about two hours and greeting all the other hotel guests who are staying on this floor. We say hello and offer candy to the children."

"Yes," Adam then took over. "We are quite pleasant. We smile, say hello, and offer candy to the children. But no child has taken our candy, and their parents seem quite rude. They just rush by us and go into their hotel rooms."

"Ah, shit," Henri stated as he ran his brawny hand down his face in disbelief. "Yeah, let's get you guys out of this hallway. And, *I'll* knock on the door. It's…um…okay if they're expecting you."

"Well, that is a new rule," Adam stated followed by Aaron's, "Yes, quite new. I never realized that there were so many rules for knocking on doors. We must start writing these rules down, brother."

Henri could only shake his head and whisper "Wow," to himself as he lightly rapped on the adjacent door. "Um, you ladies decent in there?"

"Yeah, we're coming. Keep your pants on," a surly Jules replied. Adam then said, "Oh, are we supposed to remove our pants? Did Rachel and Kayla come here to surprise us?" "Yes!" Aaron excitedly added. "Perhaps they have come here to play a surprise game of 'Hide the Sausage!' Oh, how fun."

"No boys, no," Marcus started explaining as Jules opened the door and said, "C'mon in."

"And leave our pants on, right?" Aaron inquired.

Jules just stared at him with a disgusted look on her face before saying, "Yeah. Why would you even *ask* that? Why are you two so *fucking weird*? Must have gotten it from your father, Jason. I always was a bit suspicious of him. Now get your asses in here. And why are you two even *here*?"

"Oh, well," Adam began. "You see, we have been unable to play our games for awhile and Rachel and Kayla said, now what was it they said exactly brother?" Aaron responded with, "They said that we needed to get out of the house and play our games because we are driving them fucking nuts. So, here we are to play games with you. Also, we were hoping to bring four of these men back to the estate alive."

"Why?" Jules asked. She immediately received a two-word response from the Twins who answered in unison, "Home schooling."

Jules shook her brunette head and said, "Yeah, I don't wanna know. Just come in."

Upon entering the room, Henri saw that his beloved wife was dressed in her all-black cat suit. "Sam, why are you dressed like that?" he inquired.

"Why do you think?" Sam answered. "I'm here on this mission. This is my mission attire. You know that. Why so surprised?"

"No, no, no," Henri replied tersely. "You are *not* going on this mission. This mission is in the dense forest. How the hell are you going to get your wheelchair down there? No, I'm sorry my love, but you simply aren't built for this mission. You are not going. You will stay here in the hotel, then we will all go out for a celebratory dinner. My decision is final. I am putting my foot down."

"I see," the quietly seething Sam replied. "Well, it must be *nice* to be able to put your foot down."

"Now, Sam, I didn't mean it like tha…" Henri was abruptly cut off by his wife. "Yes, it must be quite nice indeed. Do you know what I miss the most about losing the use of my legs?

Dancing. I loved to go dancing. Me, along with Maddy, Lucy, Jules, and Kristy would go out dancing almost every weekend. I had moves. I was never one for much attention, but I just loved knowing that all eyes were on my shapely legs while I was on the dance floor. And the only time that I felt almost normal was the night of Josie's sixteenth birthday party and you lifted me from my chair, and we danced together. I almost felt normal at that moment. Almost. Then, that feeling was washed away by the tragedy of Erick being knifed in the back. By Kristy, as it turned out.

"I miss the use of my legs. But what is even worse, is that every time I look down upon them, I am reminded of the hell that I went through. The rape. The beatings. The severing of my spine which has left me in this chair permanently. It all comes back. Every time you help me put on my pants. Or pajamas. Or use the restroom. Every time you put a pair of useless shoes on my paralyzed feet, that horror comes back to me. That is why I have my new Pogo. I can put a cigarette out on his head, or stick him with a knife, or beat his sexist face with brass knuckles. Then, I feel better.

"So, I do not need you to remind me that I cannot put my foot down. I do not need you to remind me of my physical limitations. And I most *certainly* do not need you to tell me what I am capable of doing. I am a fully grown woman of fifty-four. I have been on many of these missions, and it will be *my* decision and *my* decision alone as to what missions I go on. Henri, I love you. You are the only man that I have truly loved. And you are a good man. And I understand that even the best of men can make a mistake. But you will listen to me carefully. Telling me what I cannot do because of my paralysis is a mistake that you will *never* make again. And don't worry about the forest. I'll be able to navigate through that just fine."

The temperature in the room seemed to plummet as a cold silence enveloped the space. Everyone was either looking down at the floor or up to the ceiling. The silence lasted for what seemed to be an hour until Aaron said, "Well, it appears everyone is dressed." "Yes," Adam added. "You all appear to be dressed. Is it time to play some games?"

"Yeah, let's go play some fucking games," came Henri's angry response. Everyone piled into the large van, except for Jules and Sam who entered a small trailer that was hitched to its bumper. "Where are *they* going?" Gregory asked before hearing the metal door of the trailer slam shut. "I do not know, and I do not care at the moment," Henri answered coldly as he started the engine.

"Oh, joy!" Adam yelled out followed by Aarons, "Yes! Here we go! Oh brother! We finally get to play our games! Who are we playing with Gregory?"

Gregory let out a nervous chuckle before answering. "Well, boys, we are going after a small unit of the reconstituted United Autocratic Movement. There are several small pockets of them strewn around the country. These small units were held back by Vetis. They are his reserves. And they have been told to stand down and stand by and await his reinforcements. So, these pockets are just sitting in cabins in the woods, awaiting their orders. We are going to take as many of them out as we can before they can strengthen. There are fifteen of them at this location living in three small cabins. We'll get their attention, then do what we have to do. Arima will use Rachel and Kayla to track their dark souls later and dispose of them. They can't do any harm. Not in this small of a number, anyway. Plus, I guess she's helping Josie with some other top-secret mission tonight. Otherwise, she'd be here too."

The van was parked on a narrow dirt trail about one-half mile from three small cabins that could be seen through the dense brush. Jules exited the trailer and joined the rest of the group. "So, where is Sam?" Henri asked in an uncaring tone. "Eh, she'll be out in a while," Jules replied. "C'mon. Let's go get these bastards."

"Okay, Jules," Rosa said as the group neared makeshift

alarms that consisted of tin cans that were tied together on a string about three inches off the ground. "Take my hand. Focus on Sam's paralysis. Focus all your energy on what it must be like to not be able to move. To just lay there, helpless. Focus everything that you have on that. Now, boys, go get their attention."

Adam and Aaron began shaking the strings and clanging the tin cans together. "Hello, in there!" Adam yelled out. Aaron then shouted, "Yes! Hello! We are campers and we are lost! Could you please help us? How was that brother?"

"Oh, I believe that was quite good," Adam replied as they saw fifteen heavily armed camouflaged men rush out of the cabins. "Yes, they have responded. They must believe us to be campers. Oh, what a fun joke that we have played upon them."

The fifteen scruffy bearded men raised their rifles. One of them yelled out, "Hey! Get off-a our property! There's a trail about a half-mile up that-a way! Now git! Or else yer gonna have an ass full-a lead!"

Rosa's eyes began glowing red underneath her black hood as she absorbed all the focused energy from Jules. "What the fuck is *that* bitch doin'? Oh, fuck this! Fire!" the man yelled out before screaming, "What the fuck! I can't move!" There was then a chorus of men yelling out, "No! I can't either!" Hey! Why can't I move?" "What the fuck is that witch doing to us?"

"Wow, baby," Gregory said quietly to his wife. "Remind me to never piss you off. Okay, Henri, Marcus. You know what to do. Just go slit their throats and let's get back to the hotel."

There was the roar of an engine from behind them and the amplified voice of Sam saying, "I have a better idea!" They turned their heads and saw Sam's pretty, mature face looking out of the bulletproof windshield of a mini tank. The eight-foot long by four-feet wide metal box on treads came lumbering toward the paralyzed men. "Adam! Aaron! Pick out the ones you want to keep and make it quick! We don't want Rosa to use up all her energy!"

"Oh my!" Adam yelled out. "Why this is almost like trying to decide what to buy from a candy store!" "Oh, yes! This is quite fun!" Aaron answered as the pair sauntered through the brush and approached the terrified faces of the immobilized men. "How about this one, brother?"

"No, I don't believe so," Adam answered. "How about this one?" "Oh, yes!" Aaron exclaimed. "He will be quite perfect!" The pair then retrieved large ball peen hammers from white duffle bags that they were carrying and proceeded to slam them into the knees of the chosen man until there was a loud 'CRACK!' and the tortured man fell to the ground. A second man was selected and received the same demented treatment. Then a third, and finally a fourth. The four broken men lay on the ground screaming. Their screams intensified as they felt large metal hooks being thrust into their backs and into their spinal columns. "Oh, I do believe that we have found the most perfect classroom subjects, brother," Adam proudly stated. "Yes, quite perfect," Aaron agreed. "Our children will be able to learn much from them."

"Okay, boys," Sam began ordering. "Get them out of the way. I'm going to show you what games that I can play with *my* new toy." There was a thunderous bang as a small missile was launched from the tank's turret and exploded into one of the men. The forest was showered with blood and tiny pieces of bone and flesh. This was followed by the sound of rapid machine gun fire. One of the men's bodies convulsed violently as the bullets ripped him to shreds. The engine then revved up and Sam drove the tank toward the remaining nine men. They began desperately pleading as each one in turn felt the treads of the tank crush their feet. Then crush their legs. Then crush their torso. Then crush their head. There were eruptions of blood, bones, internal organs, and eyes that streamed across the forest as Sam drove over each man in succession. Once the screaming had stopped, Sam drove over all the crushed bodies one final time leaving them looking like the most grotesque and obliterated of roadkill.

Henri walked up to the idling tank and knocked on the top hatch. The hatch opened and he saw Sam's gratified face looking up at him. "Well," he began. "I know that you cannot physically stand, but I will never allow anyone, including myself, to ever tell you what you can't do. You are the most strong and capable woman that I have ever known. You are fully capable of standing up for *yourself*. I am sorry and I love you."

"I love you too," Sam replied with a slight, uncharacteristic tear in her eye. "Now just kiss me."

"Oh, fuckin' puke! You two are making me nauseous!" Jules yelled out. "Let's get these four hooked up to the tank and drag them back into the trailer. Then, let's eat. I'm kinda craving pulled pork for some reason."

Rosa rolled off the hotel bed and trudged her bloated body over to the phone. "Oh, my God," she lamented to Sam, Jules, Gregory, Marcus, and Henri. "I don't think that I'm ever eating again. That pulled pork was so good. All drippy with barbeque sauce. And that sundae with the crushed pineapple topping was to die for. I'm going to call Josie and let her know how things went.

"Yeah, hey Josie, it's Rosa. Yeah, it went fine. Sam crushed most of them with her new mini tank. Yeah, that's a good one Josie. They must have had a crush on her. Anyway, the Twins are on their way back to the estate with four alive ones. I don't know, they just said 'home schooling.' No, I have no idea what they meant. Oh, and I spoke to Rod yesterday and he thinks that he has the electrodes ready for our tests on the JQ. So, what are you and Arima up to tonight? Well, obviously Arima wanted pizza. What else? Oh, really? Well, okay. Good luck with that. We'll be home tomorrow. Bye."

"So, what are those two doing?" Henri asked. Rosa let out a

deep sigh and said, "Oh, that poor girl. She's putting her plan to get Lionnel back into motion tonight."

"Hmmmm," Henri responded. "Lionnel loved that girl very much, but he is very headstrong. Once he puts his mind to something, then that is what he is going to do. Just like medical school. He is only twenty-one and is nearly complete with his studies. He is already such a gifted surgeon. Has been since he was a teenager. But he said that he would be finished with medical school by the age of twenty-two and he is going to do just that. And he says that he doesn't love Josie anymore and that he has moved on. All that I'm saying is that Josie might be better off doing the same. But she is as headstrong as my Lionnel. So, if she is determined to try this, then she needs to be *very careful* with how she proceeds. She must be *very tactful* or else she will drive him further away. She has such a crush on that boy. I would hate to see her blow this. She *cannot* come up with some impulsive, fly-off-the-handle, hairbrained plan like her mother used to do. That *will not* work on that boy."

Chapter 105

Mixed Up, Shook Up Girl

"Um, Niece Josie?" Arima said as she walked into Josie's bedroom. Josie had just finished putting on a psychedelic polka dotted mini-dress, white go-go boots, and sparkling make-up as she turned to her aunt.

"Yes, Aunt Arima? Have you found anything out?" an anticipatory Josie asked.

"Uh, yeah," Arima answered. "Rod has found out what movie Lionnel is going to. But do you really think that this is the best move? I mean, why don't you just try to get him to go to coffee or something?"

"Oh, Aunt Arima, I love you, but you *obviously* don't know anything about men," Josie replied while chuckling. "No, this is like a *game* and we women have to be *smart* and *savvy* so that we can win. And we *win* by making men tap into their emotions. And what is one of the *strongest* emotions? Here, let me just read you Step 1:

"JOSIE PARKER'S PLAN TO WIN LIONNEL BACK
BY JOSIE PARKER

Step 1: Make Lionnel *jealous*, heh, heh, heh."

"Oh, wow, I didn't know that *you'd* be here, Lionnel!" Josie overacted as she, a hulk of a man, Arima, and their black-clad security detail of the twelve members of Rosa's Coven casually sauntered down the line outside of a movie theater. "Wow, it's *so good* to see you. So…um…who is *this* then?"

Lionnel let out a deep sigh and said in an uninterested tone, "Josie, this is my friend from medical school, Tabitha. Tabitha, this is Josie."

"Oh, well, *hello* there Tabitha!" Josie squealed as she embraced the young African-American med student. "It is *sooooo* nice to meet you! Any friend of *Lionnel's* is a friend of mine! Oh, and this rather *large* man here is Al. Al is the starting middle linebacker for the Jets. Say 'hi' Al."

"Uh, yeah, hi," a befuddled Al said as he encased Lionnel's hand within his and shook it firmly. "I was gonna go to medical school, but then I looked at how big the books are that you have to read, so I didn't. I don't read much. I really just got through college 'cause I was a big football star and my professors were told to give me a pass so that I could keep playing."

Josie burst out into contrived laughter. "Oh my, Al! You are *sooooo* funny! Always with the quips, this one. Yes, *Al* and *I* have become *quite* the item, *haven't* we Al? Just say 'yes' Al."

"Uh, yes, I guess," the perpetually perplexed Al replied. Lionnel shook his throbbing hand to shake off the pain and shook his head to shake off the disbelief of this most transparent attempt to make him jealous. "Okay, well I'm happy for you guys. Enjoy the movie and nice to see you, I guess." Josie's eyes glowed with jealous rage as Lionnel turned his attention away from her and renewed his conversation with Tabitha.

"Okay, yeah, you too!" Josie stated loudly. "Maybe we'll see you in there!" As Josie and her deadly entourage made their way to the back of the line, Josie said quietly to Arima, "Put that little bitch on my list."

"Um, Niece Josie?" Arima sheepishly replied. "Um, I really don't think that we can put someone on the assassination list just because she's seeing a movie with Lionnel. And, you know, that seems like something that your mom would do, and you want to get away from that, so maybe we should find another way."

"You're right Auntie Arima," Josie answered. "Of course, what was I thinking? The night is young. I don't need to *kill* this bitch to win Lionnel back. Nope, we'll just let step one play out through the evening. I'm sure by night's end, he will be *so* jealous that he'll be *begging* for me to take him back."

Al wore a dullard expression on his face as he asked, "Um, Jealous? What do you mean by jealous? What kind of date is thi…"

Al was cut off by an overexaggerated Josie yelling out, "Oh, Al! You are *soooo* funny! I haven't met *anyone* that could make me laugh like *you* can!"

"Uh, what did I say that was funny?" Al asked. "Just shut up, Al," Josie said bluntly as her copper curls popped out from behind the tall man in front of her and she peered down the line to see what affect her latest performance had on her quarry. She scowled, popped her head back behind the tall man, folded her arms and said, "I don't even think he heard me. He's too busy talking to *Taaaabiiiithaaaa*. What a pukey fuckin'…I mean what a pukey name. It's okay. Just be cool Josie, just be cool. You're a genius. This plan is genius. I'm sure it's worked like, millions of times before. Just be patient. But what the hell are they laughing about?"

Tabitha and Lionnel began laughing together after she

asked, "So, why didn't you tell her that we're not together. We're just friends and we're waiting for my boyfriend to join us."

"Yeah," Lionnel answered through his laughs. "It just isn't worth the time. And she's being so *ridiculous* right now, what with this *'Al'* character. I know her. They aren't a couple. She probably had Rod find out where I'd be tonight, used her connections to arrange this so-called date and is now trying to make me jealous. But it won't work. I'm over her. I'm just not ready to…um…get back out there yet."

"Uh, huh," an unconvinced and smirking Tabitha responded.

The line began moving into the theater, and Josie lost track of her prey. She had also failed to notice a second young man who had joined Lionnel and gave *Taaaaabiiiithaaaa* a warm embrace. Every few seconds, Josie would bounce her five-foot-four (and a fucking half)-inch frame as high as she could go to get a better view of the front of the line, but to no avail. She had lost him, *Taaaaaabiiiiithaaaaa,* and Tabitha's recently arrived boyfriend.

"Fuck, I mean, damn, it's dark in here," Josie whispered as she scoured the dimly lit theatre for seats. She then heard a man say, "Oh, damn. I'm sorry. My pager just went off. I'm on call at the hospital and I've got to go, but you two stay and enjoy the movie, and I'll see you back at your place, okay?"

A young man scurried past Josie who turned her attention to the direction that he had come from. She turned to her entourage and said in a wicked, deep voice, "Folks, I think I've found our seats, heh, heh, heh."

Theater patrons began relocating to other seats to find refuge from the constant barrage of "Oh, *Al*, you're so funny!" "Oh, *Al*, please hold me! I don't *like* the sight of blood! It makes me feel *woozy!*" "Oh, *Al*, I've *never* been so scared in my life! I'm *soooo* glad that *you're* here to protect lil' ol' me!" "Oh, *Al*, watch your hands there, tiger! Maybe *later!*"

Josie's frustration intensified as the heads of Lionnel and *Taaaaabiiiithaaaa* just sat motionless and continued to face the screen. There was then a bright light that was shown in Josie's face. The theater manager said sternly, "Miss, I'm going to have to ask you to quiet down or else I'm afraid that I'm going to have to ask you to leave." He then saw the intensity in her glimmering green eyes and recognized her. "I mean, I'm so sorry to disturb you, Miss Parker. I believe that I've made a mistake. Please, enjoy the movie."

"Uh, huh, that's what I *thought*," Josie said to the hastily retreating manager before thrusting her head forward between the seats of Lionnel and *Taaaaabiiiithaaaaa*. "Hey, Lionnel. You want some candy?"

"Uh, no thanks Josie. I'm just trying to watch the movie," Lionnel replied with disinterest. "Come on, man!" Josie persisted. "This is your favorite! Sorry, *Taaaaabiiiithaaaa*, but there isn't enough to share with *you*. Come on, Lionnel. Have some."

Lionnel shook his head in disgust, turned to *Taaaaaabiiiithaaaa* and said, "Come on. Let's go. I think I know how this movie is going to end."

"Okay, nice to see ya! Don't be a stranger!" a desperate Josie shouted after the departing pair.

"So, where do you want to go later?" an oblivious Al asked. "And I kinda like it when you call me 'tiger.' That was the name of my high school football team. Hey, you wanna maybe wear a cheerleader outfit?"

"Fuck off, Al. Come on everybody. Let's go. This movie sucks," a furious Josie stated as she got up from her seat and proceeded toward the exit followed by a snickering and dismayed contingent of female bodyguards.

A confused and frustrated Al sat in the center of the row of now empty seats. He was about to get up and leave when he heard a soft, female's voice say from behind him, *"I've* got a cheerleader outfit. Wanna watch me…um…*cheer?"*

"Well, *that* didn't work," a pacing Josie stated as she nervously gnawed at her fingernails. "But not to fear, Aunt Arima! That's why I have a fool-proof five step plan!"

"Please, Niece Josie," Arima pressured as she took a long drag off her joint. "Just ask him to go to coffee or something. This isn't going to work."

"Yeah, it will," a determined Josie countered. "This is *totally* going to work. What do men like to do more than anything… um…well, *almost* anything. Play the *hero*, right? So, let me read you Step 2: Play the damsel in distress by doing that thing that Aunt Blair did one time. Now give me a hit off that joint."

Lionnel was casually walking toward the apartment that he shared with his father and stepmother when he heard a woman's voice cry out, "Ow! Oh, my *ankle*! I think I've broken my *ankle*!"

Lionnel instinctively turned around and immediately slapped his forehead in frustration. Josie was sitting on the sidewalk in the middle of a spilled grocery bag holding her right ankle. "Josie, what are you doing?"

"Oh, *Lionnel*," Josie answered in a helpless voice. "Oh, it's *so good* that you're *here*! I was just walking along, and I must have caught my pretty little feet on a crack or something. Could you *please* take a look at it? I think it might be *broken*!"

Lionnel glanced up at his third-floor apartment window and saw the snickering faces of his father, Henri, and his stepmother, Sam. He rolled his eyes and shook his head in disbelief at them before saying, "Josie, you do not need my help. You have twelve security guards right over there. And why are you grocery shopping in this neighborhood anyway? Just go home Josie."

"Well, b-b-but," Josie began desperately stammering, "Yeah, I've got the Coven with me but they don't know how to fix a broken *ankle*. And, well, I *like* the grocery store on the corner and, well, hey! Don't you walk away from me Lionnel! Not in my time of need! I'm *helpless*! Oh, *I* get it! You're probably in a hurry to call *Taaaaabiiithaaaa*! Right? Well, am I *right?*"

Lionnel opened the front door of his red brick apartment building, looked back at Josie blankly and said, "No, you are not right. And your ankle isn't broken. And you've never liked that grocery store. You always said that it's impossible to find anything in there. And finally, you are about as helpless as a starving man at an all-you-can-eat buffet. Just go home Josie."

A chuckling member of Josie's security detail turned to her colleague and said quietly, "You know, for a *genius*, she *really* isn't very good at this. But I guess even being a *genius* can't overcome the broken heart and immaturity of an eighteen-year-old woman."

"Well, *this* is just starting to piss me off," Josie said to Arima as she paced rapidly on her perfectly fine ankles while literally pulling at her auburn locks. "But it's okay! Only two steps down, three to go. And I've *very cleverly* planted the seed that he can be my hero. Yeah, this time it's gonna work."

"Niece Josie," Arima responded. "It didn't work this time and it won't work the next time. Please, just ask him to go to coffee so that you two can talk. Or a pizza parlor. Or a burger joint. One with *really good* fries. And sundaes. Hey, when you call him for coffee, can I tag along?"

"No, you may *not* tag along, Aunt Arima," Josie responded gruffly. "Because asking him out for coffee isn't going to work! Don't you understand? I have to *win* him back. Talking and communicating is overrated! I need to *trick* him into falling in love with me again! Here, listen to Step 3: If Step 2 doesn't work, play the damsel in distress again by doing that *other* thing that Aunt Blair did to get Uncle Joe. Now, hand me that phone. Oh, and that joint."

Lionnel answered his avocado green rotary phone. "Hello? What is it *now*, Josie? You have a frozen water pipe that has burst, and you need me to come over and fix it? Really? Well, I don't think that's true. For starters, it's nearly seventy degrees outside, so unless your home is sitting in the middle of some supernatural polar vortex, it is impossible for your pipes to be frozen. And you have an entire department of Murder, Inc. maintenance people at your disposal. They can install alarms, booby-traps, security gates, and a million other things. Hell, they just built my stepmom a mini tank! I'm pretty sure that *they* would be able to help you more than I. *Please*, Josie. Just stop. This is over. Please don't call here again. This *isn't* going to work." As Lionnel was hanging up the phone, he heard Josie's infuriated voice shout, "Well, it worked for my Aunt Blair! Lionnel! What? You can't leave in case *Taaaabiiiithaaaa* calls? Lionnel! Don't you *dare* hang up on…"

"Huh. Well, son of a bitch," a dismayed Josie said as she hung up her pink cordless princess phone. Her green eyes began blinking rapidly and there was a noticeable twitch on the right side of her mouth. "Okay, okay, okay, not to worry. Just need to do Step 4: Do that thing from that movie. Arima, go get me my boombox and this CD from my dad's collection upstairs. Yeah, this is going to work. Because it has to. I really don't *want* to have to do Step five. But y'know, if I have to, then I *have* to. I don't *want* to, but…"

"Niece Josie," Arima interrupted. "You are driving yourself nuts. Just call him and ask him out for coffee and…" Arima paused for a moment as Josie's effervescent eyes glared at her intensely. "Okay. I'll get the boombox and CD. But this *isn't* going to work."

Lionnel was awoken by his father's banging on his bedroom door. "Lionnel, would you please get up and take care of this?" his father demanded as Lionnel wiped the sleep from his eyes. "Take care of what?"

Henri grabbed Lionnel by the collar of his pajamas and led him to the front window. "That," Henri said sternly before storming into the kitchen. "Oh, dammit," Lionnel muttered under his breath.

He opened the front window and Peter Gabriel's "In Your

Eyes" came blaring from below. Josie was standing in the middle of the street wearing a grey trench coat and holding a boombox above her head. "Hi Lionnel! I know you love this song and I'm being really romantic and shit, so just come down so we can talk, okay?"

Lionnel had known Josie since the time of her birth. They were practically raised together. They had become friends. Then they became the closest of confidants. He pined over her for years until they became an item. And finally, lovers. And throughout those eighteen years, Lionnel had never raised his voice to her. Until now. "Josie! Goddammit, stop this! This is *over*! Get it through your *thick head* and leave me the hell *alone* and go *home*! I do *not* want to see you *ever again*! Plus, this scene has been done *before* and it has been done *better*!" Lionnel slammed the window shut and heard a crash as Josie flung the boombox against a parked car. The car's siren began blaring as Henri wrapped his arm around his son and said, "Lionnel. You need to fix this. One way or another. Great. Now all the dogs are barking. And there goes another car alarm. You need to fix this, son. If you have any feelings for her, then you need to fix this. And if you don't, well…then you *still* have to fix this so Sam and I can get some sleep!"

Josie was sobbing uncontrollably on her bed. Her heart felt as though it was being crushed by a ten-ton weight and was being ripped apart simultaneously. Except for the loss of her parents, she had never felt such excruciating emotional torment. Her pained green eyes darted between a framed picture of Lionnel and Step 5 on her list. She then looked up to her ceiling and said, "D-d-dad? I-I don't k-know if you c-can hear me o-o-or not, but I-I really n-need your h-help. P-please. If there's a-a-anything that you c-can do to reach him. Anything y-you can d-do to help him f-find his w-way back to m-me. Please. I-I love him, Dad."

She let out one final stuttered breath, wiped the tears from her eyes, reached for her pink princess phone and dialed the number. "Hey there, Kayla, it's Josie. Oh, I'm sorry. I didn't realize it was so late. Anywhoooo, since I've got you on the phone, I was just wondering if you guys would like a little break? I was hoping to take the JQ on a picnic tomorrow."

Lionnel laid his emotionally exhausted head upon his pillow. He tossed and turned for what seemed like an eternity. Frustrated, he turned his transistor radio on. From the single speaker came Jefferson Starship's "Find Your Way Back." "Aw, Jesus," he muttered to himself. "I can't listen to this tonight." He fiddled with the dial. The static stopped and out of the lone speaker came Jefferson Starship's "Find Your Way Back." "What the hell? I'll try the jazz station," Lionnel said as he twisted the dial to the left until it landed on the appropriate frequency. A cool saxophone was playing and a slightly relaxed Lionnel began drifting off to sleep. Just before he nodded off, he could hear the saxophone begin to fade. He then heard static. And finally, he heard… "Find Your Way Back" by Jefferson Starship.

Lionnel burst into laughter and held his hands over his bewildered face. "*Really*, Josie? You told your *dad* on me? Well played, Josie. And well played, Mister Parker. Fine. You win. You *both* win. I'll call her tomorrow, Mister Parker. I promise. Maybe we can get a cup of coffee somewhere and talk things out. Now, can I get to sleep?" Lionnel could only shake his head in disbelief as the cool saxophone once again could be heard coming from the solitary speaker.

CHAPTER 106

———————

WIG WAM BAM

"Aunt Josie!" the four members of the Junior Quad squealed as they ran up to Josie's flower-adorned yellow VW Bus. "Hiya kids! Are you ready to have some fun?" Josie excitedly replied. "We sure are!" the perpetual ten-year-olds answered in unison. "What fun will we be having today?"

"Well," Josie began explaining as she pondered the right words to use. "It kinda depends. Is it possible for you guys to take people along with you into the past to an exact date and place?"

"No, it doesn't work that way, Aunt Josie," the quadrophonic voices replied. "We are called to the past when Vetis has chosen a soul to corrupt. We are called to a specific time and location. Then we get on our ponies and start riding until the pretty lights take us there. We are unable to bring anyone along with us and we have no control over where or when we are sent."

"Uh-huh, uh-huh," a contemplative Josie responded as she rubbed her delicate chin. "That's kinda what I thought. Time travel won't work. Okay, no problem. Step Five it is. So, do you want to go on a picnic? And do you kids want to play a little joke on your Uncle Lionnel?"

"Good morning, son," Henri greeted as he walked into his kitchen and rubbed the sleep from his fatigued eyes.

"Morning, Dad," Lionnel answered as he scraped the remnants of his scrambled eggs from off his plate into the waste basket.

"No coffee this morning, son?" Henri inquired. "Naw," Lionnel replied through a slight chuckle. "They've done it Dad. They've beaten me. I can't keep pushing Josie away. And her father has made it *perfectly clear* that I will never again get a good night's sleep until I patch things up with her. I still love her, Dad. I truly do. I just needed to do something extreme to try to wake her up. Try to wake up that sweet girl that I first fell in love with. But truth be told, I kinda like her darker side too. I've realized that it's necessary and that it is a part of who she is. And, despite some of her more *unorthodox* methods, I guess that I love *that* side of her too. I haven't slept in weeks since I broke up with her. That made me realize just how much she means to me. How much I need her in my life. Then, with these *latest* antics, heh, heh, heh."

Lionnel put his head in his hands and shook it for a moment in disbelief. "I mean, trying to make me jealous, and all the damsel in distress shit, and then that trick she pulled last night. Well, I found it to be *totally* immature and *completely* adorable. She proved to me just how much I mean to her, and I guess it made me fall in love with her all over again. Yep, I've officially fallen in love with Josephine Patricia Sommers Parker version 2.0. She still has that childlike innocence and hopefulness, but there's also a tenacity and dark drive to seek justice that I just must admit that I find irresistible. I love her, Dad. Everything about her. And so, I'm going to jump in the shower, bite the bullet, and invite her to go out for coffee. Just like *she* should have done weeks ago. I mean, what's with all the theatrics? Just ask me to go to coffee so we can talk things out. It's really not that complicated. But it is for her, I guess. That's the two sides of her that will always be in conflict. The sweet, innocent side that just wants to get back together with her boyfriend and the tenaciously manipulative side that comes up with stupid ways of doing that. She is *definitely* the product of both of her parents. And I guess that I wouldn't have it any other way."

Lionnel emerged from his bedroom wearing his usual attire of dark blue jeans, canvas tennis shoes, and a light blue oxford. His heart pounded with anticipation as he walked across the room toward the rotary phone. He found a note from his father that simply read, *Sam and I have a meeting this morning. Good luck. And son, FIX THIS! WE NEED OUR SLEEP!*

Lionnel chuckled to himself, took a deep breath, and lifted the receiver. A single loving tear fell upon the phone as he placed his finger into the dial. He was then interrupted by a light knocking on the door. *Who the hell could that be?* Lionnel thought to himself as he went to the door and looked out the peep hole. Seeing nothing, he started back toward the phone when he heard another light knock.

He instinctively picked up a large knife from under the phone stand, walked to the door and looked out the peep hole once again. Seeing nothing, he threw the front door open and immediately assumed a defensive posture.

"Hiya, Uncle Lionnel!" four innocent voices shouted from below him. Lionnel looked down and saw the four angelic faces of Sigourney, Euna, Kane, and Thanatos, who had a toy cowboy figure sticking out of his mouth. "Well, hi kids," a surprised Lionnel greeted. "Wow. You kids really *do* always dress up as cowboys and cowgirls don't you? Now, what are you guys doing here? Is everything alright?"

"Everything's fine, Uncle Lionnel!" the foursome answered. "We're here to play a game with you!" Sigourney and Euna then channeled their strength and tackled Lionnel at the knees causing him to fall backwards. Before he had time to react, Kane had flipped him onto his stomach, Thanatos had hog-tied him, Euna had placed a gag in his mouth, and Sigourney had placed a black burlap bag over his head.

"Okay, now lift!" Sigourney ordered as the giggling quartet hoisted the squirming Lionnel above their heads and carried him out of the apartment, down the stairs, and onto the street.

Lionnel stopped struggling and said *You've gotta be kidding me*, to himself when he heard an all-too familiar voice yell out, "Great job, kids! Now, just throw him in the back and don't crush the picnic basket."

He heard the purr of the VW engine and began lightly banging his head on the floor of the bus in amused frustration as he listened to Josie's rapid-fire attempt at an explanation. "Hiya Lionnel! I know this might be a bit *unorthodox*, and I really didn't *want* to do Step Five, but you see, there's no other *way*, 'cause the *other* steps didn't work and so I really had *no choice* but to do Step Five, you see that right? Plus, I *had* to get you back before that *Taaaabiiiithaaa* got her bitch hooks deeper into you, and of course, I know this is a bit *unusual* but drastic times call for drastic measures, right? I mean, it's not like I could just call you up and invite you for *coffee* or something. Nope, that *never* would've worked, so I *had* to do Step Five, which I really didn't *want* to do, but you left me no choice, so it's really *your* fault that I've had to do this, you see that right? Anywhoooo, there's *nothing* to worry about. We're just going up to the clearing near the estate and we're going to have a picnic! And I've made you all your favorites! Fried chicken, 'tato salad, ham sammiches, and chocolate pie! I was up all night cooking just for you. So anyway, we're just going to have a nice picnic and watch the kids play and once you *realize* that you still *love* me and you can't live *without* me and that *Taaaaabiiiithaaaa* is a little bitch whore, then we'll be back together and then I'll take you home. And that's Step Five. What do you think?"

The only response that Lionnel could provide was a

muffled attempt at protest. "Yep, I knew you'd like this plan!" Josie continued. "What do you kids think?"

"We think that it's a wonderful plan, Aunt Josie!" the JQ replied gleefully. "And so much fun! We hope to play this game with Uncle Lionnel again sometime."

Josie began chuckling and said, "Well, hopefully that won't be necessary, kids. But it'll always be an option. Okay! Here we are!"

The tittering children lifted the bound and gagged Lionnel out of the van and placed him on a large wool blanket in the middle of a clearing near the estate. He felt the burlap bag being lifted from his head and looked into the irresistible green eyes of his smiling love. "Hiya Lionnel," Josie softly said as she removed the gag from his mouth. "I really am sorry that I had to do this, but I *love* you and I know that you love *me*, so I *had* to do something to get your attention, and I think you'd *have* to admit that *this* was a bit of an attention grabber. And you don't have to worry about me harming *Taaabiiithaaa*. Oh sure, I've had sixteen assassination technicians following her around a bit, just in case. But that won't be necessary, right, because you and I are..."

Josie's stammering was interrupted by a smiling Lionnel tenderly saying, "Josie, just shut up and kiss me."

"Yay! We won the game!" the JQ squealed as they watched Lionnel and Josie kiss for the first time in weeks. "Aunt Josie said that if you kissed her, then we would win the game and get a special prize!"

Josie and Lionnel began laughing out loud as their foreheads touched. Josie then began untying her love and said, "That's right kids! You all get a special prize. Each of you get to select one toy from my toy box under the back seat in the bus. You can pick out anything that you want."

"Yay!" the children yelled out as they ran into the bus and lifted the back seat up. Following five minutes of silence, Josie yelled out, "Hey! What are you kids doing? Why are you so quiet? Did you find something that you like?"

She then heard the quartet say, "It's just so beautiful Aunt Josie. All of your wonderful toys. They are all so sharp and deadly. We can play so many fun games with these. It's just too hard to choose." The tender moment then ended as Sigourney shouted out, "That one's mine!" "No, it isn't, *I* want that one!" Kane shouted back. "No, you can't have it!" Euna yelled. "Sigourney claimed it and *I'm* taking this one! And Thanatos, quit putting those poison darts in your mouth!"

"Children, please just pick something out and stop your bickering," Lionnel scolded. "Pick out the one toy that you feel most connected to and let's eat. Our lunch is getting cold."

"Sorry, Uncle Lionnel," the children replied respectfully just before they emerged from the van. "Look at what *I* got!" Kane exclaimed while proudly displaying his new broadsword. "And look at *this*!" Euna shouted as she held up a set of golden, spiked scales. "Mine is the best!" Sigourney argued as she pulled back her newly acquired bow and shot an arrow towards an apple fifty yards away.

"That's so cool, you guys," a giggling Josie stated. "But what about you, Thanatos? What is *your* prize? And *what* do you have all over your face?"

"Um," Thanatos sheepishly replied as he looked down at his shuffling white cowboy boots. "Well, I kinda found your secret stash of peanut butter cups."

A tittering Lionnel and Josie were cleaning up what remained of their lunch and watching the children gallop around the clearing on their ponies. Every so often, Lionnel would gaze into Josie's deep, green eyes and give her a slight kiss upon her tender, mauve lips which would elicit yet another childish chant from the JQ. "Aunt Josie and Uncle Lionnel sitting in a tree! K-I-S-S-I-N-G!" Lionnel then said to Josie, "Listen. I'm gonna let you off the hook. I am *not* involved with Tabitha. Not in the slightest. She's just my friend and classmate. She has had the same boyfriend for like, two years or something. *He* was the guy that had to leave the movie theatre. Okay? So, you really have no reason to be jealous of her."

"Jealous?' Josie responded incredulously. "Who the hell said I was *jealous*? You want to run around with other chicks *who are involved with someone else by the way*, well that's your deal. It's no biggie. We were broken up, so you can do whatever you want. Whatevs. *Jealous*? Please, Lionnel, don't make me laugh. I'm *far* too intellectually advanced to fall prey to something as silly as jealousy. And *nooooo* I wasn't going to kill *Taaabiiithaaaa*. Just maybe *scare* her a little, y'know, if I needed to. I mean, she really wouldn't be able to chase after you with a pair of broken legs, now, could she?"

Lionnel's eyes broadened, and his mouth dropped in shocked realization just before Josie yelled out, "Joking! I'm *joking*! Come on, man! Don't be so fuc...I mean, don't be so *gullible*! You *know* me better than that! I would *never* do that to someone just for going out with the man I love!" A relieved Lionnel failed to hear Josie finish her statement as she said under her breath, "As far as *you* know, heh, heh, heh."

"Okay, you got me," Lionnel said through his chuckles. "*That* was a good one. It's just that, man, sometimes you are so much like your mother and...well, it doesn't matter. You *aren't* your mother. You are my Josie. You are the Josie that I fell in love with, and you will *be* my Josie for the rest of our lives. But you really didn't have to go to all this trouble to get my attention. Why didn't you just call me up and..."

Lionnel's thought was interrupted by the sound of gunfire coming from a short distance away. "Shit! Get down!" Josie ordered. "Who the hell are these fuc...I mean *these* guys? Members of the UAM?"

"No, they are just more of Vetis's silly assassins," the JQ answered in unison as they led their ponies toward the safety of the rear of the bus. "We'll take care of this." The children emerged from the back of the VW as the shots continued to ring out. Their brilliant blue and brown eyes began glowing with a reserved rage as they purposefully walked through the brush toward the four assassins. "Kids! Get back here!" Lionnel shouted after them. "You're going to get shot!"

"No, we won't," the children casually replied. Josie and Lionnel looked up from their blanket in disbelief as they witnessed the children wave approaching bullets away from them with their tiny, tan hands. The JQ continued their methodical approach, and the men continued their firing with an increased frenzy. Finally, the four children stood three feet away from the bewildered men and looked up at them. Each child placed an index finger into the barrel of a rifle. They then said in a sinisterly sweet, unified voice, "Do you *really* want to play this game with us? Do you? Doesn't Vetis under-stand who we *are*? Doesn't he understand what we have been brought here to *do*? Doesn't he understand that the likes of *you* cannot harm us? Do you think that you can harm us? Do you? Pull the triggers and find out."

There was a loud *BLAM*! and billowing, black smoke emerged around the four giggling children. "See?" Sigourney said in a snotty voice to the blackened men who were lying on the ground in agony. "We *told* you that you couldn't hurt us! Let's get the ponies. Now, it's *our* turn to play a game with *you*."

"Damn, baby, this really is good chocolate pie," an engorged Lionnel stated following being fed yet another bite by his cuddling girlfriend. "Where did you learn how to cook anyway? Your mother couldn't cook worth a lick."

"No, she certainly couldn't," a tittering Josie responded. "And, well, neither can I. I have a confession to make. I bought all this stuff pre-made at the grocery store this morning."

"You *didn't*!" Lionnel yelled out before playfully knocking his girlfriend onto her back and gently laying on top of her.

The pair began to kiss passionately until they were interrupted by four euphoric voices.

"Uncle Lionnel! Aunt Josie! Look at us!" the JQ shouted out as they were dragging the four would-be assassins behind their ponies. The men were pleading with them to stop while their bodies were being viciously cut by thorns and their bones were being snapped apart by harsh collisions with jagged rocks. The JQ then untied the men from their horses and whispered in each pony's ear. The Shetlands reared up and began bashing the men's skulls with their heavy hoofs. The men's brains began oozing out of the fissures and spilling onto the lush green pasture. The children continued their non-stop cackles as the full weight of Snowball, Blackjack, Flame, and Snot crashed onto their heads over and over until their faces were unrecognizable puddles of pinkish, red goo.

The children looked down upon their latest late playmates and simultaneously yawned. "Aunt Josie," Kane said in a weary voice. "May we go home now? We are sleepy."

"Of course, you can," Josie replied as she and Lionnel held hands and walked toward the four mounted children. Josie and Lionnel hugged each child before Josie said, "Thank you children. Thank you for helping me play my game with Lionnel. And thank you for protecting us today."

"It's okay," Sigourney snidely answered. "It's what we do."

Lionnel and Josie watched as the forms of the JQ, and their steeds, disappeared over the horizon. "Sooooo…the *children* are gone," Josie playfully whispered into Lionnel's ear.

As Josie and Lionnel laid naked upon the blood-soaked blades of grass in between the four crushed corpses, Lionnel said, "Seriously, Josie, why didn't you just invite me to go to coffee and talk things out?" Josie rolled on top of her beau, stared at him with her intense emerald eyes, smiled demurely, and replied, "Yeah. Like *that* would've worked."

Chapter 107

School Days

"You're a fucking disappointment, Gobbo!" Vetis roared as his razor-sharp whip slashed Gobbo's tenderized demonic skin for the twentieth time. Black bile gushed from the gaping wounds as Gobbo plead for mercy. "P-please, Master! T-the children are just too powerful! Even on Earth! And they are growing stronger with each passing day! With each victory over one of our kind, they are rejuvenated further! It won't be long now until they are at full strength and are powerful enough to defeat you! Please, Master, mercy! I have done all that I can!"

Vetis tossed the dripping whip to the corner of the fiery room, sat upon his skeletal throne, and pouted. "I suppose you're right, my most faithful Gobbo. It's just that I feel it all slipping away, and that's starting to *piss me off*! We have lost almost all our dark souls here in Perdition to the failed war against Enlightenment. And there are fewer and fewer of them remining on the Earth. And those that *do* remain are destroyed by that little witch, Arima. And then there's her half-sister. The one that was to be our savior. The one that would fight alongside her copperheaded mother and Pastor father. *She* was to be the one to tip the scales in our favor. And where is she *now*? Just sitting in Enlightenment, eating her fucking ice cream happy as a fucking lark, *that's* where! Does she *care* that she has nearly destroyed me? *Noooooooo.* Does she *care* that Perdition is practically defenseless because we have no remaining forces? *Noooooooo.* All she cares about is her *happiness*, and the *happiness* of her loved ones, that selfish little bitch.

"The only thing that is protecting us is the Great Door. Those fucking Enlightenment goodie-goodies can't get through that. They could send a million of their pure souls to storm it, and the door would remain steadfast. But if that door were ever to be opened, and just *one* of those assholes makes their way in, then not only will they have prevented us from taking over the Earth and Enlightenment, but they would be able to conquer our only refuge in this God-forsaken corner of the universe. But that would be impossible. No one would be stupid enough to open the Great Door, right Gobbo?"

"O-of course, Master," the trembling Gobbo replied as he sat at Vetis's red, calloused feet. "The Great Door is *never* to be opened. And *you* are the only one with the key. We may not have much, Master, but we will *always* have Perdition."

"I suppose you're right, Gobbo," Vetis stated in a disappointed tone. "But its just so fucking boring here! It isn't enough! *Nothing* is ever enough! I *must* conquer the Earth and I *must* conquer Enlightenment and I *must* get rid of those fucking JQ brats somehow! But how? I cannot destroy them on Earth, and I cannot lure them here. If I cannot destroy them, then I will be unable to corrupt another soul on Earth to lead my parallel movement and overwhelm the forces of Arima and that other red-headed disappointment. Oh, how I wish to hang her fucking green eyes from my lobes. It would actually look quite nice, don't you think, Gobbo?"

"Oh my, yes, *quite* nice," the submissive Gobbo answered. "Accessories are *everything* when it comes to fashion. Her green eyeballs hanging from your ears would be the *perfect* complement to your dark red flesh. I dare say, you would be *quite* the talk of the town, Master."

"Then I want *that too!*" Vetis roared. "I want that bitch's green eyes! But how? I cannot get them from her now. If I pop them out of her spiritual head, they'll just disintegrate, and she'll conjure new ones. No, I would have to take them from her human body. But that is impossible now. Yes, quite…um…impossible…um…there would be no…um…way to…Oh glory be, Gobbo! I have it! I have the answer to all our problems! This is fucking brilliant! Give Poppa Vetis a big-ol-hug, sit on my lap and listen to my ultimate plan!"

Gobbo let out a slight giggle as his frail, boney frame was encased in four six-foot long scorching hot arms. "Yes, Gobbo. This time, my plan is foolproof. Now just listen closely. This might get a bit…um…complicated. We don't *have* to get rid of those fucking JQ kids! Hell, we don't even *have* to start a parallel movement! Think about it, Gobbo. What tipped the scales towards righteousness? Give up? That red headed bitch. And what event led to that eventuality? Give up? Her first kill. It was her first kill that put her on the road to what she calls *Twisted Humanitarianism*. It was that first kill. That first taste of blood that led her down the path of revenge killings to protect the downtrodden. Then her joining and leading Murder, Inc., which eventually grew so powerful that they, along with the great democracies of the Earth, could defeat us. It was her first kill, Gobbo, that led her to her half-sister. Her *first kill*. So, if we can go back in time, and tell her first kill to not drive his sabotaged car home from the bar, then he will not die, and then I can corrupt his soul into our movement."

Gobbo reluctantly replied through a shaking voice, "B-but, Master. The four children. They will destroy every soul that you wish to corrupt before you can get to them."

"That's what's so brilliant about my plan!" Vetis yelled out as he thrust his mighty frame off the chair, hurling Gobbo's frail body across the room and into the jagged, flaming wall. "Don't you see, Gobbo? If those little fuckers aren't successful in killing this douche, and he doesn't get into his car that night, then I will have his soul to corrupt, and that little bitch will be deprived of her first kill! And if they *are* successful in killing him, then she would *still* be deprived of her first kill, because his death would not be at her hands! It's a win fucking win! Either way, *she* doesn't kill the guy and *she* doesn't start on her path of righteous killing against the oppressors, bullies, and terrorists of the world! We will have taken this bitch off the board without her even knowing it! Then, when I defeat the Earth, it will be my greatest pleasure to pop those fucking green eyes right out of her skull.

"Oh, Gobbo, I do not believe that I've ever been happier. Come. Sit back on my lap. I need to strengthen my essence to travel into the past and whisper into a man's ear. And let's watch those fucking kids and see what they're up to. They don't have *any clue* that they have just been rendered inconsequential. And get that fat, orange cocksucker in here! He's good for relieving my…tension. Yes, Gobbo, let's watch these oblivious little fuckers enjoy their final days. Because their today is going to look *much different* tomorrow, heh, heh, heh. Huh. They *are* fucking weird. What the fuck are they *wearing*? And what the fuck are they *doing*?"

"Hiya Aunt Rosa! Hiya Uncle Gregory! Hiya Uncle Rod!" the Junior Quad squealed out as they were flailing their arms and clapping their hands in the living room of the estate. "Hello, children," Gregory greeted. "What on earth are you four wearing? And what are you doing?"

Kayla pushed 'pause' on the ancient DVD player and giggled as her twin sister Rachel began explaining. "Well, today is the children's first day of home schooling and we have many subjects to cover. That is why you are here today. As we are giving them their lessons, you will put electrodes on their heads and Rosa will connect with their energy to see just how powerful they are. As for what they are wearing, don't they just look *adorable?*"

Gregory, Rosa, and even the stoic Rod could not help but let out a chuckle as they looked down upon the foursome. Sigourney and Euna were wearing matching pink sweaters, pink satin jackets, pink poodle skirts with white polka dots, bobby socks, and saddle shoes. Thanatos and Kane were wearing denim dungarees that were rolled up just above their white, canvas tennis shoes, white T-shirts, and black leather jackets. Thanatos took a black comb from his back pocket, put it in his mouth, then used it to grease back his white hair.

Euna then spoke. "Yes, don't we look adorable? And we are having our first lesson of the day. This is our dance class, and we are learning how to do the hand jive. Mothers, will you please start the movie again so that we may finish our lesson?"

"Of course, dears," Kayla answered, and Sha-Na-Na's "Born to Hand Jive" came blaring out of the television speakers. The children immediately began flailing their petite arms and clapping their hands perfectly in the prescribed sequence to the song's rhythm. Upon the song's conclusion, Sigourney looked at her sibling and cousins and said, "Yep, we got it. That was easy. C'mon. Let's get dressed for our next class."

The quartet came back into the living room ten minutes later in their customary all-white, fringed western outfits. "Okay, we're ready Uncle Rod," Kane stated as they all took a seat on the couch. As Rod was sticking the electrodes onto Sigourney's forehead, she looked Rod directly in the eyes and said in her high-pitched voice, "You are a very nervous man, aren't you, Uncle Rod?" "Um, um, yes, I am, my dear. P-please don't stare at me like that." The children giggled and Rod proceeded to go down the line of tan foreheads. The electrodes were placed onto the children at the very tip of their lightning bolt birthmarks without incident until Rod reached Thanatos. "No, no," an exasperated Rod requested. "Please, Thanatos, do not put that in your…and not that one either. We must not get these wet. And, no, please Thanatos, you already had that one in your mouth."

"Thanatos!" Kane shouted. "Stop putting electrodes in your mouth! It's not healthy! Let's get this over with! I want to see what games our fathers are going to teach us later."

"Fine!" Thanatos yelled as he spit the final electrode out into Rod's awaiting, shaking hand. "Okay, now Rosa, when I tell you to, just hold onto this metal bar that is connected to the electrodes," Rod requested. "And children, please just shut your eyes for a moment and relax. Try to think of your most relaxing memory. We need to get a baseline reading. Then, as you begin your lessons, we will be able to measure the increase in your energy depending upon the subject."

"Well, we all have to think about the same thing," Sigourney stated. "So, *I* want to think about the bedtime story that Aunt Maddy told us about her shoving an arrow through a pedo's ass!"

"No!" Kane countered. "*I* want to think about Aunt Maddy's bedtime story about her blowing Aunt Vai's father's head off with fireworks!" "Yeah, that one's fun," Thanatos contributed. "But *I* want to think about Aunt Maddy's bedtime story about Aunt Blair eating a man that they cooked for a Halloween party." "Okay, let's be reasonable," Euna interjected. "Those are *all* fine stories, but don't you think that we could all agree that Aunt Maddy's *best* bedtime story was when she rigged the brakes on that man's car and his head was embedded in a tree? Won't it be relaxing to think about how she cut the brake line then feel the car speeding down the highway until it crashes?"

The four children began laughing uncontrollably before Sigourney said, "Yeah, that *will* be relaxing. Okay everybody, let's think about Aunt Maddy's first kill. But I think we're going to blow Aunt Rosa's mind."

"Very good, children. Very good," Rod complimented. "Good. You appear to be very relaxed. Now Rosa, please grab this metal bar and…" There was a violent explosion the moment Rosa touched the metal bar. Her body was flung across the room into the adjacent wall. "Rosa!" Gregory yelled out as he rushed over to the smoking body of his wife.

"I-I'm okay," Rosa said in a weary voice. "Wow. And that is when they're *relaxed*. How much energy will they have when they actually start using their little brains? I'm sorry, Rod, but this isn't going to work. They're too powerful. They overloaded my system with the slightest connection to their energy. Unless we come up with something else, I suppose we'll *never* know just how powerful they are. But I can tell you *this*. I can absorb a lot of energy. I mean, *a lot*. And for my system to be overloaded *that* easily, they *must* be at least as powerful as…a nuclear generator. At *least*."

There was a nervous silence in the room before Sigourney turned to her sister and cousins and said snottily, "I *told* you guys that we'd blow her mind." The four members of the JQ nodded before looking at Rosa and saying in their most innocent voices, "Sorry, Aunt Rosa."

"That's okay, children, it wasn't your fault," Rosa replied as her husband lifted her off the floor. Gregory then whispered into her ear, "So, you're saying that we are dealing with four ten-year-old walking nuclear power plants? What the hell happens if they ever *melt down*?" Rosa looked into her beloved husband's worried eyes and said with soft trepidation, "the apocalypse."

Thirty minutes later, Rachel, Kayla, Rod, Rosa, and Gregory stood in silent amazement as the JQ placed their final book upon the pile in front of them. "That one was easy, too," the foursome said in unison. "We have read and absorbed all the knowledge in all these books. Poetry. Literature. Algebra. Geometry. Trigonometry. Botany. Chemistry. Astronomy. World History. Civics. What will be learning about tomorrow?"

"Um," Rachel began. "I'm not *sure*. We'll have to go back to the library. Maybe some more literature. Or statistics? Theology? I don't know. I think we'll just go to the local college bookstore and buy everything that they have. *That* might kill a couple hours. But hey! Our children are like, super geniuses or something!" Rachel then looked at her sister and they both yelled out, "*Woooooooooo!*"

"Well, I certainly hope that tomorrow's books taste better than today's," Thanatos replied as their fathers, Adam and Aaron walked into the room.

"Hello children," Adam greeted followed by Aaron's, "Yes, hello. We hope that you have had a fun day of school. Now it is time for us to teach you games you can play."

"Yes, indeed," Adam added. "Games that you can play with bad men. We have four of them from our camping trip in Indiana out in the stables. Are you children ready?"

"Yay!" The children squealed as they stampeded out the back door and into the stable. They instantly began giggling and pointing at the four naked and bruised men hanging from their arms from an overhead rafter. "P-p-please, children. P-please let us down. Please h-help us," one of the beleaguered men begged.

"No, we will not!" Kane shouted out. "You are our game pieces, and we are going to have fun with you!" Adam, Aaron, and the rest of the "faculty" entered the stable. Adam and Aaron stood in between the bound, pleading men and began their lesson.

"Oh, children, this will be quite fun," Adam began. Aaron then said, "May I have a volunteer for our first game?" "Me! Me! Me! Me!" The children began yelling out with raised hands. "Hmmm, how about Euna for this first game," Adam said.

"Yay!" Euna squealed out. "That isn't right!" Thanatos shouted. "*Girls* don't get to go first! Only *boys* get to go first!" "Yeah!" Kane agreed. "One of us *boys* should go first!"

"Oh, well, we were not aware of that rule," Aaron said. "Is that correct, Kayla?"

An annoyed Kayla shook her head and said tersely, "Nope. Not even close. Thanatos, do you and Kane want to do *all* the laundry *again* this week?"

Kane and Thanatos looked at one another with defeated faces and reluctantly said, "No. Girls can go first."

"Excellent," Aaron said. "I am so glad that we cleared up that rule. Now Euna, my brother and I are not strong enough to play this game, but perhaps you are. Do you think that you can do this?" He then bent down and whispered something into Euna's ear. Euna's excited smile widened, and she went up to the hanging 'chad.' Her blue and brown eyes began glowing just before she snapped the man's leg in two just below his knee. Her all-white cowgirl outfit became saturated with blood as she dug underneath the anguished man's tendons and muscles and pulled his jagged, broken shin bone from his lower leg. She then broke the bone in two, jumped up and thrust the bones into the wailing man's eye sockets. The whimpering man's body shook for a few moments before shuddering for a final time.

"Excellent, Euna," Adam stated followed by Aaron. "Yes, that was quite good. And remember children to always keep the bones. Do not discard them. They can be made into wonderful game pieces. Now, I believe it will be Sigourney's turn."

"Don't you *dare* say it," Sigourney said as she got up from her seat while glaring at her male cousins. "Yes, Fathers, what game shall you teach *me*?" Adam whispered something to his brother who smiled and nodded. He then bent down and whispered into Sigourney's ear. "Yeah, *I* can play *that* game," Sigourney haughtily said as she approached another pleading man. Drool and snot was running down the beaten man's face. Sigourney lowered his ropes until he fell upon his purple, broken knees. She looked deeply into his pleading eyes, smiled demurely, then began viciously biting through the flesh on his neck. Within seconds, she had chewed through his spinal column and his head popped off like a cork. The entire group was showered with blood as the head plopped onto the lap of Thanatos. "That was cool, Sigourney!" Thanatos yelled out just before he licked the blood from the severed head. "Meh, it's not bad. Needs salt," Thanatos stated flatly as he tossed the head to the side of the stable.

"That was excellent," Adam praised. Aaron then said, "Now Kane, I believe it is your turn." A snickering Kane listened intently to the whispered instructions. He pulled a step ladder from the side of the stable and placed it behind the trembling man. "You are quite lucky, sir," Kane said. "You ae going to be one of Aunt Alexa's masterpieces." His eyes began glowing and his sharpened fingernails began growing. In an instant, Kane had sliced the flesh from the screaming man's back in one sheet. Kane howled with laughter as he then cut through the back muscles and pulled them from the swaying torso. His giggling was uncontrollable as he thrust his fist all the way through the man's back and out his chest, spraying the impressed crowd with a fresh layer of fascist blood.

"Very well done, Kane," Aaron stated. "Yes, quite wonderful," Adam agreed. "Now, children, it is time to teach you our favorite game. And Thanatos, you get to go first, since you have been so patient. This is a special game that we taught your mothers just before they taught *us* a game. Oh, Rachel, Kayla. How will the children ever learn how to play 'Hide the Sausage'? That is not something that we can teach them."

"Nope, not necessary," Rachel replied sternly. "They're going to be perpetually ten years old. That is *not* a game that they will *ever* have to learn. Understand, boys?"

"I suppose so," Adam and Aaron replied in unison before

tying the last man to a long, metal bench, injecting him with adrenaline, and splitting his chest open.

"What is going *on?*" Vai asked as she, Jessie, a healing Cliff, Sam, Jules, and Jamie entered the stable. "We just came up here because Josie said she has a big announcement and wants everybody here for a meeting. Arima and Marcus are on Kaneko's private jet and bringing Paciano, Stellan, and their two-year-old-son, Zihad back home. They should be here in an hour. So, we might want to clean up. This is a mess." Taking the cue, LucyFur jumped from Jessie's arms and began lapping up the fresh blood from the floor.

"We are learning how to play operation, Aunt Vai!" the JQ gleefully responded. "Would you like to play with us?"

Vai hesitated for a moment before pulling up a chair. She smiled and said, "Yes, dears. Yes, I would very much like to play. Gallbladder."

As Thanatos was pulling the screaming man's gallbladder from his slimy cavity, the children looked at one another, nodded and abruptly began exiting the stables. "Children! Where are you going?" Kayla cried out after them. As the adults watched their mounted, giggling, hand jiving children be absorbed by a swirl of colorful lights, they heard the JQ say in unison, "We are going to Madison, Wisconsin on June 7, 2017. You may want to ask Aunt Maddy to come for us this time. She may want to see this."

Chapter 108

Street Kids

"There's Aunt Maddy now!" Thanatos shouted out to his brother and cousins as the lethal quartet watched a twenty-nine-year-old Maddy Sommers crawl under a back parking lot chain link fence and disappear under a grotesquely-orange 1969 Dodge Challenger. "Let's go say 'Hi' to her!"

"You *know* we can't do that," Sigourney replied in her customary haughty tone. "That is Aunt Maddy from 2017. And she is still alive. And she won't even know who we are. Plus, we aren't to interfere with any events except for the assassination of our target. Anything other than that could disrupt the course of natural events in unpredictable ways. Let's just watch her. This is the bedtime story that she told us. Her first kill. The time when she cut the brakes on the car of the man who murdered Uncle Joe."

"Wow," Euna contributed as she was feeding Blackjack a carrot from the shadows of a nearby tree line. "Look at how quickly she did that. And how quickly she discarded her black clothes and tools into that garbage bag. It was just like her story. We all know that Aunt Maddy has a tendency to…um… *exaggerate* a bit. But not about this. Even on her first kill, she was very efficient. And very effective. We could learn much from her."

"Which leads me to a question," a pondering Kane stated. "If Aunt Maddy was already going to kill this guy, then why were *we* summoned?" The JQ stood in contemplative silence as they watched Maddy's darkened car silently pull out from behind a dumpster, onto the street, and away from the run-down tavern. "I think that we need to watch for a while before we make a move. Something doesn't feel right. And Thanatos, quit putting old cigarettes in your mouth."

The children waited for over an hour. They watched with intensity as drunken patrons would step outside for a smoke or to slur sweet nothings into the ear of a potential conquest. The children would quietly giggle and roll their eyes at one another as they heard a steady stream of men saying, "Damn, baby, you're all grown up now aren'tcha?" "You know what would look good on you? Me!" "Wanna come over to my place and watch my new big screen? I've got some fun movies we could watch."

Their attention turned to a large, black sedan that had pulled into the parking lot and backed next to the orange monstrosity. They silently watched the man sitting behind the steering wheel. Every few seconds, there would be the tell-tale glow of a cigarette and a plume of grey smoke emerge from the open driver's side window. "There he is. There's our guy," Euna whispered as a man wearing a dirty T-shirt and jeans staggered out of the bar and began approaching the sedan.

"Are you sure? They all kinda look alike," Thanatos replied. "Yeah, I'm sure," Euna answered. "Look at all of his stupid tattoos. He has the confederate flag, swastika, the number 14, and a weird frog like image all over him. Plus, I can sense his evil. Yep, that's him alright. Hey, the guy in the car is getting out and greeting him. Let's focus our hearing on them and listen in."

"Well, well, well, if it isn't the great, grand, all-powerful

Detective Edmund Simmons." The spindly, skin-headed man said as he walked up to the sedan. "Now, to what do I owe this great pleasure? Well, I bet I know. I bet you have a few goodies for me, don'tcha? At least you had better. I ain't goin' down for that dude's murder. You said it would be alright. You said that it would be called self-defense. But I hear the cops are looking into it. Sayin' that maybe I murdered the guy, which of course, I did. But only because you *hired* me to do it. You hired me to slap that bitch around. You hired me to lure that big oaf out of the bar. And you hired me to shoot him when he tried to play hero. What a dumb son of a…"

The man was silenced by a fierce slap on the side of his face by Detective Simmons. "Don't you *ever* say one bad word about that man. That man *was* a hero. The world would be *lucky* to be filled with men like him. Brave. Smart. Just. He was truly a great man. And he was my best friend. I've just come from his visitation. His funeral is tomorrow. So, I will not listen to one harsh word about him, you fucking piss-ant."

"Well," the man countered. "If he was so *special*, why did you off him? Did he know a little *too much* about your business? Or maybe he was playin' around with your wife. That's it isn't it? Dipping his wick in the wrong wax."

Detective Simmons harshly slapped the man once again, causing his cheek to turn bright red. He looked down and noticed a trail of brake fluid snaking from underneath the man's Dodge Challenger and said, "Nothing like that. Joseph Angelo Argento would never mess around on his wife. Or betray his friend. Unlike me. My reasons are my own and I'm sure as hell not going to share them with you. Don't worry about the cops. I'm the lead investigator and I have ways to ensure that it'll be ruled self-defense. But just in case, and to ensure your safety from any wanna-be neighborhood vigilantes, you need to follow the plan and get out of here. I've got the briefcase with your papers. It has everything you need for your new identity, and the deed to an apartment in Brooklyn.

Once there, you will find an address and key for a safety deposit box. That's when you'll get your money. That's when you will disappear. And I *never* want to see your fuckin' trashy face ever again. Understood?"

"Yeah, I understand, *Detective*." The man snidely replied. "Just remember. If the money ain't there, then I might just have to sing a little song. You got that?"

"Yeah, I'm not too worried about that," Edmund replied as he hid a slight smirk. "Just have a few final drinks with your friends, drive on home, get a good night's rest, and get your ass out of Dodge tomorrow. Just get in your car and drive to your God-forsaken destiny. Oh, and I wouldn't take this briefcase into the bar with you. You wouldn't want it to come up missing now, would you?"

"You got a point, there, *Detective*," the man said through his laughter. He took the briefcase, opened his car door, and tossed it onto the passenger seat. He slammed the door shut and said with a grin, "Now, how 'bout a twenty? A little goin' away present?"

Detective Simmons smiled, pulled a twenty-dollar-bill out and handed it to the grinning man. "Sure, sure. Here you go. It's *my pleasure* to buy you one last round. Now get the fuck away from me. I have a friend to bury."

"Let's do it now!" Thanatos said. "No, not yet," Kane urged. "There's something wrong. Let's just listen for a while longer. That detective guy is getting his phone out. Let's listen in."

"Yeah, it's Simmons. Yeah, it's done. No, he won't be a problem. This is going along just as we had planned. My heart has never felt this heavy, but you're right. It's time to light the fuse for the next generation. It's time for his niece to get her first taste of blood. Then, we'll monitor her development, and, in time, she will join our ranks. I just hate that I had to sacrifice my best friend for this. But it had to be done. We had to do something to light this first ember. And, knowing Maddy the way that I do, this will be the event that will launch her very deadly career. And this will be the event that will eventually bring her into our fold. Yeah, she cut the brake lines. He's in for a bumpy ride. No, I'm not worried about Blair. There's no way that she'll ever find out. And, she'll have *my* shoulder to cry on. I'll get her through this. Plus, she needs me to cover for Maddy. She won't be a problem. Yes, I'm sure. I don't know why you all worry about her so much. Her bark is *way* worse than her bite. She's never had the stomach to get her hands dirty. That's why she had Joe. And now, she has me. I'll check in with you after the funeral. And this asshole's autopsy."

"This doesn't make any sense," a confused Kane stated. "Aunt *Maddy* is going to kill him. We aren't needed, unless… unless…I think I know what's going on. I think that we were brought here to kill him *instead* of Aunt Maddy. And if Aunt *Maddy* doesn't kill him, then she will never tell us this bedtime story. Maybe she won't have *any* bedtime stories to tell us. The future will be altered. Vetis is very clever. But not as clever as *we* are. Okay, gang, listen up. I think that I know a way around this."

"I shouldn't do *what*?" the racist murderer screamed as he sat at the sticky bar finishing his drink. "What the hell are you yellin' about?" the bartender said. "You've had enough. Time to go. Get your drunk ass outta here. We'll see ya tomorrow."

"No, you won't, heh, heh, heh," the man slurred in response. "Hey, I'm getting the feeling that I shouldn't drive tonight. It's weird. I just had this little voice in my head tellin' me that it wasn't a good idea. It was a nice voice. A powerful voice. Anyway, I'm feelin' a bit woozy. Anybody here wanna give me a ride? We can stop off for some burgers or somethin'. My treat. I just got this feelin' that I shouldn't drive tonight. What with the cops lookin' at me and everything."

"Yeah, I can give you a ride," a rotund, overly made-up woman nearly three times his age said suggestively from the corner of the bar. "Well, hell, yeah, baby!" the tittering man responded as his intoxicated eyes peered down at what appeared to him to be a mid-twenties super model. "Yeah, *you* can give me a ride. This'll be fun. I just need to get something out of my car. I'll grab a cab and pick my car up tomorrow. Now, you just sit right there, you pretty little thing, and I'll be right back. Y'know. For that *ride*, heh, heh, heh."

The woman blushed and she felt a familiar dampness as her best prospect in years staggered out the door. The buffoonish man zig-zagged over the cracked concrete toward his prized car. He was whistling and looking into his wallet. "Shit. I used my last condom the other night on that crack whore. Oh well, what do I care? If this bitch gets knocked up, then she gets knocked up. Its not like she'll ever be able to find me. Not after tonight, heh, heh, heh.

"Nope, after tonight, I'm on easy street. New name. New city. My own fancy apartment. And six figures sitting in a safety deposit box. And all I had to do was squeeze a trigger. All I had to do was get rid of another libtard. Fuckin' (derogatory term omitted) lovers. I hate those pricks. The only thing that's worse than a (derogatory term omitted) or a (derogatory term omitted) or a (derogatory term omitted) is a White man who *loves* those godless vermin. They've invaded our country. Taking over the news and the movies and the schools. Fuckin' our White women. Or turnin' our kids gay or some shit. They're a cancer. I'm *glad* I shot that son of a bitch. And I'm *really* glad to now have the money to start my *own* movement. A movement to fight against these fuckin' leftist, snowflake pricks. A movement to take our country back and put it into the hands of the *true* patriots. The *true* Americans. White Christian men. *We* are the ones who should be ruling everything! Not the (derogatory term omitted) or the (derogatory term omitted) or the (derogatory term omitted). Us! And if we have to bring this whole fuckin' democracy down to do it, well, then, so be it. Hand me the fuckin' flame thrower. Then these other so-called *people* can work for *us.* Be our slaves. Or they can fuckin' die. It's gonna be paradise on Earth. And *I'm* gonna have a front-row seat, heh, heh, heh."

The deplorable man looked up when he heard the soft voices of four children say, "You say bad things. That makes us want to play with you."

"W-w-what the fuck are you (derogatory term omitted) kids doin' on my *car?*" he screamed out as he saw four children dressed in blood-stained white western outfits sitting on top of their Shetland ponies, who in turn were standing on the roof and hood of a nightmarish-orange Dodge Challenger. The vintage metal creaked under the weight of the unwelcome passengers as the frantic man came rushing towards the car.

"Get your assess off of there!" He screamed at them. "Okay," the children replied in unison. They nudged their heels into the sides of their friends and the ponies dutifully pounced down upon the pavement. The children looked up at the approaching man and smiled innocently as he yelled out, "I'm gonna beat your fuckin' little assess! Just look at the dents! Oh, I'm gonna *kill* you little sons-a-bitches! I don't care if you're kids or not! You'll just grow up to be takers and rapists anyway! I'm gonna do the world a favor!"

"Gee," the tittering children responded as they slowly trotted away from the car. "You radical right-wing men sure are funny when you get angry. Your eyes bulge out and your white faces turn bright red. You should be careful not to get so heated. You don't want to melt now do you...snowflake? So, would you like to play a game with us? How about tag?" The four children's voices then dropped, and their faces grew dark as they finished with, "You're it."

"Snowflake? How *dare* you call me a...oh, I'm gonna play a fuckin' game with you, alright!" the man yelled as he jumped into the driver's seat and turned the ignition. "I'm gonna play roadkill! And *you're* gonna be it!"

"This is going to be fun," a giggling Sigourney said as the JQ tapped the sides of their steeds.

A lonesome tear fell down the cheek of the hopeful woman looking out the window of the bar as she heard four galloping children scream "Wooooooo!" followed by the roar of a powerful engine.

The chrome front bumper of the muscle car would come tantalizingly close to the back hooves of the Shetlands before the children would look back, stick their tongues out, laugh, and rapidly accelerate. "Wheeeee!" the exuberant children exclaimed as they guided their impossibly fast steeds along the rural road. Their blondish-white hair and bloodied, white fringe streamed straight back from the rush of the warm June air. The scene was repeated over and over through the winding curves on the outskirts of Madison. The drunken and increasingly irate driver would floor the accelerator only to once again be denied his bloodlust by a galloping and giggling cloud of dust. His anger hit a frenzied pitch and he was sweating profusely. He saw an approaching sharp curve. *Well, they're gonna* have *to slow down now,* he thought to himself as he flashed a devilish smile and slammed his foot down on the accelerator. His deafeningly loud machine was inches away from the back pounding hoofs of Snot when the road abruptly veered to the left. He watched in amazement as the laughing children's steeds effortlessly glided around the sharp corner. The RPM needle was buried in red as he desperately turned the steering wheel. There was the horrific, high-pitched sound of skidding rubber.

CHAPTER 109

I Love the Sound of Breaking Glass

There was a brilliant flash of white light along the edge of a narrow highway that wound its way between the lush trees of a dense forest. The nearly full moon cast its eerie light down on two black-jeaned, black-hooded figures that had emerged from the brilliant spectacle. "Whooooa, that was *trippy*, man!" Erick exclaimed to his wife. "Is that what dropping acid is like?"

"I dunno," an annoyed Maddy replied.

"How 'bout shrooms?" Erick inquired further. "Is that what doing 'shrooms is like?"

"I dunno," Maddy answered more tersely.

"Well, how about…" Erick tried to ask again before he was abruptly cut off by an increasingly agitated Maddy. "I don't fucking *know*! I haven't *done* that shit! All I've done is smoke a little weed and then, well, I don't *even* want to talk about my little adventure with heroin. That shit nearly killed me. Now, would you like to hear all the different ways that I'm *pissed off* right now?"

"No, not really," an uninterested Erick replied following a deep sigh and eye roll.

"No, you don't?" Maddy persisted. "Well, you're fuckin' *gonna*! Here's all the reasons that I'm *really* pissed off right now! Numero-Uno: I *told* you that if we let Uncle Joe train us on how to go back to Earth through time that we would be bothered! I fucking *told* you! And guess what? I was *right*! Here we are! Numero-Two-O: I was *just about* to relax with a bowl of my delicious, conjured ice cream when Arima told me about this little escapade. So, I'm missing out on *that*! Numero-Three-O: Where the fuck *are* we exactly? Why are we standing in the middle of the fucking boondocks? Stupid fucking Gwen probably led us into the middle of nowhere on *purpose*. That's just the type of vindictive *bitch* that she is. Numero-Four-O: Here we are all dressed in our murdering finest and guess what? We can't fucking *kill* anybody! What's the point of *that*? All we can do is find the JQ and bring them home! Which leads me to Numero-Five-O: Where the fuck *are* they? Do you see the JQ? *I* sure as fuck don't see the JQ! Are we supposed to go tromping through the *fucking wilderness* to find those hell spawn brats? Well, what do you have to say, Mister?"

"Shhhhhh," Erick replied after ignoring his wife's diatribe. "I think I hear something. It sounds like…um…it sounds like…thunder." From around the sharp corner came a galloping, giggling blur of four children riding impossibly fast Shetland ponies followed by the intense roar of an engine. There was then the horrific, high-pitched sound of skidding rubber and an explosion of crumpled metal and shattering glass as the Dodge Challenger lodged itself into the trunk of a centuries-old Oak tree.

"Wow," a dismayed Maddy stated to her equally surprised husband. "That was *cool*. Is there any better sound than shattering glass? They say that when a door closes, a window opens, right? An open window with glass that you can crawl through to your next opportunity in life. *If* you have the balls to do it. Glass represents the world outside that you can look at but not touch. Not experience. You can only watch the world go by. You are safe behind the glass, but *staying* behind that glass gives you no real-life experiences. No love. No loss. No real emotional connection to anything. No impact upon the world. You're just sitting there, taking up space and resources. You're not contributing anything. You're just sponging off everybody else's hard work and experiences. It's a really sad, lonely life. But when that glass *breaks*? When it shatters, you have *no choice* but to experience the real world! You have *no choice* but to be in it! To belong to it! Because your glass fortress has been shattered and you're exposed to the raw elements of the world, whether you want to be or not. Maybe it'll be a good thing for you. Maybe that shattering glass has given you the excuse you always needed to get out and actually live a life. And maybe that new life will be a positive for other people that you are now forced to interact with. Or maybe not. Like *this* fucker. *His* shattered glass just allowed his head to be planted into that tree. Wow, man. His head is fucking *buried*!"

"What the fuck are you talking about? Are you *sure* you don't drop acid?" a confused Erick asked before hearing the quadrophonic voices of the Junior Quad. "Hiya Aunt Maddy! Hiya Uncle Erick!" the foursome squealed.

Maddy looked upon the approaching children through her tearful effervescent eyes and yelled out, "Oh my God! Kids! It's so great to finally see you! Come here and give us a hug!" The children squealed with delight, jumped down from their ponies and launched themselves into the warm, awaiting arms of Maddy and Erick. "Oh, just let me look at you," Maddy stated through her stuttering, emotional voice. "Oh, my lord, you are all so cute! You are the *perfect* combination of your parents. It's just so great to be able to actually hold you. We've been wanting to do this since you were born, but all we could do is watch. Well, and tell you bedtime stories in your dreams. Have you heard all my bedtime stories?"

"We sure have!" the foursome responded enthusiastically. "We just *love* them!"

"Well, of course you do," Maddy retorted through her giddy chuckles as Erick rolled his eyes once again. "So, tell me. Which story is your *favorite*? Oh, I bet I know. Is it the one about me and your Uncle Erick burying that murdering fuck alive in a frigid hole? Oh! Or is it the time that I dismembered those rapists then hung their heads and torsos in that construction site? And then I said, 'Now you're hung enough for me!' Was it that one? Or how about the time I tied that prick up and cut pieces off him while dancing around? Then I cut off his dick, stuffed it into his mouth, decapitated the fucker, and hung his head on the wall. I bet it's *that* one isn't it, hmmmmm?"

"Well, not exactly, Aunt Maddy," Sigourney answered. "No, those are all great stories, but they aren't our favorite," Thanatos contributed. "I mean, *all* of your stories are *just* wonderful," Euna chimed in, "but there's *one* story that we enjoy over all others." "Yes," Kane concluded. "Our *favorite* bedtime story doesn't have *you* in it at all. The story we love the *most* is when Aunt Josie shot her first boyfriend and his father with arrows, then threw them in a pool filled with piranha. *That* one is our favorite!"

"What the *fuck* are you little bastards talking about?" an agitated Maddy roared. "That fuckin' story *suuuuucks*! And those piranhas were *mine*! She *stole* them, the thieving little bitch! Plus, she made a joke at the end of it that referenced porn, and children should *not* be exposed to that. I just can't believe that my daughter would tell you about that. That's just wrong." Maddy's tone then changed to a contrived, innocent manipulation as she looked down upon their tender faces and said, "Come on kids. I *know* that one of *my* stories is probably your favorite. It's okay. Just tell me, then we can all go home. It's okay. Take your time to think about it. I can wait. I have *all* the time in the world. Literally."

Euna, sensing the need for diplomacy replied, "Well, I suppose that if we were to choose one of *your* stories, Aunt Maddy, then it would be *this* one." The other three children nodded emphatically in agreement while awaiting their opportunity to change the subject.

"What do you mean *this* one? *You* killed this guy. *I* didn't. What are you talking about?" Maddy asked while wearing a confused expression upon her slightly befreckled face. "Don't you recognize the car, Aunt Maddy?" Sigourney asked.

Maddy walked across the highway with her husband while staring at the twisted metal. The front end was completely wrapped around the tree and the smoking engine block had crushed the driver's feet, legs, and torso into the back seat. Blood dripped from the bark that encased his obliterated head. Maddy reached over the jagged metal and gently stroked what remained of the victim's shaved scalp and said softly, "Oh...my...God. I'm in Madison. It's June 7, 2017. This is one of the saddest nights of my life."

"Who *is* this?" a concerned Erick asked. "This," Maddy quietly replied, "is the man who murdered Uncle Joe. This is the man who destroyed my family for a time. This is the man whose brakes I cut. This is the first man that forced me to kill him."

Erick put his arm around his beloved wife, and she laid her copper locks upon his shoulder. He felt his black hoodie become saturated in her tears and said tenderly, "Are you okay?"

Maddy responded by bouncing into the middle of the highway while clapping her hands and laughing. "Okay? Are you fucking *kidding* me? I've never *seen* this before! I knew that I caused him to crash his car, but I never had the opportunity to *see* what I did! And just *look* at it! It's fucking *beautiful*! Look at his body! It doesn't even *exist* anymore! It's just a bunch of mush! And his head is fucking *pulverized*! And look at all the beautiful blood on the pavement and clear up in the tree! Oh my God! Do you know what I'm thinking about? I'm thinking about his final thoughts. Can you *imagine*? Can you *imagine* knowing that in a split-second you're going to fucking crash into a tree? Can you *imagine* knowing that in a split-second your entire body is going to be destroyed? The thought of all the *pain* that you're going to experience just before you fucking *die*? Can you *imagine*? Okay? Fuck yeah, I'm okay! This is fucking awesome!

"But wait," Maddy said in a more reserved tone as she turned her attention to the beaming smiles of the JQ. "If *I* killed him, which I did, then why are *you* four here? Why were *you* called? I had it handled."

"Well," Kane began explaining. "It seems as though Vetis is trying to be a bit cute with time and future events. He used his influential powers to tell this man to not drive his car home tonight. And, if he *hadn't* driven home, then he would not die, and you would not have had your first kill. And if you *didn't* have your first kill, then perhaps you don't go on to your career as a vigilante serial killer and freedom fighter. And you would not have connected with your half-sister, Aunt Arima. And if you *don't* do any of that, then perhaps Vetis would not have been defeated in the year 2042. You were the key to it all, Aunt Maddy, and Vetis tried to make you irrelevant."

"Yes," Euna contributed. "And *we* were called because this bad man was to be Vetis's next soul to darken. So, *we* were to kill him. But we realized what was happening. We realized that if *we* killed this man instead of *you* killing him, then Vetis would succeed in his plan. So, we had to *make sure* that the man drove his car tonight. That is all we had to do. Make sure he drives his car with the cut brakes. And that was quite simple. We just played 'Tag' with him. He was 'it.'"

"Yes!" Sigourney exclaimed. "And it was fun! We had such fun allowing him to almost catch us then speed up until…"

"BOOM!" a giggling Thanatos yelled out. "So, you see Aunt Maddy, you still killed him. There will be no record of our being here. As far as your 2017 self knows, he died completely at *your* hands. As will so many others now from this point on. And then, we will hear all your wonderful bedtime stories."

"Huh," a chin stroking Maddy said as she pondered what she had just heard. "Well, *that* was a pretty fucked up thing to do. That Vetis is a real prick. We really need to find a way to destroy him once and for all, so I don't have to worry about being bothered while eating my ice cream."

"Oh, we have a plan, Aunt Maddy," the quartet stated in unison. "And you are going to play a very important part in it."

"Whaaaat?" Maddy answered dismissively. "No, no, no. This is *Earth's* problem. When I said 'we' I really meant 'you.' I've got shit to do. Just have Arima tell me when you've got it done."

"Well, *I'll* listen to your plan, kids. Why are *you* always the one that people plan with?" an incredulous Erick asked. "I mean, I've killed people *too*! I've planned the murder of a *bunch* of fuckers! In a lot of *fun ways* too! Jamming toy soldiers up that pedo's ass, for example. Remember *that* one? Or, how about when I had to infiltrate the brownshirts? Sure, I didn't *kill* them, but I had to infiltrate them so that you *could*. Or, how about the guy that almost killed you and our unborn child? I ripped *that* fucker's heart right out of his chest! Why don't *I* get a bit more respect for *my* contributions in saving the world?"

Maddy looked into the hurt eyes of her beloved husband. She knew that she had to find the right words to soothe his bruised ego. She knew that she could not fuck this up. Maddy fucked it up. "Well, because I'm the *star* of this book series, duh. *That* was a stupid fuckin' question."

"Well, you *used* to be the star," an offended Erick countered. "You *used* to be the focal point of this story. But now, the *main* story lines involve our daughter and the JQ. Face it, you're nothing more than a *secondary* character now."

Erick immediately looked down to hide his knowing grin

from his enraged wife. *This is so easy*, he thought to himself just before he heard Maddy shout out, "You motherfucker! *Secondary* character? *Secondary* character? Oh, I'm no fucking *secondary* character! I was, and still *am*, the *star* of this half-baked shit! If it wasn't for *me*, Josie and the JQ and Arima and all the *rest* of these fuckin' poseurs wouldn't even have a story to *be* in! I'm the fuckin' star and will *continue* to be the fuckin' star or else my name isn't Maddy *fuckin'* Sommers! And *that's* my name, so *that's* just how it's going to be! Okay kids, you got my attention. It's time that I shatter my own pane of glass, stop watching this shit, and get back in the game. So, what's your plan. And just whisper it to me. Your Uncle Erick doesn't need to know. He's just a *secondary* character, anyway."

"Maddy, come on. Don't be like that," Erick pleaded. "I didn't mean anything by it. Come on. Please let me hear the plan."

"Well, I don't know," Maddy responded in her "hurt" voice while staring down at her shuffling feet. "If it was your goal to hurt my feelings tonight, well, congratulations sir. You have accomplished that. I hope that you feel proud of yourself."

"Maddy, I didn't mean to hurt your feelings," a back peddling Erick answered. "What is it that you want? What can I say to make you feel better?"

"Well," Maddy's lilting voice responded. "I *suppose* that I *might* feel better if you were to retract that horrible *lie* that you just told and admit that *I'm* the star of these books. That *might* make me feel better."

Erick let out a deep sigh, shook his hung head in disbelief and said in a defeated voice, "Fine. I'm sorry that I said that. You are the star. Are you happy now?"

"Yep, sure am!" Maddy cheerfully replied. "You know, one of the things that I love about you is that you know when to admit that you're wrong. Okay kids, how about that plan? And speak up so that your Uncle Erick can hear it too."

A swirling bright white light emerged from the tree line next to the highway as sirens could be heard approaching from the distance. Just before Maddy, Erick, and the JQ entered, they heard a soft, feminine voice say, "Please, Maddy. Please don't go just yet. Just give us a moment." A blonde-haired woman and bald man emerged from the glare of the kaleidoscope. Their eyes were filled with tears as they rushed towards the children.

"Oh, fuckin' Gwen," Maddy muttered to her husband. "She's such a fuckin' softie." Maddy then turned to the figures who were embracing the children as they sat upon their ponies. "But make it fuckin' fast, bitch! We gotta get out of here before the cops show up. I can't be seen here."

"Who are you?" the JQ asked in unison. The chuckling woman wiped tears from her blue eyes and said, "Well, my dears, I am your Grandmother Kristy Anderson. And this is your Grandfather Jason Anderson. We are the parents of your fathers, Adam and Aaron and of your Aunt Alexa and Aunt Vai. We have been pleading with the powers in Enlightenment to allow us to come here and hold you just one time. I have done some very stupid and destructive things in my life, and my penance was to never be able to be in contact with my loved ones. Until now. Thank you, Maddy. Thank you for forgiving me and allowing this visit."

"You did *what*?" a shocked Erick asked. "*You* set this up? I'm so *proud* of you right now."

"Yeah, yeah, yeah," Maddy stated as she looked away from the group. "It's not a big thing. I just thought that they might want to meet their grandkids, that's all. Nothing to make a big deal over."

Erick lifted his wife's head up with his index finger and looked into her tearful eyes. He smiled at her and gave her a slight nod. Maddy let out a relieved chuckle and yelled out,

"Oh my God Kristy, I've missed you so much!" The pair of reunited friends embraced tightly as Maddy continued. "And of *course*, I forgive you. I mean, I stole your kids and drove you away. What *else* could you do but allow yourself to be possessed by my bitch mother and murder me?"

"Oh, I've missed you too," the joyful Kristy replied. "But I'm still sorry that I murdered you. And Erick! I really shouldn't have stabbed him in the back. My beef was with you, not him."

"It's okay," Maddy answered which prompted Erick to say, "Um, no it's not. She fucking stabbed me."

"Just get over it!" Maddy ordered before taking Kristy and Jason by their hands and leading them back to a bewildered JQ. "Listen to me, kids. These are your grandparents. And they are wonderful people. They are my friends. You can trust them, and you can love them. Just as I do."

As the figures dissipated into the bright, swirling light, there was the sound of tires screeching to a halt over the shattered glass on the pavement. "That really *is* a great fuckin' sound," Maddy said as they were carried away to the estate in 2042.

CHAPTER 110

ANYTHING YOU CAN DO (I CAN DO BETTER)

"Well, everybody's here except for the JQ and I guess we can't get started until they get back and we know that they're safe," Josie stated as she looked upon the multiple faces of her friends and most trusted members of Murder, Inc. on this cooling June evening. Each were seated in folding chairs in a cleared pasture behind the estate in pre-assigned groups. Everyone then gasped as they noticed a bright white light explode from behind them.

"Oh my God, is it them?" Rachel cried out. The group then began chuckling as they heard pounding on the front door of the estate and a demanding woman's voice shouting, "Hey motherfuckers! Anyone home? We have your fuckin' kids!"

"Yeah, it's them," Josie stated as she rolled her eyes. The group got up from their seats and rushed to the front of the house where they found Erick, Maddy, Kristy, Jason, and the JQ on their ponies. "Oh, thank God!" Kayla yelled out as she and her twin sister rushed to their respective children.

Tears of joy were plentiful as the group embraced one another in this unexpected reunion. "We're sorry that we snapped your neck, Mother," Adam stated followed by

Adam's, "Yes, quite sorry. We did not enjoy playing that game." "Oh, just shut up and come here!" Kristy exclaimed as she and her husband Jason were enveloped in the embrace of Adam, Aaron, Alexa, and Vai.

"Dad!" Josie squealed as she launched herself into her father's awaiting arms. "Uh, what the fuck am I, chopped liver?" an annoyed Maddy said. Josie looked at her near-mirror image, sauntered up to her and said softly, "Hello, Mom. It's great to see you. Thanks for helping with this." Erick took the opportunity to approach Lionnel. "Helloooo, Lionnel," Erick said nonchalantly. "Um, h-hello sir, I mean, M-Mr. Parker, I mean sir," a nervous Lionnel replied. "Soooo," Erick continued. "I hear that you've been listening to some Jefferson Starship." Lionnel let out a nervous chuckle and replied, "Yes sir. It's a new discovery for me. And one that I found to be…um…inspirational." Erick wiped a tear from his eye, approached the nervous young man and hugged him tightly. He then whispered into his ear, "I love you like a son, Lionnel, but don't you *ever* break my Josie's heart again, do you understand?" "P-perfectly, sir," Lionnel replied before they were joined in a group hug by Maddy and Josie.

Kristy and Jason made the rounds as they were introduced to everybody by the uncharacteristically emotional Sam and Jules. Maddy approached the rightfully suspicious Rachel and Kayla and said, "So, here ya go. Here's your fuckin' brats. So, just try to keep track of them from now on, okay? I have shit to do, and I don't even *like* these little fuckers, so just leave me out of it from now on."

The JQ then said in their unified, innocent voices, "That isn't true Aunt Maddy. You like us. Love us even. That is why you tell us bedtime stories every night."

"What the fuck are you four talking about?" Maddy yelled out, garnering the attention of the entire group. "Bedtime stories? Me? Fuckin' kids and their imaginations. Listen kids, I've got nothing against you *personally*, it's just that I *told* your parents that you four would be a fuckin' *nightmare* and look at all the *shit* that you've caused." She then looked over to her husband who gave her a single look. It was just the two of them silently communicating with one another as Erick's look said, *Maddy, you don't have to be right all the time and you don't have to be tough all the time. Let down your guard and allow yourself to express the love that you have in your heart for these children.* Maddy chuckled, nodded, and said, "Oh, fuck it! Come here you four! I love you all so much! And you can call me whenever you need me, okay? If you need anything at all, just let Arima know, and I'll be here for you. I'll be like your lil' redheaded guardian in the sky!"

"And we will be *your* guardian here on Earth, Aunt Maddy," the JQ replied. "Should we tell them about our plan now? Your mission will not be over, and you cannot go back to Enlightenment until we tell them."

"What plan?" Josie inquired. "Oh, just a little something that me and the kids have cooked up," Maddy answered haughtily. "And since we have the entire murderer's row here, I guess its as good a time as any."

"Okay, but *I* have a plan to announce *first*," Josie stated bluntly. "Uh, well, I'm sure you do," Maddy countered. "But since *I* am the slight elder here, and *my* plan is probably a bit more *important*, then *I* think that *I* should go first." "Mother," Josie's stern voice replied as she pasted a fake smile upon her youthful face. "Once again, and for the *last time*, I am in charge of Murder, Inc. and *I* am leading this meeting. So, I will call on *you* at the appropriate time. Thank you for your understanding. I'm glad that's settled."

"Why, you ungrateful little bit..." Maddy attempted to counter before she felt her husband's warm hand clasp her mouth. Erick then said, "That will be fine, dear. You just let us know when it's time for her to speak. And take your time. I'm enjoying being here with you."

"This is fucking ridiculous," an annoyed Maddy stated to

her husband as she angrily kicked her crossed leg with her arms tightly folded. "How come I have to go second? Oh, I bet *I* know. It's because I'm now a *secondary* character, right?" "Just let it go and shut up," an annoyed Erick answered before Josie got up and stood in front of her assembly.

"Thank you all for being here," Josie began as her flowered summer dress waved subtly in the cooling breeze. "And thank you for your continued support for our organization. I know that I've been a bit...um...out of sorts lately. But I'm back on my game and ready to lead this entire group with the respect, dignity, and empathy that you all deserve. Now, to our little plan.

"As we all know the Underground Autocratic Movement, or UAM, still has some fighters hiding out in various rural areas in this country. There are a handful of pockets throughout the world, actually, but we will target the members in *this* country first. The world takes its cues from America. So, if we complete the eradication of them *here*, other countries should follow suit. Well, once we get rid of a few turncoat foreign dignitaries, that is. But that's another discussion for another time. This country can be a shining beacon for all the world, or it can be a toxic, hate-fueled cesspool that drags *everyone* down into darkness. We've done much to turn the tide, but our battle is not yet over. My friends, we *will* turn this country into the humanitarian shining beacon that all *true* freedom and peace-loving patriots aspire for it to be. And we will do it by doing to them what they wish to do to us. We're going to rip these fascists apart and crush them once and for all.

"I have divided the country into five quadrants. Each of you will lead groups of Assassination Technicians to flush the traitors out and destroy them. Alexa has been producing a stockpile of Lucy's toxins that you will have at your disposal along with your other customary...um...toys. The specific locations and assignments are in the packets that I have given you. Here are the teams. Quadrant One will be Jessie, Cliff, and...um...LucyFur, I guess. Quadrant Two will be Sam and Henri. Quadrant Three will be Kayla and Rachel. Yes, ladies, it's time for you two to get back in the game." Rachel and Kayla looked at one another, smiled and yelled out, "Wooooooo!"

"Oh, for fuck sakes, that's annoying," Maddy muttered under her breath before being jabbed in her ribs by her husband's elbow.

"Quadrant Four will be Rosa and Dragenstein. And finally, Quadrant Five will be Vai and The Twins. It's time for you boys to start playing your games again. Go there, kill them in any way you find most appropriate and enjoyable. But bring at least one of them back alive from each quadrant. I want a few that we will interrogate. We'll dispose of them after we obtain all the information that we can from them. As for everybody else, Gregory and Marcus will fly Aunt Arima to each quadrant as the missions are completed so that she can absorb and destroy their dark souls. Kaneko, Stellan, and Paciano will remain here and care for Zihad and the JQ. And Rod, Lionnel, and I will work on the most important part. None of this will end as long as there is pure evil in the universe that is influencing humanity. As long as Vetis exists, he will continue to whisper into the ears of the willfully ignorant and continue to build hate-filled, self-absorbed armies of dutiful dullards. We must find a way to destroy him, and that is what we are working on right now. How we on Earth can reach and destroy him in The Realm of Perdition. We don't know how to do that yet, but we're working on it."

"Well, good luck with *that*," Maddy stated in an arrogant tone. "Mother, do you have something to say?" Josie asked as her intense, green eyes glared at Maddy. "Well, I was just *thinkin'*," Maddy coyly responded. "That it would be *great* if someone *here* had a plan for that. But, y'know, it really doesn't seem to be that *important*, seeing as how *I* have to go *second* and everything, so I guess I'll just keep it to myself."

"Mother," and increasingly frustrated Josie replied. "If you would like to share your plan with us, now would be the time." "Oh, I dunno if I'm in the *mood* now," Maddy replied as she looked up into the starry night while twiddling her thumbs. "I mean, I *was* in the mood, but seeing as how your plan seems to be *primary*, I guess my *secondary* plan just isn't all that important."

"Oh, Jesus Christ!" Erick bellowed to his wife. "Would you just get the fuck up there and tell them what the JQ's plan is?" "Fine! I will!" Maddy snapped back. "But not until our *genius* daughter admits that this is the most important part of the plan!" Erick looked at his proud daughter with pleading eyes before Josie finally broke down and said in a cold, tense voice, "Fine, Mother. Your plan is the most important part of this. Are you happy now?"

"Yep, sure am!" Maddy exclaimed as she jumped up from her seat and bounded to the front of the dismayed but amused group. "Thanks dear for the introduction and thanks for admitting when you're wrong. You may be a genius, but there's nothing that can replace good old-fashioned experience. Oh, please don't sit in my chair, dear. I think there's one towards the back. Yep, right over there. Thank you for your consideration. Okay gang, here's the deal. There are two parts to this. One battle will be waged on the Earth and the other will be waged in the Universe. And when the smoke clears, that fucker Vetis is going to wish that he had *never* fucked with humanity, heh, heh, heh."

There was nervous silence as Maddy took a bow following her overly animated presentation and gestured to her daughter to come to the front. "The floor is now yours, dear," Maddy said in a conceited tone with her nose in the air. "Thank you, Mom. Really, thank you," Josie said as she reassumed her position in front of the group. "Wow. Well, that's the plan then. Kaneko, we're going to need a lot of your luck to rub off on us for this to work. Okay, a few final thoughts. This operation will take a few months. We will have to sacrifice a bit and be away from each other for long periods of time and I just want to express right now how much I love you all and will miss you. We also need to have this completed by Alexa's art show. We will use her incredible art as a final celebration of our victory. When will you be ready, Alexa?"

"Well," the bubbly blonde began. "At the pace that I'm working, I'm looking at February 14 of next year, 2043." Josie chuckled and said, "February 14th. Valentine's Day. My birthday. My parents' anniversary. Of course. It's perfect Alexa. Thank you. Okay folks, that's it. Let's have these fascist, demonic assholes all wrapped up in a bow by next Valentine's Day. Oh! But that's not the most *important* part!" Josie squealed. "*Some* of you may have *noticed* that I arrived here with a certain *handsome man* on my shoulder. So, no need for rumors. That's right! Lionnel and I are back together! Isn't that great?"

The entire group stood and gave the couple a standing ovation more from relief than actual adulation. Marcus whispered to Arima, "How exactly is that the most important part? I mean, it's nice and everything, but saving the world and the universe seems a bit more important." "Yeah, I know," Arima calmy answered. "But teenage girls, y'know. What are you gonna do? Hey, did you see how our weed is doing in the back garden? This is gonna be a fun summer."

A bright white swirling light appeared just behind the seats of Erick and Maddy. "Aw, shit, we have to go," a somber Erick muttered. Following tearful hugs good-bye, the forms of Erick, Jason, and Kristy walked into the vortex. Just before following them in, Maddy grabbed her daughter and said, "Listen. I know that I can be a bit…um…*difficult* sometimes, but just know that I love you and I am proud of you, okay?"

"Okay, Mom. I love you too," Josie replied in her choked up voice.

"Damn, this never gets easier," Josie said through a forced smile as the reflection of the white vortex disappeared from her tears. "But that's our reality. And at least we know that our loved ones are still with us. Alright, let's shake this off. I think we need to have some fun before we call it a night. Kaneko, would you please bring out the libations? Stellan and Paciano, could you grab the snacks? And Adam and Aaron, would you please bring out our entertainment for the evening?"

With each awkward step that they took as they were being led by a heavy chain by the Twins, Pogo II and Larry shrieked in pain. Wooden "feet" had been nailed to their stumps where their knees once were, causing intense misery with every forced step. Holes had been drilled into what remained of their arms and serrated kitchen knives had been lodged into the tender wounds. Their soiled diapers leaked urine and excrement as the screaming pair were lifted by the Twins and placed into a large playpen. Rachel and Kayla placed mouth-guards over what teeth the pair had remaining, for safety reasons one would assume, looked at each other and yelled out, "Woooooo!" Sam and Josie wore lascivious little grins as they approached their trembling, tortured mini gladiators. Sam looked down and said, "Okay, Pogo II. This is your chance. Despite your torture of innocent women over the years, I am giving you this chance to redeem yourself. If you win this match, I'll stop putting cigarettes on your head for a while and I'll change your diaper more than once a week. Now, get in there and kill this bastard!"

"Huh," Josie snorted before turning to her Larry. "Well, Larry, you are *just* as much of a dickwad as Pogo over there. But if *you* win, I'll have *your* diaper changed *daily* and I'll stop using your *chest* as a dart board. Pretty good deal, huh? Now cut this little prick up!"

Josie took her place at the side of the cartoon-adorned

"ring" next to Lionnel who looked straight up to the sky while trying to pretend this wasn't happening. "Hey!" Josie yelled out. "They aren't doing anything! Zap 'em!"

"Alright Josie," Adam said as he pressed a button on a remote causing Pogo's shock collar to rip electricity into his neck. "Yes, alright. What a fun game you have chosen," Aaron said as he pressed his button causing Larry to squeal in agony. The pair of reluctant warriors stared at each other for a moment then began flailing their arms.

"Oh, wow," Jules said in amazement. "Look at how fast they can twirl their little arms." "Yeah, my Pogo's going to kick his ass," Sam cooly replied. "No, he won't," Josie retorted followed by the pair going back and forth with, "Yes, he will," "No, he won't", "Yes, he will," "No, he…oh shit! Lionnel look at *this!*"

Larry had managed to bowl Pogo over with a butt of his shaved, scarred head and was now straddling his face. Pogo was choking on the pungent feces that he was being smeared with and was dripping into his open, screaming mouth. The entire group, including Lionnel, burst out into uncontrolled laughter. "Okay, this is pretty messed up, Josie," Lionnel said through his howls. "But I have to admit, that's pretty funny. Especially for a pair of deplorables like them. Come on Pogo! Are gonna take that shit? I mean, literally! Are you gonna take that shit? Get up!" "Hey!" Josie yelled out. "Whose side are you on anyway?" "Oh yeah, sorry," Lionnel said. "I kinda forgot whose was whose. Fascists all look the same to me. Come on Larry! Stab him in the eye!"

"Eat shit and die!" Jamie yelled while Dragenstein said in her Monroe-esque voice, "You know, it seems like only yesterday that I snapped Larry's limbs off and now look at him. I'm so proud." A red-faced Cliff turned to his beloved Jessie and whispered, "Oh man, I'm going to hell just for being here. Are you *sure* you can't behold any evil in this group?" Jessie's brilliant blue eyes remained locked on the vile carnage as she replied, "Nope. Not one bit. No evil here. Just vengeance. And popcorn. Hand me the popcorn, Cliff."

The group's laughter became louder as Pogo spun out from underneath Larry, bounced upon his wooden "feet" and slashed the entirety of Larry's face from his forehead to his chin with his left "arm." "That's my Pogo!" Sam yelled out. "That's cheating! Where's the ref?" Josie screamed as she jumped to her bare feet. "Oh man," Marcus said to Arima. "Is this really happening right now, or am I tripping balls?" "I dunno," his wife answered through her haze. "Looks real. But I'm pretty baked right now so…hey pass me those brownies, wouldja? They're nice and gooey, just how I like them."

An ashamed Rosa and Gregory looked upon the scene while trying to conceal their amusement. "Well, she had to find *some* sort of outlet," Rosa said to her husband. "I guess this is better than those power trips that she went on." A shocked but entertained Gregory could only smile and nod as his eyes were transfixed upon the comedically horrific scene.

Larry struggled to see out of his left eye as blood poured into it from his forehead. He grimaced, then plunged one of his knives into Pogo's thigh. They both lost their balance and tumbled backwards. The laughter continued as the pair rolled about on the blood, urine, and excrement-soaked padding of the playpen. "Oh, Jesus Christ, this is funny!" Henri bellowed. "Look at them! They look like a pair of fucked up turtles!" "Come on! Get up!" Jerry yelled out before the entire group began enthusiastically clapping and chanting, "Fight! Fight! Fight! Fight!"

Josie once again yelled out, "Zap them!" Their tiny bodies convulsed as the electricity shot through their torsos and what was left of their extremities. "Shit! That didn't work!" Josie screamed. "Zap 'em again!" Following six more painful electrocutions, the pair of trimmed, bloodied, and filth-covered combatants continued thrashing about on the mattress in vain. "Shit!" Josie screamed. "They can't get up! Someone go pick them up or roll them over or something!"

"No, no, no," Rod responded. "I'm sorry Josie, but that would be interference and the rules state that no one from outside the playpen can interfere." "Well, shit," Sam muttered. "What do we do in the event of a tie?" Rod looked over the rules that Josie had scribbled out just before the match and showed them to Jules. "Yeah, okay. I've got this," Jules said as she focused her attention on a nearby grove of trees. Two majestic white tigers came strutting out of the wooded area and approached the playpen. The group looked on in anticipatory silence as the tigers lunged down and bit the heads off the weeping and pleading sex traffickers. Blood from the severed necks sprayed the enthralled onlookers while the small, headless bodies continued to convulse. The satisfied felines licked their whiskers and gave a nod to Jules before lumbering back to their home. *Wow, that was cool*, LucyFur thought to herself as she lapped blood splatter from Jessie's face. "I win!" Kaneko yelled out to Stellan and Paciano. "Pay up bitches! I had my money on it being a tie and their heads being eaten by tigers. Don't know why, but that was my bet." "Yes, you did. We thought you were insane. How did you even know that was a possibility? Here's your ten dollars, dearie," Stellan said as he begrudgingly handed the money over.

"Well, so much for Pogo II and Larry, but rules are rules. Not exactly what I had planned, but it was still fun, right?" a cheerful Josie stated. The entire captivated audience stood up, cheered, whistled, and applauded as they watched the battered, headless bodies shudder one final time and come to a rest. Josie looked at the blood and filth covered playpen, turned to Lionnel, and said, "Do you think we could clean that up and get a couple bucks out of it at a yard sale?" Lionnel looked at his love and solemnly shook his head. "Well, *that* sucks," a disappointed Josie replied. "Stupid Pogo and Larry.

That was a perfectly good playpen. The JQ only used it for like four days and now its ruined!"

"Oh, my fucking *God*, that was *funny*!" Maddy shout-whispered to her husband. "I thought we weren't supposed to say anything?" Erick asked. "Oh," Maddy answered, "Arima's so baked right now, she has *no idea* that we've entered her soul. Besides, what a fun way to spend an evening! You know, I'm pretty good at torturing people, but I have to admit, our daughter can do it better. I'm so proud of her."

Chapter 111

Walk Unafraid

It was always the first thing that she noticed. The faint scent of iron as the sticky thick molasses gently dribbled off her claws and onto her awaiting tongue. She felt a slight sense of satisfaction as her furry ears positioned themselves to intensely listen to the faint exhalation of air passing through her latest victim's mouth which was now permanently formed into a silent scream. Then, the sound of the blood droplets hitting the floor. Slowly at first, like an annoying leaky faucet. *Drop....drop....drop....*then faster as the taught skin surrounding his jugular gave way completely to unleash a crimson waterfall which hit the hard wood floor as though someone had poured an entire gallon of milk upon it. She pulled her claws completely from his throat while loosening her fangs' grip from his hair. Then the familiar thud as the lifeless body succumbed to gravity completing the merciless fait accompli.

A mischievous smile forced the upward curling of the right side of her mauve lips and whiskers. *This was successful. This was liberating. This was justified,* she thought to herself as she positioned herself on the man's chest and began eagerly lapping up the blood that was gushing out of his slashed throat. She looked down upon the mess that he had created as the pool of newly released blood expanded outward like a growing hurricane churning above warm water. She heard two sets of familiar footsteps approaching. The door opened and she looked up innocently at the two pairs of frantic eyes that were staring down at her.

"Oh, *there* you are sweetie!" a relieved Jessie exclaimed as her shoes sploshed across the hardwood floor to her cherished pet. "We have been so *worried!*"

"Yup, there she is," Jules dryly stated. "And *here's* the asshole that tried to escape. Nice job, cat. You kinda made a mess, though."

"Not as much of a mess as *we're* making downstairs," Jessie playfully replied. "Oh my God! Can you believe how *loud* these pricks can scream? I mean, I thought all the *previous* fascist fuckers were loud, but this *new* batch has them beat. By a mile. And man, do they piss their pants! At least LucyFur's…um… *friend* didn't last long enough to piss everywhere. This won't be *nearly* as big of a clean-up job as ours."

The two friends could not help but let out an amused giggle as they watched LucyFur's blood-soaked face mew up at them, then return to her evening's meal. She began purring loudly as she continued her ravenous feeding.

The women's giggles turned into unbridled, full-throated laughter as they watched this blood-soaked furball's euphoric feeding. "Well," Jules observed. "At least we won't have to feed her tonight."

"What are you talking about?" Jessie shot back. She bent over her beloved pet and picked her up. A new coat of fresh blood was squeezed out of LucyFur's matted hair and saturated Jessie's designer top as she hugged the enraptured cat. "Oh, my sweetie *always* needs her nummy-num-nums, now, *don't* you?"

LucyFur's purring continued as she lovingly rubbed her drenched face against that of her "owner." The pair giggled and purred until Jessie said, "And once dinner time is over, I think I know a certain little *someone* who is going to need a B-A-T-H."

Upon hearing the ominous four letters being uttered, LucyFur shrieked with intense fear and began thrashing her paws violently into the air until Jessie was forced to let her go. The shoes of Jules and Jessie were splattered with blood as LucyFur's plump body cannonballed into the crimson pool. LucyFur looked up at Jessie with disdain, turned her back and returned to her morbid meal.

"Yeah, *that* shit's not happening," Jules replied. "And she *really* should have been named 'Maddy,' because that's one blood-lustful little bitch."

"Yeah," Jessie agreed before concluding with, "or Josie."

"Yeah, she's really fucking those three up downstairs," Jules stated. "And making a mess all over the hard-wood floors of the living room in this beautiful estate. And on Christmas, no less. It's kind of a shame. Well, one down, one to go. I'll go check and see if Sam has found the other one. Then we really need to figure out how those two escaped from the stable. Josie really shouldn't have let all the assassination technicians off for Christmas, but oh well. I'll see you in a while after we find that other asshole. Don't let Josie have all the fun."

Jessie entered the living room and found the rest of the inner circle of Murder, Inc. sitting around three bloodied, urine-soaked men tightly bound to chairs. "Oh, you *really* want to screw with me?" Josie was screaming as she glanced up at the blood-stained portrait of her parents hanging over the fireplace. "Do you *know* who I am? Do you *know* who my parents are? Do you *know* what I'm capable of? I know that Vetis has been whispering his plans to you. We know that he has to keep you somewhat updated as to his progress so that you'll stay in the fold. We found you in your little hidey-holes. We exterminated the rest of you vermin in your camps, and we have allowed you five to keep breathing for one reason and one reason only! Information! So, you *will* tell me everything that Vetis has told you and I will allow you to keep on living. For awhile anyway. Or you can keep your mouths shut and watch as I take tiny pieces off of each of your bodies! Oh, hey Jess. Have you guys found the escapees yet?"

"Yeah," Jessie answered as she kneaded the back of Lucy-Fur's soaked neck. "LucyFur took out one of them upstairs. It's kind of a mess. Jules is looking to see if Sam has found the other one. Don't worry. He couldn't have gotten far. Not with the big cats roaming around."

"I don't like Sam out there by herself," Henri muttered to Gregory who whispered back, "She's fine. Have you learned nothing? I'm telling you, if you say one overprotective word to her, you're going to be in the doghouse."

"Okay, nice work, Jess," Josie cheerfully replied before giving the rest of the group a dark glare. "But *someone* in this group needs some additional training on tying knots. Those two were tied up *way* too loosely. But I'll deal with that later."

Lionnel looked sheepishly up at his beloved girlfriend and stammered, "Um, I-I'm sorry Josie. That was *my* fault. I used the wrong type of rope on those two. I swear they were bound up tight, but I ran out of the good rope and thought that the thinner stuff would do the trick. I was wrong. They were able to wriggle out of it. I'm so sorry."

Josie cocked her copper-topped head and looked at her boyfriend for a moment before grasping him around his neck and declaring, "Oh, that's okay baby! Mistakes happen! Okay, now back to you three." Josie's brilliant green eyes darted at the three trembling but defiant men. She raised her knife and sauntered over to the man in the middle and said sweetly, "*C'mon* now handsome. You don't *really* want to die like *this*, do you? And for *what*? A *traitor*? For someone who is a *traitor* to all of humanity? Don't you understand that this is all about *him*? Don't you understand that he doesn't *care* about you? That you're just a *pawn* to help him gain *power*? And he doesn't even want power because he thinks that he can make things *better* for people. He only wants power to soothe his *tender little ego.* We just kicked his *ass,* and now its all about vengeance. Because his *tiny little antichrist ego* is bruised. Well, sweetie, our little group here kinda wrote the *book* on vengeance. He may be a demon, but we have righteousness on our side. And righteousness will *always* defeat pure evil. *Always.* We defeated him once and we will do it again. In glorious fashion. That's going to happen with or without your help. So, waddayasay? How's about you just open that pretty little mouth of yours and tell us what we want to know. Then, we'll all just relax and have a nice Christmas. Okay, sweetie?"

The beaten man smiled at Josie as though he was in a trance and said, "That ain't true bitch. Vetis is the chosen one. He has been anointed by God to save this world from your kind. He's come to save the world from all the (derogatory term omitted) and (derogatory term omitted) and (derogatory term omitted). And all of you who love those Godless scum. He will rise to power with our help, and the Earth will be ruled by the *true* patriots. The *truly* blessed. And even if you kill us, our souls will still be here to help him. You *can't* kill us. He has promised us immortality."

"Wow. You poor, brainwashed bastard," Arima stated. "That isn't true at all. We can kill your physical body and I can destroy your black soul. Easily. And I will. Hey, are there any more of those Christmas tree cookies left? You know, the white ones with the green frosting and sprinkles? Those were so good."

"No, sorry Aunt Arima," Josie answered. "You and Marcus ate all those last night. I think there's still some fudge though. Okay, now where were we? Oh yeah. So, you *see* sweetie, we *can* kill you. There will be no victory for you and there will be no immortality. Just excruciating pain and suffering. So, just be a *good* little fascist bigot and tell us what we want to know, alright?"

The unblinking man continued to stare straight ahead with the same plastic smile before saying, "I ain't telling you shit. Now get the fuck away from me, bitch." He then spat blood and saliva into Josie's befreckled face.

"Well," Josie said calmly as she wiped her face with her hand. "I guess it's a good thing that all my vaccinations are up to date because there's no *telling* what kind of *diseases* you knuckle draggers are carrying." She then shot her effervescent glare at the white-suited Twins while her mauve lips twisted upward into a mischievous little smile. "Okay. I tried to be nice. Boys, do you want to play with your Christmas gifts?"

"Oh, my yes, thank you Josie," Adam replied followed by Aaron's, "Yes. We love our gifts. Thank you so much." The quivering man watched as the Twins went behind his chair and approached the Christmas tree. He heard the rustling of paper, boxes, and Styrofoam padding. He gulped hard and broke out of his indoctrinated stupor as he heard the high-pitched whirring of two drills. It was the last sound that he ever heard. Arima floated above the floor, absorbed the recently released dark soul, and placed it into a large piece of fudge. She and Marcus giggled as they bit into the rich, dark chocolate. "Yeah, he'll be totally flushed away in a couple hours," a satisfied Arima stated. "And man, is he delicious."

LucyFur suddenly jumped down from Jessie's lap and ran out of the pet door in the kitchen. "What the hell is *her* problem?" Jerry asked. "I don't know," Henri replied. "But I think that we'd better go check on our wives."

This shit's starting to piss me off, Jules thought to herself as she trudged through the pure white snow toward a shed on the outskirts of the estate. *But this has to be where they're at. There's bare footprints. And Sam's tread marks.* Jules raised her sword and cautiously opened the creaking, wooden door. She saw the back of Sam's treaded wheelchair. "Sam! What the fuck, man! Did you take care of this fucker or what?" Jules shouted out as she walked toward the wheelchair. She dropped her sword and gasped as she found Sam staring at the ceiling. There was a slight trail of blood coming from her ebony lips and a pitchfork coming from her chest.

"Oh, Jesus Christ, Sam!" a pained Jules screamed out as she fell to her knees and clutched her dear friend's face. Sam's eyes drifted slowly and focused on the beautiful face of one of her best friends. They had known one another since their freshman year of college. Despite their differing personalities and constant bickering, they truly loved one another. They loved one another as deeply as they loved the rest of their tight-knit clan from those days. Lucy. Kristy. Maddy. They had shared countless triumphs and tragedies. The pair were sadly destined to share one final tragedy together on this night. Sam forced a smile and said through a bloody gurgle, "Y-you owe me th-three dollars. P-put it in the swear j-jar, heh. L-look out. B-b-behind you."

The entire group of Henri, Jerry, Josie, Lionnel, Rachel, Kayla, Alexa, Adam, Aaron, Stellan, Paciano, Jessie, Arima, Marcus, Cliff, Jamie, Gregory, Rosa, and Kaneko followed Lucyfur's tracks to the shed. They flung the door open. Henri fell to his knees and let out an anguished scream as the remaining members of Murder, Inc's. inner circle saw two black panthers, two white tigers, two lions, and Lucyfur feasting upon the decapitated body of the final escapee. Streaming tears froze onto their traumatized faces as they also saw the corpses of two best friends holding one another in a final embrace. Sam had been impaled by a pitchfork. Jules's throat had been slashed open.

LucyFur left her feast, jumped upon the wheelchair, let out a mournful mew and lovingly licked the face of Jules. She then pounced down, looked at the big cats and said to them, *My friends, we have just lost one of our true friends on this Earth. And now, ladies and gentlemen of my pride, I am here to declare that there is a new sheriff in town.* The panthers, tigers, and lions looked at one another mournfully, let out tortured cries, and crouched reverentially at the oversized feet of LucyFur.

"You motherfuckers!" Josie roared as the group re-entered the living room with the bodies of their fallen friends. "I'm not fucking around anymore! Give me that fucking drill!" Adam quickly handed Josie the drill while Aaron forced one of the trembling men's mouths open. There was the shriek of the drill's motor followed by a morbid grinding sound as Josie thrust the drill all the way into the violently shaking man's mouth and out the back of his head. Blood and skull shrapnel pelted the cold bodies of Sam and Jules who had been delicately laid on a table next to the Christmas tree.

Josie tossed the bloodied drill onto the couch and grabbed another of the Twins' presents. She approached the final fear-stricken man and said in a deep growl, "Okay, motherfucker. Show and tell time. I *really* wouldn't fuck with me right now."

"Okay, okay, okay, I'll tell you!" the hyperventilating man yelled out. "I'll tell you everything! I know what Vetis has planned! I'll tell you! P-p-please just don't hurt me!"

Following the man's hysterical confession, Josie's glowing green eyes fell upon the tiny bodies of the JQ. "Hey, kids!" Josie bellowed. "That shit gonna be a problem for you?" "No, Aunt Josie," came the unified voices of Sigourney, Euna, Kane, and Thanatos. "Good," Josie stated before turning her burning emerald eyes once more to the trembling man.

She lifted the axe that she had been holding and began smashing it relentlessly into the man's body. She was wielding the axe with an unbridled fury and deep gashes were cut into the man's legs, neck, and torso. She wore a demented smile on her blood-spattered face as she lopped off each of his arms with one blow each. A river of blood was flowing out of the screaming man's multiple wounds. His agony finally stopped as Josie buried the axe between the man's treacherous eyes.

A physically and mentally drained Josie dropped the axe and looked around the room. The tinsel, ornaments, and needles of the Christmas tree were dripping blood and skin fragments. Henri and Jerry were holding one another while sobbing uncontrollably. Her Lionnel was rocking in a ball in the corner while muttering, "It's all my fault. It's all my fault. It's all my fault." Everyone was embracing one another as their faces were covered with anguish and tears.

Josie reached deep inside herself and said a private prayer to her mother. "Jesus Mom, what am I supposed to do now?" She closed her eyes and listened to her heart. She then righted her spine, looked at Arima and said, "Aunt Arima, put their fucking dark souls in the Christmas turkey. We're gonna fuckin' roast them. They're going to burn for hours. Then, we're *all* going to enjoy them for our Christmas dinner. And they're going to burn again in our stomach acid. Something good just *has* to come out of this."

"O-okay Niece Josie," Arima stammered before she lifted off the floor. Her eyes rolled back into her head. She opened her mouth. The only voice that could possibly bring any sense of comfort to Murder, Inc. in this moment came out. "Oh, Jesus, you guys," a remorseful Maddy stated through Arima. "I am so sorry for your loss. Henri, Jesus what you must be going through. I'm so sorry. And Jerry. You loved Jules so much. I'm so sorry. Lionnel. Pick yourself up. This wasn't your fault. This wasn't anybody's fault except for Vetis. His narcissistic evil has taken two more loved ones from you. But never again. We got this. The plans are in the works up here. And please take just a little comfort in knowing that I now have my final two best friends alongside me. Please don't worry about them. They are with me and Erick and will stay here until they learn how to conjure their own homes. And Henri, I know this isn't much consolation, but Sam can walk again. And man, is she pissed."

CHAPTER 112

WE GO TOGETHER

"Finally, we have a plan that will work, Gobbo!" Vetis roared with self-satisfaction. "Finally, we will get rid of that pesky fucking JQ and proceed with our domination over the Earth and Enlightenment! Finally, we will be able to move out of this dreary Realm of Perdition. It's so fucking depressing that this is the only place in the universe that I am safe since my defeat. Which was *rigged* by the way! I did *not* lose my war! They *cheated*! Anyway, I hate being secluded here. All these horrible souls milling about. I need fresh blood to conquer and dominate! I need fresh minions to worship at my feet! Perdition is not enough! It has never been enough! Plus, I hate what that slithery, copper headed bitch did to the place while I put her in charge up here. I mean, what's with all the tapestries everywhere? In a world of fire? In a world filled with dark souls? It just looks ridiculous. An embarrassment, really. Gobbo, get one of the enslaved to take down the tapestries. And have them paint all the walls black. I want to leave this place just as I discovered it. Dark and menacing. And more skulls! Why did that bitch take down all the skulls? That will look nice. Then, my loyal Gobbo, once I am the ruler of the universe, you shall be granted dominion over this dreadful place and all the few remaining dark souls that reside here. Then, you can decorate it however you like. But for right now, I want it dark and menacing! Got it?"

"W-why Yes, Master," the groveling Gobbo replied. "Of course. I will get someone on it right away. Have you had a chance to look at my suggestions, Master? Are you ready to choose our four warriors from Earth's past to eliminate the Junior Quad?"

"Yes, I have made my choices, Gobbo," Vetis sneered back. "And it doesn't matter when or where they are. I have no other use for them than to destroy those fucking brats. And it was quite the masterful plan on my part. They are too powerful together. But separately? Heh, heh, heh. Separately they can be defeated as long as I find the right assassins. And I have. Four of the most ruthless child-murderers ever to walk the Earth. They are vile. They are evil. They are perfect. All I have to do is send my signal that they are the next that I will attempt to convert. Send the signal about all four of them. Then, the despised JQ will have no choice but to separate and try to defeat them one on one. Which they won't be able to do! They draw their strength from one another! Without their soul mates, they are nothing more than ten-year-old children. They are no more menacing or threatening than kids running around on a playground. And the beautiful part, Gobbo? They won't see it coming! They will still think that they are invulnerable! Then, my hand-picked assassins will carve those little fuckers up. I hope they do it nice and slow. This is a moment that I wish to savor. All of that is correct, right Gobbo?"

"Why, yes, Master," Gobbo replied. "It was all in your daily briefing. I do wish that you would take the time to read that, Master. And, well, actually, this plan was *my* pla…"

Vetis slapped Gobbo across the room and roared at him. "*Your* plan? Were you about to say that this was *your* plan? Were you about to take credit from your *Master*? And fuck your daily briefing. It's boring. And there's too many big words. That's what I have you for. To give me the information that I need to make decisions. Now, whose plan was this exactly, Gobbo?"

"I-it most certainly *was* your plan, Master," Gobbo meekly replied as he lifted his boney frame from off the cold stone floor. "It was *your* plan to separate them, thereby eliminating their ability to draw strength from one another, thereby eliminating their powers. It was *your* plan to falsely identify these four child-murdering assassins as your next to be indoctrinated, thereby luring the separate members of the JQ to their ghastly fate. And it has *always* been *your* plan to eliminate the JQ so that you may conquer the universe without having to go through the Great Door. You can do all of this while commanding your troops from the safety of your throne in Perdition. Because, if you were to go out the Great Door, your physical form would be vulnerable upon the Earth. And, as imposing as your physical form is, Master, going through the Great Door is a risk that someone as great as you should never be exposed to. This was *your* plan, Master. And I am in awe of it."

"Of course you fucking are," Vetis answered with a tone of self-satisfaction. "Everyone should be in awe of me. And they will be. The entire population of Earth will cower at the very mention of my name by my hand-picked dictators. All the goodie-goodies in Enlightenment will *beg* me for the privilege of serving me. Everyone, Gobbo. It makes me feel warm and fuzzy. Now, hand me those names. Allow me to concentrate on each one. Then, let's watch Sigourney, Euna, Kane, and Thanatos be sent back to the hell from whence they were summoned. This is going to be fun."

"Hey! This isn't fun!" Sigourney screamed out. "Let me out of this cage!" A tall man emerged from the shadows of a dingy basement in the year 1897 wearing a tattered cowboy hat and a haggard smile. The sound of sharpening knives being rubbed against one another created a high-pitched squeak. The man looked at the confined ten-year-old girl. His eyes traversed her entire tiny body. He savored every aspect of her. Her white, fringed cowboy hat resting upon her nearly pure-white strands. Her caramel face with a birthmark resembling a lightning bolt that streaked between one brown eye and one blue. Her little white cowgirl shirt, fringed vest, and long skirt. He began laughing as he peered down upon the tassels on her white cowboy boots.

"Oh, my dear," he began with a lascivious sneer. "I had a dream about you. A dream of a little girl dressed all in white. A very *powerful* little girl whose powers would be stripped from her. A little girl who would provide me with my latest and greatest feast. It was such a wonderful dream. And now, my dream has come true. Here you are. My little delicacy. All locked up in my little cage. Just waiting to have tiny ribbons of your flesh sliced off, battered, and deep fried. Oh, I'm going to feast on you for weeks, little girl. And with each bite, I will listen to your pleas. I will chew your flesh and laugh as you beg me to stop. It will be so satisfying to get rid of one more bitch from this world. One less bitch to look down upon me. One less bitch to tell me what to do. One less bitch who would deny me. Yes, you will just grow up to be a little bitch, just like *all* the women that I have encountered. I have travelled from town to town getting rid of little bitches just like you. But *you* will be my favorite. Because I was told in my dream that getting rid of *you* in a most unpleasant manner would grant me powers. And immortality. And I have no reason to doubt that. Because *you* were in that dream. And now, here you are. And now, I am going to prepare my first taste. Stick your arm out of the bars, little girl. Let me have a taste."

Sigourney folded her arms defiantly, tilted her head and said in a snotty tone, "No. I don't want to. I don't *want* to play this game. You are a very bad man. I understand why Vetis chose you. So, I don't *want* to play this game. I have another game in mind. But, if you do me one favor, perhaps I *will* play this game with you."

The man bent over laughing, nearly dropping his knives before saying, "What is it my little treat? What is the favor that you are asking of me?"

"Just look deeply into my eyes," Sigourney answered in a sweet voice. "Look deeply into my eyes and if after doing that you still want to carve me up and eat me, then I'll play your game."

"Sure, why the hell not?" the chortling man replied. He bent down so that his eyes were directly in front of hers. His smile turned to painful shock as Sigourney's eyes began glowing. He fell to his knees and began screaming in agony.

"That's what I thought," Sigourney stated bluntly as she pulled the iron bars apart, stepped out of the cage and looked down upon the tortured man. "Do you know what you are experiencing? You are experiencing all the innocent souls who died at your hands. You are experiencing their conquest of you. They are all inside of you. They are tearing you apart from the inside out. Are you enjoying my game?"

The man's tortured screams continued as tiny, glistening hands began ripping their way out of the man's flesh. There was the echoing laughter of female children as their souls tore through his chest, legs, arms, and back. His internal organs flopped onto the dirt basement floor and blood flowed freely from wide lacerations in his entire body before the hysterical man looked up and peered into the intense eyes of his executioner one final time.

There was a clopping sound that came down the basement stairs. Sigourney climbed upon the back of Snowball. She opened her mouth. The dying, disgusting man then heard the voices of four distinct children saying in unison...

"Hey! Let me out of these shackles!" Kane demanded in German as he stared at the approaching Nazi scientist in 1941. "This is uncomfortable!"

"Oh, my special little friend," the evil, nearly hyperventilating scientist said as he snapped rubber gloves around his wrists. "Oh, how I have waited for you. A child such as yourself. I have dissected and studied so many children over these past several years. I have been looking for the secret powers of the human mind and body. Secrets that I believe that only the untarnished minds and bodies of children possess. Secrets that I can harvest and develop into a master race for my Fuhrer. Secrets that I can use to help him dominate the world. I must admit, I have become a bit despondent. I have studied over one-thousand children, but no secrets have been revealed to me. At first, I thought that it was because I was dissecting the wrong children. Vermin children. So, we started our breeding program. We created children that were spawned from the most healthy and pure of our race. I had great hopes as I sliced their wriggling little bodies open. But they held no secrets for me either. I was actually about to report that my research was a failure when *it* happened.

"I dreamed of you last night, my little friend. I dreamed of a little child, all dressed in a white American West outfit. A child who held the secrets of not only humankind, but secrets of the universe! This morning when I woke up, I of course thought that it was just my sub-conscious playing cruel tricks on me. Then, I checked my traps in the forest where the local children like to play. And I found *you* all wrapped up in a tidy metal package. So, here we are, my young friend. *You* will be responsible for unlocking our secrets. And *you* will be responsible for the glorious victory of the Third Reich! It will be my *great honor* to cut you open. To listen to your screams as I inspect each of your organs. To listen to your incoherent ramblings as I slice little pieces of your brain from out of your precious little skull. I would *like* to say that I'm sorry that you must remain awake for this ordeal, but I'm *not*, heh, heh, heh."

"Well, okay then," Kane responded casually from his position laying on the cold, metal operating table as the man bent over his head with a scalpel. As he was leaning forward, the maniacal scientist's eyes briefly locked onto the glowing eyes of Kane. His sly smile immediately transformed into shocked horror. He fell upon his knees and clutched his anguished eyes with his hands. Kane lifted his arms and legs, snapping his iron restraints. As the shrieking man continued to clutch his face, Kane whistled. The forty-inch-high Flame came bursting through the door and trotted to his friend's side. Kane climbed upon his faithful steed and looked down upon the tortured man.

"Do you know what you are experiencing?" Kane inquired with his sweet voice. "You are experiencing the horrors of war. War that you have contributed to. You are experiencing images of blown-apart bodies. And you are experiencing the pain that each of the innocent victims of war feel just before their passing."

Kane continued to look on as pieces of the scientist's body were being blown off him as though micro bombs were carpeting his flesh. Geysers of blood and pieces of bone shrapnel were violently showering the laboratory. Just before the man let out his final anguished breath, this murderer of the innocent heard the voices of four distinct children saying in unison...

"You better let me out if you know what's good for you!" the chair-bound Thanatos shouted to the pinstripe-suited gangster standing in the dark corner in front of multiple bottles. "Yeah, that's not happening kid," the gangster stated as he came from out of the shadows and stood in front of the young cowboy under a single overhead lightbulb. "I don't know why the competition keeps sending you kids around to snoop on me. I enjoy killing kids as much as I enjoy killing anyone else. You know what I love, kid? I love my booze. I love *selling* my booze in my speakeasy. I love getting broads drunk. But what I *really* love is that look on someone's face just as that bullet hits them right between the eyes. Man, woman, kid. It doesn't matter. I love that look of fear and pain. I love the look of *death*. Now, how about you tell me who sent you? Maybe I'll make it painless for you."

"No, I don't think so," Thanatos answered. "Hey! What's in those bottles back there? Does it taste good?"

"Still trying to get information, huh?" the wise guy said through a respected chuckle. "Well, you've got balls, I'll give you that. I guess you're not going to tell me, so I guess I'll just have to put one between your eyes. I gotta get going anyway. I have new showgirls to audition." The gangster pulled a revolver from his jacket, pointed it at Thanatos and stared directly into his latest victim's shining eyes. The man's body was suddenly thrown backwards against the wall of bottles as a barrage of bullet holes ripped through his flesh.

"Well, that was easy," Thanatos stated as he flicked his wrist and broke the ropes. Thanatos whistled and the pale green form of Snot came barreling into the liquor cellar. Thanatos climbed upon his friend and had him trot over to the remaining bottles on the shattered shelves. "What's this? Gin?" he shouted out before taking a huge swig from the bottle. "Blech! What's this? Whiskey? Blech! What's this? Vodka? Blech! What's (hic) this (hic)? Rum? Oh, I don't feel so well."

Thanatos looked down upon the riddled man as he gasped for breath. Blood flowed out of countless bullet holes on his body and face as Thanatos said, "Do you know what you're experiencing? You are experiencing your favorite thing. You are experiencing the pain of everyone that you have murdered. You are experiencing death. *Your* death and *their* deaths. All of them, combined into one painful experience. Thanatos then smiled and opened his mouth. The last thing that the dying criminal heard were the voices of four distinct children saying in unison…

"Hey! This isn't funny! Let me out!" Euna screamed to the dark, towering figure in the attic of a townhouse in 1963. She looked around the space from her chair that she was tied to and saw soiled stuffed animals and toys strewn everywhere. The insane, giggling man approached her and said, "Oh good. You're awake. Oh, thank you for coming to my door and asking for candy. Thank you so much. It is a pleasure to have you here."

"Yeah, well it's not *my* pleasure so let me go!" Euna ordered. "Oh no, no, no. I can't *do* that. I can't *do* that," the giddy man answered. "Oh no, no, no. You are my new *toy*. I need to play with you. And you look so…so…healthy. I must *play* with you. Oh, how I have played with so *many* children. It is so fun. But I haven't been able to play for such a long time. Not since I was defrocked. Oh, how I found so *many* wonderful playmates at my churches. So many trusting families that just let me play with their precious children. Even after it was revealed what I and so many others like me had done, those families continued to go to that church and trust another. Then another. Then another. It was so *easy* to move from church to church and find my toys. Fun, cute little toys who I would play my games with. But that was taken away from me. I haven't had anyone to play with in so long. It has been so sad for me just watching all these toys that I long to play with walk past my house every day. Why, there's the Jacob's little boy. He just started kindergarten. I just love to watch him walk in his tight little jeans and I dream of playing with him. Then there's the eight-year-old girl of the Robinson's. She looks so cute in her little dresses. Oh, the games that I wish to play with her. She could be my little dolly. But I can't. No one comes to my house. I was about to hang myself, until last night.

"Last night I was awoken by the most wonderful dream. I dreamed of a tanned-skinned little girl dressed in an adorable cowgirl costume. I dreamed of playing cowgirl and Indian with her. I dreamed of tying her up and doing things to her. I dreamed of her cries as I made her do things in my teepee.

Her wonderful, innocent cries! I heard the doorbell ring, and I woke up. And there you were. So cute. So eager to feast upon my poisoned candy. So ready to be played with. So ready to be kissed."

The perverted former priest bent down to kiss Euna's tan lips. He smiled as he locked his eyes upon hers. Euna's brown and blue eyes began radiating. The man shrieked, ended his attempted debauchery, and fell into the fetal position on the floor. Euna shrugged and the ropes that were binding her snapped in half. She whistled and the clomping of hooves came bounding up the attic stairs. Euna looked down upon the whimpering man as she climbed upon the back of Blackjack.

"Do you know what you are experiencing?" Euna asked in her innocent voice. "You are experiencing the emptiness that all your victims experienced. You did not just cause physical trauma, which was horrible enough. You caused never-ending emotional and psychological trauma. That is what you are now experiencing. The feelings of famine that ravaged their souls every moment of every day from what you did to them. Those horrible things that you put them through caused them to feel guilt. Shame. Embarrassment. For the rest of their lives, they were empty of any feelings of joy. Happiness. Love. Trust. Their souls were incapable of being nourished. For their entire lives they were emotionally famished."

Euna watched as the man's body and face began to sink in. His eyes began bulging out and his tongue hung from his gasping mouth. His bones became visible just under the thin layer of now ashen-grey skin. He lifted his head slightly, looked at Euna with his sunken in, emaciated eyes and listened as the voices of four distinct children said in unison, "Silly Vetis. We do not *have* to be physically together in order to be connected. We are *always* together. We will *always* have our love of each other and the love of good souls to strengthen us. We cannot be destroyed. We are invulnerable.

We are immortal. And we have been called here once again to rid this world of evil men like you. We possess the souls of the Four Horsemen of the Apocalypse. But not an apocalypse of the Earth. An apocalypse of the *evil* upon the Earth. Thank you for playing with us. It has been fun. We have to go home now. Our parents are probably worried, and we don't want to be grounded. Plus, it's dinner time and it's taco night. Good-bye."

"Stupid Gobbo! What kind of stupid fucking idea was that?" Vetis screamed as he repeatedly slapped Gobbo's face mercilessly. He tossed Gobbo's limp frame to the floor, stroked his crimson chin with one of his four hands and said, "So be it. I now know what I must do. I should have done this long ago. They are powerful, yes. But I am a demon. I contain all the evil in the universe. I must do this personally. I must go to Earth in my physical form. And I will use each of my four arms to rip each one of those little bastards apart. Here Gobbo. Here is the key to the Great Door. You will guard it with your very existence until my return. And I *will* return. With the four tiny heads of the four horsemen. *And* the heads of their little ponies *too*."

CHAPTER 113

ACROSS THE UNIVERSE

Vetis let out a deep sigh as Gobbo placed the iron key into the Great Door. There was a loud THUNK as the locks disengaged allowing the vast iron hinges to squeak open. "Gobbo," Vetis said sternly. "You let me back in as soon as you hear me knocking on this door. You know that my time on Earth is limited. If I stay too long, then I will be trapped there in my physical form and I will be vulnerable. Yes, as powerful as I might be, I could actually perish upon the Earth. But that won't be a problem. I'm going to vanquish the fucking JQ once and for all. And I'm going to enjoy every moment of it."

Vetis righted his nine-foot, crimson red frame with false bravado and stepped outside the safety of Perdition and into the cosmos. He mournfully looked up at the obscenely large gold letters that spelled VETIS hanging over the door, then gulped as he heard the Great Door slam shut. He chuckled nervously and concentrated on the glowing blue ball that was orbiting a bright yellow star. He concentrated further, trying to pick up the essence of his unsuspecting quarry. He smiled as he felt the sensation being emanated from the souls of

Sigourney, Euna, Kane, and Thanatos. He took one step forward with his massive, clawed right foot.

A dense, dark red fog appeared in a clearing near the Sommers-Parker estate in upper New York State. Vetis emerged from the sinister shroud. He threw his horned head back defiantly, roared, flexed his four biceps, and looked down where he saw the smiling faces of Arima, Jessie, Jamie, Rosa, Vai, Adam, Aaron, Kayla, and Rachel. They were standing around a long, pure white hearse wearing knowing smirks with their coated arms casually folded. He heard giggling coming from around his feet. His fiery eyes looked down further and he saw the mischievously grinning Junior Quad looking up at him while sitting on their faithful Shetlands. Vetis's heart began beating rapidly as he watched the children's brown and blue eyes begin to eerily glow. He could feel his blood pressure rise as he heard the seemingly innocent voices of the four children say in unison, "Hello Vetis. We have been expecting you. We have seen this day. Thank you for coming. Thank you for coming to play with us. We are going to have great fun with you."

The hyperventilating Vetis clutched his fear-stricken heart and declared, "Oh fuck this! Maybe just ruling Perdition isn't so bad after all! I'm outta here! Fuck you guys!" Vetis's massive frame disappeared back into the dark red fog as the children mocked the retreating spineless bully. "Vetis!" the children shouted after him. "Come back! You are so big and powerful. We are just children. What's the matter? You can't fight your own fights? You have to hide behind your demonic army? Come on back, Vetis! You big pussy!" The final thing that Vetis heard as his massive, wilted frame re-entered the cosmos was the deriding laughter of four ten-year-olds followed by an admonishment by their mothers for using the word 'pussy.' Lava tears of embarrassment streamed down his disgraced red face as he approached the promised sanctuary of the Great Door.

There was a violent pounding upon the Great Door as a booming voice yelled out, "Hey Gobbo! Let me in!"

"Y-yes?" Gobbo replied with trepidation. "W-who is it?"

"Who the fuck (*clink*) do you *think* it is? The fuckin' (*clink*) pizza guy? Let me in!"

The iron key was heard being inserted into the lock. There was a loud THUNK as the locks were once again disengaged. Gobbo pulled the door open and gasped at the sight that stood in the doorway in front of him. A joyful, black tear fell from one of his yellowed eyes as he bowed at the feet of the five intense women who stood confidently in front of the backdrop of the kaleidoscopic universe.

Lucy was dressed in an all-black cat suit holding a conjured box of test tubes and other "science shit" that the rest of her friends did not care to understand. Next to her stood Kristy in a flowing yellow sundress holding a freshly conjured bundt cake. Jules stood to the far left of the group wearing conjured faded blue jeans, black boots, and a black leather biker jacket. Sam was proudly standing on her tone, caramel legs that were enveloped in a tight, pin-striped pencil skirt that accented the rest of her business attire which included a bulging designer purse. Gobbo looked up at the figure that was standing in the middle. She slowly lifted her head, allowing her piercing green eyes to meet his. Her slender mauve lips curled up in a mischievous smile as she removed the black hood from her copper bangs. Maddy Sommers let out a low, devilish laugh and clutched her right hand around a pair of well-worn brass knuckles before saying, "Took you long enough. We've got shit (*clink*) to do!" Maddy looked behind her college friends at the rest of her beloved entourage. "Come on everybody! Let's get to work! It's going to take awhile to conjure this fucking (*clink*) place into shape! And what the fuck (*clink*) is that fucking (*clink*) clinking sound?"

Sam wore a haughty smile as she retrieved a large glass jar

from her purse. "This," she began explaining, "is the source of that clinking sound. This is our new swear jar. Every time somebody swears, a good deed that they must perform will be deposited into it. And, I must say my old friend, you've already racked up quite a tab. You see, Maddy, not everybody is comfortable with foul language, and we want this to be a place where everybody can live throughout eternity in blissful comfort."

"Fuck (*clink*) that!" Maddy roared back. "No fuckin' (*clink*) way! That isn't heaven! That's fuckin' (*clink*) hell!"

Sam chuckled, patted Maddy on her auburn head and proceeded to lead the group into Perdition. "Okay now everybody," Sam began as she pulled a large notebook from her bag. "As you will see from my schematics of Perdition, everybody has an exact equal amount of space to use to conjure your homes. And Jules, could you please keep your space tidy this time? We *really* don't want a repeat of your college closet. Now, the diner and ice cream shop that Uncle Joe and Aunt Blair requested will be in *that* area over there. And the rock club where Aunt Patty and Jacklyn will book musicians to play will be *here*. Now, Herbert, or Mister Botanist. Could you and your lovely wife, Iris, and your adorable daughter begin sprucing up the place? These rocks are just so depressing. And let's get rid of those skulls hanging all over."

"It will be our pleasure," Herbert answered as he held hands with his family and closed his beady eyes. Throughout Perdition, exotic plants and flowers began growing and blossoming out of the jagged, fiery stone. Fresh blades of lush green grass covered the entire surface, and a stream of clear, blue water replaced the flowing lava in the river. In a matter of moments, morbid darkness had been replaced by an explosion of colorful life.

"Very, very nice," Sam stated to the proud Botanist. "Now, Louise, Abdalla, and Gwen, this area over *here* will be your spiritual amplification center where we can all go to reach out to our loved ones on Earth. And Clyde Manfre...um... Manfren... Manfrengensen, this area over *here* will be your vintage clothing and jewelry shop. But please. No more bullet holes. Please conjure fresh vintage clothing, okay? Thank you. Sean, Charlie, and Rosetta, this area over *here* will be your karaoke bar. And believe me, we ladies are going to get a *lot* of use out of that!"

"Wh-what about *my* request?" a hesitant voice stated from behind the group. "I don't suppose you have anything in that notebook for *me*, do you?" Sam let out a deep sigh, rolled her brown eyes and hastily flipped through the notebook. "Yes, here it is," Sam replied with resignation. "Okay, do you see that dark path between those jagged rocks? Just go between there, then keep walking until you run into a wall. Then turn left and keep walking. There will be a very narrow rock passageway. Cross that, then keep walking. Turn left at the fried chicken stand. Keep walking. You will eventually come to a completely barren area. That is where you may conjure your pegatorium, Howard."

"Oh, thank you!" Howard exclaimed as he embraced Sam's frame. "And you are welcome to visit anytime you like, my dear. We could have some...*ahem*...fun together."

"Gross. Get the fuck (*clink*) off of me," came Sam's terse reply before continuing. "Let's keep moving, people. Now, Abana and I will be conjuring a Complaint Center in *this* location. We believe that Henri will be pleased that both of his deceased wives will be working together to process any infractions of our rules. And helping us will be Marcus's parents, Lillian, Mr. and Mrs. Roper, and Amanda Denhart. Erick, Jason, and the rest of you men can conjure your sports bar in *this* location."

"I didn't ask for a fuckin' (*clink*) sports bar," Erick whispered to his increasingly annoyed wife who had her arms tightly folded while impatiently tapping her size six left foot. "Shit, (*clink*) that jar's really fuckin' (*clink*) sensitive."

"Okay, may *I* now ask a question?" Maddy inquired in a lilting voice as she tilted her head slightly to the side. "Why, of course you may, Maddy," Sam replied. "But please make it quick. I have much more to go over."

"Oh, *this* won't take very long," Maddy replied as she innocently batted her copper eyelashes at her overbearing friend. "I just have *one* question. And that question is…" Maddy's voice trailed off for a moment before she got into Sam's face and screamed, "Who the *fuck* (*clink*) put *you* in charge? *I'm* the one that the JQ had make contact with Gobbo! *I'm* the one that convinced him to let us in as soon as Vetis hit the bricks to try to kill the JQ! *I'm* the one that promised him that he and the rest of the dark souls would be allowed to live here in peace as long as they played nicely with us! *I'm* the one that promised them no more torture and a chance for redemption of their black fuckin' (*clink*) souls! Is this fuckin' (*clink*) place called 'Samville?' Fuck (*clink*) no, it isn't! It's called 'Maddyville!'

"Maddyville?" Erick inquired of his wife. "Where the fuck (*clink*) did you come up with 'Maddyville?"

"Well," Maddy began excitedly explaining. "I figured that we needed a new cool name for our new home in the universe. I mean, we can't keep calling it 'Perdition' now, can we? That's fuckin' (*clink*) depressing. And I just thought since *I'm* going to be the mayor, then it should be called 'Maddyville.' Pretty cool, huh?"

"No, it isn't cool," her beloved husband responded dryly. "And who said that *you* were going to be mayor? What, are you just going to self-appoint yourself and surround yourself with a bunch of feckless yes-men who will mindlessly do your bidding, then disparage anyone that has even the *slightest* disagreement with you? And then, claim that everybody's out to get you and everything's rigged against you so that you will be an all-powerful martyr for all eternity? Was *that* your brilliant fucking (*clink*) plan?"

"Well, yeah, kinda," an embarrassed Maddy answered as she looked down upon her shuffling feet. Erick took his admonished wife into his arms, lifted her head with his index finger and said softly, "You don't *need* to be in charge. You don't *need* to be in control of everything. Just look around you. You are surrounded by the kindest souls in the universe. You can finally let your guard down and allow yourself to completely trust others. You don't have to be prepared for battle anymore. We can just live together in peace. We will *all* play our part, and we will run this place *together*."

"Buuuuut," Maddy tentatively began asking in her "hurt" voice. "Can I still run the group meetings? I've always been *really good* at that."

"Of course you may, my love," Erick answered before Lucy interrupted. "Hey! I've got an idea for a really cool name! How about 'Mel?'

Erick and Maddy looked at Lucy for a moment before simultaneously saying, "No." Erick's face then beamed with a huge smile as he said, "I think I have it! I think that I have our cool new name for this place! How about 'Unison?'"

The entire group cheered and applauded the suggestion with one notable exception who muttered under her breath, "It's *okay*, I guess, but it doesn't have the same ring as 'Maddyville.'"

She then perked up and said, "Okay fine. I'll run the meetings, but rules will be made by a vote of everyone living in Unison. Erick, Uncle Joe, Aunt Blair, and Aunt Patty will be my consiglieres."

"But...but...wait...you're still putting yourself in cha..." Erick attempted to interject before being sharply elbowed in the ribs by Lucy. "Do you really think that you're going to get a better deal than this? Just let her have it. Besides, it's not like there's a rules enforcement mechanism. Just do whatever you want."

Maddy glared at the disruptive pair before continuing. "Lucy, Jules, and Kristy will be in charge of rules enforcement."

"Yay! This will be fun!" Lucy yelled out. She then intensely looked Erick in his brown eyes and said, "You'd *better* be good. *I'm* going to be a hardass. And you *know* that I distrust men, even you. So don't fuck (*clink*) with me." Erick could do nothing but shake his head in amazement and laugh to himself at the absurdity of the situation. *Wow*, he thought to himself. *The more things change, the more they stay the same. Nothing's going to change their world.*

"And Sam," Maddy continued, "can be in charge of organizing shit (*clink*) and processing the fuckin' (*clink*) complaints. And there's *one* fuckin' (*clink*) complaint I'm going to take care of right fucking (*clink*) now! Come on Erick! Let's go behind those trees in our new forest!"

The group stood in silence and awkwardly stared up at the brilliant stars as they listened to the tell-tale sounds of passion coming from the grove of trees. Maddy emerged from the forest as she was pulling her pants up, strode over to Sam and said, "We don't really need these fuckin' (*clink*) things to prevent pregnancy or diseases, but they sure as fuck (*clink*) come in handy to get rid of fuckin' (*clink*) swear jars! And there's a helluva (*clink*) lot more where this came from, so don't try me, bitch (*clink*)!" Maddy then threw a used condom into the jar. All the glowing good deeds that had been collected disappeared as they were covered in Erick's spiritual seed. "Fine!" Sam yelled out before slamming the jar to the ground, causing it to disappear. "Just watch your language! It's not ladylike!"

"What fuckin' ever," Maddy replied dismissively. She then paused for a moment and listened for a clinking sound that never came. Satisfied, she began again. "Okay, now that *that's* settled, Gobbo, go round up your dark souls. We're about to have our first *official* meeting in Unison!"

Erick could only hold his bewildered head in his hands as he heard his wife's triumphant voice shout out, "Here ye! Here ye! Here ye! There's a new sheriff in town, heh, heh, heh."

CHAPTER 114

LONG WHITE CADILLAC

"Awwwww, this is the life," a finally serene Maddy slurred as she stretched her petite, bikini-clad frame out on the lounge chair next to their newly conjured swimming pool. "Just hanging around, sipping on conjured tropical cocktails, taking a dip in the pool. Yeah, this is the life. I never thought that eternal bliss would be so..." Maddy halted in mid-sentence and turned her fierce green eyes towards the bushes that had suddenly began thrashing about. "Howard!" She yelled out. "You had *better not* be perving on us and jerking off in the bushes! What is it with guys who jerk off into plants? I mean, what the fuck did the plant do to deserve being covered in some freak's jizz? And what's erotic about that anyway? I mean peaches, sure, that makes sense. They kinda look the part. But innocent house plants? That's just wrong."

As Maddy was completing her somewhat coherent diatribe, the thrashing in the bushes intensified. "Oh fuck, I shouldn't have mentioned peaches," Maddy regretfully stated. "Howard! Get your ass out of there you fuckin' perv!"

"I'll handle this," the pale green-skinned Iris stated. She

flicked her wrist and vines from the bushes wrapped around the waist of their quarry and lifted him into the air.

"I-I'm sorry, Maddy," a nervously excited Howard began mumbling as he gripped his engorged penis in his right hand. "But you ladies all look so…um…look so…um…*sexy* in those bikinis. You, and Sam, and Iris, and Jules, and Kristy, yes, *especially* Kristy and…and…" Howard's exclamation ended as he shot his climax several feet, cannonballing perfectly into Maddy's Mai Tai.

"Motherfucker!" Maddy screamed in disbelief as she wiped the splashed goo from her left eye. "Get the fuck out of here! And you are *soooo* fucking banned from the pool area! For all eternity! I have decreed it! Go back to your pegatorium and do weird shit with a dark soul!"

"I-I'm sorry, Maddy," Howard said as he slinked off toward his dark hole. A black, viciously scarred form carrying a round tray approached the pool-side table and said, "Here. I have conjured a fresh drink for you Maddy."

"That's *Mrs.* Sommers to you, you fucking creep. Thanks for the drink," Maddy replied. "Of course, Mrs. Sommers. My mistake and my apologies," the dark spirit of Detective Edmund Simmons answered before turning his attention to the rest of the group. "Would anyone else care for anything from the bar?"

"Naw, get the fuck out of here, you fuckin' douchebag traitor," Joseph Argento replied in a surly tone. Blair whispered something into her husband's ear. Joseph then said, "Wait. Come back here and drop that tray." Detective Simmons reluctantly returned to the table of anxious observers. Joseph lifted his brawny frame from his chair, looked his former best friend in the eye and struck him squarely under his chin. Edmund's demonic teeth flew out of his mouth in a stream of black bile. "*Now* you can go, asshole," Joseph stated. He picked up the dislodged teeth, placed them in a napkin, and handed them to his adoring wife.

"Okaaaay then," Maddy said. "I guess *that* little feud is going to last awhile. Well, let's change the subject. Hey, Aunt Patty! Who did you get to play the opening night of the newly conjured LOHAD? I bet it's somebody really cool, right?"

"Hey! I have a question!" Erick interjected. "I get that you wanted to replicate the club you had on Earth but what's the point of having the 'No Drugs! No Guns! No Assholes!' sign? I mean, we're in paradise. *Our* paradise. There isn't any of that shit up here."

"Oh yeah, there is," came Patty's immediate and terse reply. "There are *definitely* assholes up here. Assholes that would wear a conjured Barry Manilow T-shirt into *my* fuckin' club! And that shit ain't happening! Got it?"

"Yeah, I got it," Erick replied softly as his wife pursed her lips tightly to keep herself from laughing. "Okay, now back to the question Mads asked," Patty continued. "So, I've reached out to all kinds of cool artists. And do you know what they told me? That the club wasn't big enough, and that they don't want to go slumming, and they don't want to travel all across the universe just to play a forty-five-minute set and blah, blah, blah. Fuckin' prima donnas. But I found two fucked up, don't give a shit motherfuckers to play a double bill! Lux Interior and Mojo Nixon! How fuckin' cool is *that* going to be?"

"Wow," the entire group stated in unison before Maddy exclaimed, "Hold on a minute! I think Arima's trying to get ahold of me! Yeah, Soul Sister, this is Lil' Red! I can hear you fine! Over and out!"

"Okay, hey Mad…I mean Lil' Red? I mean, you really don't have to yell so loud and say, 'over and out' after every sentence, okay?" Arima said.

"Yep! Copy that, Soul Sister! Over and out! So, what's the sitch? Is Vetis dead yet? Over and out!"

"Um, no," Arima answered. "He came down here, took one look at the JQ and split. I'm sure he's on his way back there.

I'm not sure how long it takes to travel through the universe, but he should be there at any time."

"Figures. Fuckin' pussy," Maddy muttered. Arima responded, "Um, hey Lil' Red? Maybe you shouldn't say 'pussy' around the JQ anymore. They just got in trouble for using that word and they spilled that they heard it from you, so Kayla and Rachel are kinda pissed right now."

"What's with all the fuckin' language police, anyway? Over and out!" Maddy yelled as she glanced over at the haughty face of Sam. "Oh fuck you, Sam. Like you think you know everything," Maddy stated before turning her attention back to Arima. "Yep, okay, Soul Sister! We kinda figured he would puss...um...I mean that he'd back down! That's cool! We're all set up here for when he shows up! We're almost done conjuring our little slice of heaven! All we have to do is not let him in the Great Door, then his time will run out, and he'll be sucked right back to the last place on Earth that he'd been, and his physical form will be trapped there! Then the JQ can fuck him up! Over and out! Oh! And one more fuckin' thing! You need to have a talk with your perv friend! Do you know what he just did? He was looking at us women and jerking off in the bushes and blew his fuckin' wad right into my drink! That shit isn't cool, Soul Sister! You need to set him straight, or I will, got it? Over and out!"

"Yeah, okay Lil' Red. I'll have a talk with him," a slightly embarrassed Arima replied. Maddy then said, "Oh, and just one more thing! Is my lovely daughter there? I want to say hi to Josie! Over and out!"

"Naw," Arima answered. "She took Lionnel to Bermuda for a few days. His friend Tabitha has been calling him wanting him to come over and help her study and Josie's getting really jealous and pissed about it. She said that if she doesn't get him away from that little skank that she's going to cut her head off and that would piss Lionnel off, so she doesn't want to do that."

"Huh," Maddy replied. "Well, I can't see as I blame her. Chicks gotta protect her property. If that little whore doesn't back down, then she'll leave Josie no choice. Well, okay then! Keep me updated Soul Sister! Hug everybody for us and we'll talk soon! Well, maybe not Rachel and Kayla if they're being uptight little bitches, but hug everybody else! Maddy out!"

Maddy settled back into her lounge chair just as there was a frenzied pounding at the Great Door. "Gobbo!" Maddy ordered. "Get your sniveling ass over here! It's showtime!"

Maddy, Gobbo and the rest of the group got up from their pool side seats and approached the Great Door while snickering.

"Gobbo!" Vetis roared. "Let me in! Shit didn't work out!"

"Whooooo iiiis iiiit?" an exaggeratedly high female voice responded followed by giggling.

"Who is it?" Vetis yelled back. "Who the fuck do you *think* it is? The pizza guy? It's Vetis! Let me in!"

The female voice lowered and replied through her chuckles, "Vetis isn't here, man." Vetis fumed as he heard uncontrolled laughter coming from the other side of the Great Door. He then looked up and noticed that the grand golden letters that had spelled out his name had been removed. In their place, in bright yellow, red, green, blue, pink, and purple, it read 'UNISON.'

"What the hell is going on in there?" Vetis screamed out. "Gobbo! Stop fucking around and open this door, right now Goddammit!" Vetis heard the slight creak of hinges as the rectangular peep hole in the Great Door was being opened. Vetis's dark red eyes peered into the opening. He then gasped at what he saw. Peering back at him were a pair of glowing green eyes. "Hey, hey, hey, what the fuck are *you* doing in there, bitch?" Vetis began stammering. "Gobbo! Kill this bitch now and let me in!"

"Oh, I'm sorry, Vetis," Maddy coolly replied. "But you *see,* Gobbo and the *rest* of the dark souls got tired of putting up

with your shit. So, they invited us to come over and...um...
redecorate. And that is what we have done. And I know that
Gobbo told you that the Junior Quad could be destroyed if
you separated them, but that was a little fib. Actually, he didn't
lie to you completely. All the *accurate* information was in your
daily briefing. There's really no excuse for not having read
those. And...Hey! Don't drop that! Do you know how long it
took me to conjure that fucking thing? Jesus, take a little pride
in your work, wouldja? Sorry about that. These fucking dark
souls don't give a fuck about anything. Anywhoooo, where
was I?

"Oh yeah. And I'm not the *only* one here from Enlightenment. I've brought a *whole group* of Pure Souls with me. Sorry,
but you're just going to have to face it. This place is under new
management. And we have called it 'Unison.' Why? Because
we are so much stronger when we work together as a group
than when we work against one another individually. You
know when you're in a conversation and everybody's talking
over one another and everybody eventually gets pissed and
not one fucking thing is accomplished by it? See, that's the
world that *you* tried to create. A world where everybody is
suspicious of one another and hates one another then wants
to actually kill one another. But through your defeat, people
have realized that they have much more in common than they
have differences. They have realized that hating one another
doesn't do anything to benefit *anybody*. They have learned that
by working together, that *everybody* has a chance to live a long,
happy life both on Earth and in Enlightenment. Yes, Vetis,
they have learned to work in Unison."

"That's not *actually* why I thought of it," Erick whispered
up to his wife. "I just thought it sounded cool at the time and it
was better than 'Maddyville' and it kinda played into how the
JQ always speak in unison and shit like that. I didn't think
about any of *that* stuff until you started your little speech."

"Shut up, Erick! I'm on a roll here! And it is *not* cooler than

'Maddyville'!" Maddy shot back before glaring once again into the forlorn eyes of a spineless demon. "So, you see, Vetis, you *really* aren't welcome here. In fact, a vile piece of shit like you isn't welcome *anywhere* where there are good, decent people. They have rejected you. Oh, and your tiny little army of twenty-three UN dignitaries that you think will lead a new war on Earth? Well, don't worry about *them*. My *daughter* is going to take care of *them* really soon. Too bad you won't be around to see it. But, if you're lucky, maybe they'll let you *hang around* for a while and watch the grand finale of our sordid little tale. So, I'm sorry, but we can't let you in. Plus, the place is still a *bit* of a mess and we *really* aren't prepared to entertain. But, hey! Thanks *so much* for stopping by! It means the *world* to us! Seriously. It *literally* means the world to us! Okay, then! Safe travels! Byeeeeee!"

Vetis roared in frustration as the peephole door slammed shut and he once again was forced to listen to the howls of mocking laughter. "Motherfucker!" Vetis screamed. "Oh shit! I can feel it! I'm being pulled back! Gobbo! Gobbo, please! Come on little buddy! Let me in! I'll do anything! You can rule Perdition! Anything! Please GobboNooooooooo!" Gobbo could not help but smile as he heard the voice of his eternal oppressor finally fade out of his tormented life. "Fuck him," Gobbo defiantly stated.

"Hey!" Maddy yelled out. "Watch your fuckin' language! There's kids around! Jesus Christ, were you raised by heathens or something? Show some fuckin' class!" Gobbo then wondered if he had made the right decision.

"So, why are *we* here exactly?" Vai asked her friends as they were sitting around folding tables next to the long, white hearse playing cards and watching the delighted faces of the Junior Quad. The foursome was prancing around the field on their ponies playing polo. They were using dismembered legs as mallets and a decapitated head as the ball that had been provided by their fathers. "Goooooooaaaaal!" Sigourney shouted out. "See? We *girls* are better than you *boys* at *everything*. Even *polo*," Euna snottily stated. "That's not true!" Kane shouted out followed by Thanatos. "Yeah, that's not true! We let you win! You cheated! We're better!"

"Boys!" their mother, Kayla scolded. "You did *not* let them win! They won fair and square. Now apologize to them! Or do you want yet *another* week on laundry duty?"

"No Ma'am," the boys answered meekly as they hung their heads. "We're sorry. You won fair and square."

"And girls," Rachel added. "It really isn't polite to rub the noses of your opponents in your victory. It is unsportsmanlike. Now, you two apologize for that. Or do you want to do dishes for the next month?"

"No, Ma'am," the girls replied. "We're sorry we pointed out to you that we girls are better than you boys at everything, including polo, and that we are the stronger sex and…"

They were suddenly cut off by their mother. "Girls! That is *not* an apology! Try again, or so help me, you will *both* find yourselves so grounded that you couldn't fly even if you're in an airplane!"

Sigourney and Euna let out a deep sigh, looked at one another and said, "Okay. We're sorry that we are better than you."

"Nope. Try again," a frustrated Rachel said as she began walking towards her all-powerful daughters. "Okay, okay, sheesh," Sigourney stated. Both girls then said, "We're sorry that we were poor sports and sore winners, and we won't do it again."

"That's better," a satisfied Rachel said as she walked back to the group. "So, anyway, what was the question again?" a tripping Arima asked. "Oh yeah. Why are we here? Well, Maddy's taken over Perdition and locked Vetis out, so he'll end up being trapped back here so the JQ can take him out and…oh yeah. Why *are* we here?"

"We are here, dearies," Jamie answered, "Just in case our little gladiators need some backup."

"We won't!" came the children's unified voices from the field as they continued to bat the head around with the dismembered legs. The group began chuckling before Rosa said, "Well, Jess, Arima, and I are here for a specific purpose. Arima just smoked some of her 'Killer Weed.' That will allow her to absorb the dark soul of Vetis. But instead of destroying him, I am going to manipulate his energy while he is in Arima. I am going to bind him in his own evil energy. Then, Arima will release his bound soul, Jess will recite her incantation and his great evil will give her great strength. His evil soul will perish as soon as it is transformed into Jess's permanent strength. Vetis will be no longer. And Jess will never feel the pain of evil again. And she will *always* be able to kick its ass."

"Oh, how fun," Adam stated followed by Aaron. "Yes, quite fun, indeed. Plus, we need to assist in putting the pieces of the body in the hearse. Oh, what fun Alexa will have playing with his body parts. But they will be quite heavy. I wonder if we will need more help."

At that moment, an out of breath Dragenstein came running into the field. Her white, chiffon dress was blowing up, exposing her large phallus and she was carrying her size eighteen white pumps. "Oh my, that was quite a trek. Have I missed anything?" she asked in her breathy voice. "No," Vai answered. "What the hell are *you* doing here? I thought you were on a drag tour. And would it kill you to wear some underwear? I mean, its really chilly out here."

"Teehee," Dragenstein tittered as she demurely covered her mouth. "Sorry about that. It's just that undergarments are so restrictive, and I tend to run a bit warm blooded. And I just *couldn't* miss this! I just *couldn't* miss the grand finale!"

"This isn't the grand finale," the trailing Kaneko stated as she picked up Vai's hand of cards and looked at them. "Gin! I win again! Nope, this isn't the grand finale. There will be blood, but not enough of it. Plus, if you've been counting the chapters, we're only on the twenty-second chapter of this book. There's always twenty-three. Always. So, this isn't the grand finale. But it sure as hell is going to be fun, right kids?"

"It sure will, Aunt Kaneko!" the enthralled children responded before Euna yelled out "Gooooooaaaal! That's twelve to nothing boys!"

"Awwww shit, here he comes," Jessie stated as she buckled over in intense pain and chanted, "Malum tuum dolorem facit. et dolor meus es fortitudo mea, (*your evil causes pain. my pain is my strength*). Okay that's better. I'm ready."

A dark red cloud oozed from out of nowhere in the clearing. The nine-foot-tall, horned-headed, four-armed Vetis threw his head back and roared once again. "Okay, you little bastards. I'm back. Earlier I just thought I'd let you off the hook, but I've changed my mind. I'm going to destroy you."

"That's not true! You are lying!" the JQ replied in unison. "You are frightened of us. You know the power that we wield. You were forced to come back to us because Aunt Maddy has moved into your home, and you have nowhere else to go. You do not wish to play with us, but we wish to play with you."

"But not just yet!" Thanatos said before yelling out, "Gooooooaaaaal!" "Hey!" Sigourney yelled. "That doesn't count! We weren't paying attention!" "It does so count!" Kane yelled back.

Vetis stood and watched the children in confused disbelief as there was a barrage of, "No it doesn't!", "Yes, it does!", "No, it doesn't!", "Yes, it does!"

Finally, Vai ended the verbal and pointless stalemate when she said, "Children, would you please stop your bickering and take care of Vetis?"

"Oh yeah, him," Thanatos answered. "Bring it on, you little fuckers. I can take anything that you throw at me," Vetis growled with fake confidence.

"Okay," The four children stated before casually looking at

Vetis's knees. Their eyes glowed for a moment and Vetis's kneecaps exploded. Vetis screamed in anguish as he watched his dark red flesh and black bones fly across the field in a stream of black blood. He fell to the ground, lifted his four arms, and began concentrating on the four cute blonde heads that were bobbing towards him.

"What is he *doing*?" Kane asked. "I think he's trying to blow up our heads," Euna answered. "Really, is that what you are doing?" Sigourney asked of the desperate demon. "That's silly. You can't blow up our heads. You have no power over us. We know that you can blow up dark souls and the bodies of humans. But you cannot blow *us* up. Here, let us show you how to do it. Thanatos, would you like to do the honors?"

"Sure would," Thanatos stated. His eyes began glowing as he focused on the four-foot-long abdomen of the legless creature. Vetis let out a tortured wail as his internal organs exploded out of his frame, showering the onlookers with black blood and squishy, slimy intestines.

"Huh," Vai whispered to Rosa as she threw a piece of gooey flesh off her head. "It kinda *seems* to be enough blood for a grand finale." "Nope," was all the enthralled Rosa could say in response as she chewed her popcorn.

"How, how are you *doing* this to me?" the hysterical Vetis exclaimed as the JQ were binding his arms to the saddles of their Shetlands with leftover intestines. "This isn't supposed to happen to me! I am all-powerful! I control *everything*! I *am* everything! I can do *anything* that I want! I *never* have to face consequences!"

"No, you are *not* all-powerful," the children said in unison as they climbed upon the backs of their friends. "You are pure *evil*. You may be able to get your way by bullying and lying to others for a while, but eventually your debt will have to be paid. Eventually your evil deeds will catch up to you. Eventually you will be vulnerable. And eventually, *we* will be called. We are the four horsemen of the apocalypse, and we were sent here to help the human race extinguish pure evil. The pure evil that you possess and plant into the hearts of others. We are going to destroy you now. You are *not* all-powerful. You are nothing but a big pussy. HYAW!"

Upon hearing their cue, Snowball, Blackjack, Flame, and Snot began galloping at full speed in different directions, ripping Vetis's four arms from his body. Rivers of black blood flowed out of the gaping sockets as the children trotted back to the suffering body.

"Don't forget to save the head, children," Adam reminded followed by Aaron's, "Yes. Please save the head. Alexa would like to play with it."

"Okay fathers," the children replied. They began to giggle uncontrollably as their eyes glowed again. Vetis pleaded for mercy as he could feel razor-sharp slashes cutting through his throat. His screams turned to pathetic gurgles as the slashes penetrated ever deeper until his head was completely removed from his torso. The red, horned face of Vetis was frozen in an expression of eternal shock and fear as the remaining blood flowed out of his neck and pooled around his impotent horns.

"Got him!" Arima yelled out as she floated several feet above the scene. "And I have him bound in his own evil," Rosa answered. "Jess, are you ready?" "Fuck yeah. Give him to me," Jessie answered. Arima released the dark, bound soul of Vetis into the awaiting soul of her dear friend. Jessie could feel the anguish that Vetis was experiencing as his evil was being transformed and consumed by her feminine strength. Jessie flexed her muscles, smiled, walked over to the fragmented torso of their enemy, and carried it to the hearse with one arm.

The members of the Junior Quad were giggling and whispering to one another. "What are you four talking about?" Kayla asked. The four looked at her and said in unison, "We were just trying to make sure we remembered the joke that

Aunt Maddy wanted us to tell after his arms were ripped off him. We are supposed to say, 'Well, I guess he won't be grabbing any more pussy with *those*.' Then we're supposed to say, 'Funny, right?'"

"That's enough!" Rachel yelled out. "That is now the *third time* that you have used the P-word!"

"But Mothers," the JQ began pleading. "Aunt Maddy said that it would be funny."

"Well, it *isn't* funny!" Rachel countered. "It is *not* funny to hear those filthy words coming out of the mouths of children! We are going to go home and wash your mouths out with soap! Then, you are going to bed early and you are grounded for a week! Do you four understand?"

"Yes, Ma'am," the four despondent children replied as they began placing the slimy remnants of Vetis into the back of the long, white, Cadillac.

Maddy and Erick silently departed from their observation perch in Arima's soul. Maddy turned to her beloved husband and said, "What the fuck is *wrong* with those uptight bitches? That was gold! Pure fucking gold! Sure, I could have delivered it *better*, but having kids say that? That was funny as fuck! I *told* you we never should have let the Twins get involved with those two. Nope. They've been nothing but trouble."

The only reply that a beaten down Erick could provide was, "Okay. You're right. I'll go conjure up the ice cream."

CHAPTER 115

IF YOU WANT BLOOD (YOU'VE GOT IT)

The air temperature outside the estate was beginning to plummet in the early evening of February 13th, 2043. Inside the cozy home, two increasingly frustrated mothers were frantically trying to get ready before their departure to an art gallery in Brooklyn. "For the last time children," Rachel was saying sternly as she applied glittery makeup to her ebony face, "You are *not* going to the art show tonight!"

"But why not?" the four pleading voices answered in unison. "We'll be good. We promise."

Kayla put her hair dryer down and looked into the seemingly innocent eyes of Sigourney, Euna, Kane, and Thanatos. "Because, children, we will be up very late, well past your bedtimes. Now please leave us alone and let us get ready. Go with Kaneko and get your dinner. Then, I'm sure she can teach you some fun games to play. Or do we need to have yet *another* week without TV?"

"Yeah, c'mon kiddos," Kaneko enthusiastically stated. "I've got four frozen cheese pizzas in the oven. And each of you gets your own. Then, I'm going to teach you all how to play poker. You do have piggie banks, don't you?"

"Okay," the children said in a resigned tone as they sorrowfully began trudging out of the room. "But we're *not* happy about it."

"Oh, and children," Rachel added. "No time travel or murdering tonight, understand? Just stay at home and play games with Kaneko, got it?"

"Yeah, we got it," the disappointed children replied. "You don't have to worry about us time traveling anymore. It isn't necessary now that Vetis is dead. Okay, mothers. Have a nice evening. We'll just go eat our pizzas and be good."

Kaneko left with the tikes. Rachel and Kayla heard their pattering footsteps descend the stairs. The twin sisters looked at one another, smiled and let out a loud "Woooooooo!"

"Oh, this is going to be so much fun tonight," Rachel said. "You bet," Kayla answered. "I just can't *wait* to see what the guests think about Alexa's artwork. Oh, I hope it goes over well. She has worked so hard on it these past few months." "Don't worry, my dear sister," Rachel replied. "I'm just sure that tonight will be a *hit!*" The pair looked at one another and once again yelled out, "Woooooooo!"

Josie was firmly gripping Lionnel's hand as she excitedly opened the door to the art gallery. The pair were immediately stopped by a brick-wall of a man. "Sorry folks," the man stated in a dullard tone. "I have to check your IDs before you can come in."

"Al!" Josie exclaimed. "You *know* who we are! And what the hell are *you* doing here anyway?"

"Well," the six-foot-six-inch behemoth began explaining. "Alexa said that if I worked security tonight, she'd dress up in her cheerleader outfit for me and um…make me cheerful. So, here I am."

"Okay, first off, gross," Josie replied as she shook her curly copper locks in disbelief. "Secondly, you will *not* be working door security tonight. We have the Twins and the twins for that. How about you go into the kitchen, hmmmmm? You can be…um…food security. Your job is to keep Aunt Arima from the…" Josie's voice trailed off as she saw Arima in the corner popping something into her mouth. "Aunt Arima!" Josie yelled. "*Please* don't eat all the hors d'oeuvres! Those are for our guests!"

"Oh, hey, Niece Josie," Arima calmly answered. "Yeah, sorry about that, but these little bacon wrapped ones are just so good." "Aunt Arima," Josie said as she sauntered over to her aunt wearing an amused look on her youthful face. "*That* isn't bacon." She then leaned over and whispered something into her ear. Arima clutched her mouth and dashed into the nearby restroom.

"Okay, everybody," Josie announced to the gathering of her murderer's row. "Let's get ready. And remember, Alexa has been waiting for this night for months, so let's all just have a good time and make this an enjoyable and memorable evening for everyone. Okay?"

There was raucous applause and backslapping before the group assumed their positions for the event. A few minutes later, the hands on the clock struck twelve. The date was now February 14th. Valentines Day. "Happy nineteenth birthday, baby," Lionnel whispered into his love's ear. He shed a slight tear as he looked upon the five-foot and four-and-a-half-inch frame of his fiancée that was draped in a full, flowing red gown. "I hope you get everything that you have ever wished for tonight." "Oh, Lionnel," Josie purred. "You have *already* given me everything that I want. And more. Come on. Let's let them in."

"Welcome everybody!" Josie exclaimed as she unlocked the door and hung a sign that read, 'No Guns! No Drugs! No Assholes!' on the outside window. "Please, won't you come in and join us on this most special evening."

Twenty-three male dignitaries from all over the world began making their way through the entrance. They were stopped and thoroughly patted down by the all-white suited

Adam and Aaron before handing their invitation to the awaiting Kayla and Rachel. The twin sisters would look carefully at each golden ticket which read,

Welcome to Alexa's premiere art show, Hanging Chads: The Lineage of our Ascension. Tonight you will be greeted by an explosion of artistic delights. And tonight, will mark the first evening of unison between the servants of Vetis and the members of Murder, Inc. Tonight, all debts will be settled, and we will become one in harmony. We are pleased that you have joined us. And we are pleased to join you. Welcome and enjoy the show.

Each dignitary let out a slight impressed gasp as they looked upon the artwork on the walls that were painted upon odd-looking canvases. There were nearly photographic renditions of treasured faces from the lives of the Argento, Azar, and Sommers families. Henri, Gregory, Jerry, Marcus, and Cliff wore all black tuxedoes with red bow ties as they circulated around the room carrying trays of hors d'oeuvres. They would approach the dignitaries and say, "Would you care to try our bacon surprise? They really are to die for." More than one dignitary commented on how tasty the treat was while also noticing its unique texture. Rosa, Jessie, Jamie, Vai, and Dragenstein wore tight black knee-length dresses with red scarves around their necks. As they circulated throughout the party, they offered glasses of a thick, dark black liqueur. "Hmmmm, tastes a bit like licorice," they would frequently say following their first sip.

"What the hell are you looking for?" Lionnel asked Josie as she nervously peered out the front window. "Oh, um, nothing," Josie anxiously replied. She suddenly felt at ease as the front door opened for a final time and a young Black woman entered the gallery. "Oh, *hellooooo* there, Tabitha!" Josie squealed as she ran up and hugged the unsuspecting guest. "Um, Hi," Tabitha responded. "I was a little surprised by getting this invitation. I mean, I'm not sure what this gathering is about or this whole Vetis thing, but I'm glad to be here."

Lionnel looked confused as he watched his beaming Josie say in her overly friendly voice, "Oh, I wouldn't want *you* to miss *this*. Please just accept this as *my apology*. I know that I've been acting a *tiny bit* immature about your friendship with my Lionnel here, and I just wanted to make it up to you. Here, *please* let me show you around." Josie gave the perplexed Lionnel a mischievous wink as she locked her arm around Tabitha's and began leading her down the row of artwork that had been meticulously painted with brushes made from human hair on canvasses of skin.

"Now *this* painting is of my Great Grandparents, Hank and Betty Sommers standing in front of their new Buick. I never got the chance to meet them, nor did my mother, as they died in a car accident several years before she was born. They were leaving a key party, and he was drunk and *SMASH*! I heard they were nice, though. Now this is Charlie and Rosetta who taught my dad how to sing. Well, kind of, heh, heh, heh. And this is Robbie. He was a transexual friend of my parents who died at the hands of two rapists. And these two bloody torsos hanging in this construction site are what was left of them after my mother got ahold of them. Pretty cool, huh?

"*This* is a beautiful portrait of my grandfather, Freddie. Look how proud he looks. This portrait was painted from a picture taken just a few days before he passed away from cancer. My mom said that she had never seen him so calm and proud of himself after he left his wife. And here she is! This is my so-called bitch grandmother and biological grandfather, the Pastor. See how intricately painted the snake scales are on their faces? Alexa's just so talented. Come to find out, they weren't just *servants* of the demon Vetis, which I know you don't know about. They were *actually* his *children*. That's why they're snake-like. His Earthly offspring are always serpentine in some way or another. So, my mom is *actually* the product of incest between a demonic brother and sister. I know, gross right? Explains a lot about her, I guess.

"And speaking of the Pastor, here is a portrait of his *other* child, my Aunt Arima, surrounded by her mother, Abdalla, and her grandmother, Louise. Look at how they're glowing behind her. This is one of my favorites. And here is Aunt Arima's most handsome husband, Marcus, with his Moms and Pops. He loved them so, and he still goes to New Orleans to visit them at their gravesite at least once a year. He's right over there carrying that tray of bacon-wrapped hors d'oeuvres. You should try one. They're to *die* for! Anywhooo, *this* picture might be a bit confusing. I know its just bloody teeth on the pavement, but these are the teeth that my Great-Uncle Joe knocked out of the Pastor's mouth and took home as a present to my Great Aunt Blair.

"Now, this is Clyde Manfrengensen, Aunt Arima's boss at the morgue she and Marcus worked at. And these are the spirits of the most wonderful couple, Mr. and Mrs. Roper, who helped Aunt Arima before they ascended into Enlightenment. And speaking of Enlightenment, this is Herbert, also known as the Botanist, with his green wife, Iris. Look at the explosion of colors of all the flowers surrounding them! Alexa said it took her *hours* to mix the bloo…um…the *paint* to get the colors on this one right.

"Oh wow, memories. This really large canvass is a before and after. This is a bloody rendition of my Great Aunt Patty's club LOHAD the night she and everybody in the club were executed. See the detail of the bullet holes in Sean's flesh? He was my mom's manager at the bookstore that my mom owned. And the next picture is the kids-only club and diner that I turned it into following that tragedy. Oh, the fun games we played in that basement, let me tell ya. Oh! This is *also* one of my favorites! This is my first boyfriend being eaten alive by piranha! See how the calm, blue water in the pool is turning into a violent red? Yeah, I planned it that way. It's like, symbolic or something.

"What's next? Oh! These fine-looking ladies are my mom's best friends that she met in college. This is Sam, Jules, Lucy, and Kristy. We just lost Sam and Jules recently and we're still struggling to get over that. I pray that you never have to learn what it is like to lose a loved one. Especially a parent, like I've had to do. Okay, sorry. Let's not get all teary-eyed and lift our spirits a bit. This is a really cool painting of Larry, Pogo, and Pogo II. They were rapists and murderers that we kept around for our um…amusement. See all the little holes in Larry's chest? Yeah, I used to use him as a dart board. He was so fun. I kinda miss him. Now, *this* handsome couple is Stellan and Paciano, our friends and caretakers at our estate. And this is Kaneko, the luckiest woman to have ever lived.

"Now *here*, we have Adam and Aaron with their respective brides Rachel and Kayla. Look at the detail of the dripping blood on their smiling faces. They are always so happy when they get to play their games. You met them at the front door and don't worry. They wouldn't harm a fly. Well, unless I tell them to. Alexa said that she kept trying to paint a portrait of their children, but the image would disappear off the fle…um *canvass* as soon as she finished.

"This portrait is of Aunt Arima's best friends, Jamie, Cliff, and Jessie. Oh, and LucyFur is on Jessie's lap. She's kinda nuts. Don't piss her off. She's around here, somewhere. And this is Rosa with her coven. They were rescued by my dad from a bunch of white-supremacist dicks who enslaved them. Big mistake on their part. Rosa and her group have taken out *hundreds* of these assholes since. And this is Rosa's husband Gregory giving a speech at the UN. That's where all of tonight's guests are from. They're *actually* servants of Vetis and we're…um…joining them tonight. And finally, this *last* portrait is of my dad's friends, Pastor Tim and Jeremy. Their souls now live in the oceans of our world and their love for each other, and all humankind, has blessed every body of water upon the Earth. Whew. Man, that was a lot of work."

Tabitha, Josie, and Lionnel came to the end of the presentation and were standing by a wall that was draped in a long, red velour curtain. "Um," Tabitha began inquiring. "These are really great. And I'm really happy that you seem to have settled with these Vetis people and everything, but why aren't there any portraits of your parents? The show just seems to be a bit, um, incomplete."

"Oh, don't worry about *that*," Josie demurely said as the smiling Alexa joined her and took her hand. "We have *one more piece* to show everybody. And I *do believe* that its about time." Josie and Alexa stood behind a podium that was positioned in front of the large red curtain. "Here ye! Here ye! Here ye!" Josie boomed. The entire group turned their attention to her and fell into a bemused silence.

"Once again," Josie began, "thank you all for coming here. Thank you for allowing us to join with you on this glorious evening. And thank you *Taaaabiiiithaaaa* for joining us as well. You are our *most* special guest. You see, *I* know that *you* know everybody here. Because *I* know that *you* have been placed on this Earth to lead Vetis's next attack. But you aren't just a *servant* of Vetis, now, are you? No, you are *much more* special than that. I would like to now present our *final* piece of the exhibit. I love *all* this work, but *this* one is *by far* my favorite. I like to call this one...," Josie dramatically paused for a moment, looked directly at Tabitha with her jealous, green eyes, smiled wickedly, and concluded in a demented growl, "Who's Your Daddy?"

"Hit it Rod!" The goggle-lensed Rod slicked back his greasy hair and pulled on a wide, golden rope. There was a loud gasp as the crimson curtain succumbed to gravity and pooled on the floor. Josie's petite, mauve lips curled up in a morbid smile as she watched Tabitha's eyes begin to stream tears. Hanging on the wall was the violently dismembered body of Vetis. His torso had been split open, and all his internal organs had been rearranged in the cavity in a 'Peace' symbol. His long, black tongue hung out of his decapitated head that was lodged on the end of his erect penis. Alexa had lettered "DICKHEAD" on his forehead beneath his sawed-off horns. Streaks of black blood drizzled over the entire piece, making it look like Pollack had obscenely bastardized a demented work of Picasso. The four arms of Vetis had been screwed into the wall and were jutting out toward the aghast audience. Each of their hands were turned upward and held a large gold frame containing a painted canvass made of human flesh.

The arm on the far left held the portrait of the beaming faces of Uncle Joe, Aunt Blair, and Aunt Patty holding a smiling, three-year old, copper headed girl. The arm on the far right held the portrait of a proud and tearful Erick Parker cradling his daughter for the first time in the hospital. The arm on the bottom of the piece held the portrait of a flower-dressed and barefoot Josie embracing her husband-to-be, Lionnel. And jutting out from the chest cavity in the middle of the grisly peace sign was the fourth arm. It held the largest painting depicting a young, auburn-haired woman wearing a black hoody, and a devilish smile. The intense gaze of the brilliant green eyes of Madeline Ruth Sommers penetrated the dark souls in attendance causing them to shiver in fear.

"You know, *Taaaabiiithaaa*, Josie began again. "It's *one* thing to try to turn our world into a demonic, fucking hell-hole. But it's quite *another* to try to steal my *boyfriend* to do it! Fuck *you*, you skanky little snake!" Josie reached behind the podium, took out a sword and decapitated Tabitha with one stroke. A geyser of black blood-bile serpents came shooting out of Tabitha's gaping hole. Her body began to wilt and deflate until it was a pile of flaccid skin lying upon the white-tiled floor.

"Huh," a blank-looking Lionnel said. "I really thought that

that she was just my friend." "Eh," Josie responded with a shrug. "Don't worry about it. We'll talk about it later." Alexa then shouted out, "Slaaaaaashdaaaaance!" Rod pressed a button on a remote and AC/DC's "If You Want Blood (You've Got It)" came thundering through the speakers embedded in the ceiling.

On cue, the jubilant members of Murder, Inc. sprang into action. Dragenstein ripped the arms off the nearest dignitary in one violent motion. She then began spinning the screaming man in a tight circle, sending streams of blood around the room as though he were a lawn sprinkler from hell.

Rachel, Kayla, Adam, and Aaron grabbed conveniently hidden axes and began chopping at the tops of the skulls of four others. They shrieked in agony as they fell to the floor with their blood and skull fragments showering the ceiling and artwork on the wall. Rosa slashed a throat, forced the gurgling man to his knees, pulled his head back violently, and released a torrent of blood which came shooting out of his gaping wound. Jessie grabbed a man by his neck, and thrust upwards, liberating his head and spinal column from his body. Blood gushed out of the man's sliced open back, creating a crimson, iron-scented mess all over the previously white tile.

An outside police cruiser stopped suddenly, and the driver started to exit the vehicle after he had seen sheets of blood spraying the inside window of the gallery. His partner grabbed the rookie by the arm and pulled him back into the cruiser. "Huh-uh," the experienced officer said. "That's a party being thrown by Murder, Inc. We don't get involved. Just keep driving."

The carnage was incomprehensible as the gleefully demented members rid the remaining forces of Vetis from the Earth. The skin and future canvass of each corpse was carefully cut away and removed by the meticulous Lionnel as his loving fiancée looked on. Josie's glimmering green eyes reflected the torrent of blood being unleashed within the hall.

Cliff and Al, who had been relieved from food security, took turns beating a dignitary's face repeatedly until it resembled ground beef that had been mixed with pink play dough, put into a blender, poured into a cocktail glass, and garnished with a tomato. Gregory held one man down while Henri and Marcus used a two-man tree saw to viciously saw through his quivering abdomen. Intestines and organs came tumbling out of the exposed cavity and laid in a pool of depraved justice.

The smiling Vai quietly directed the slaughter as axes, knives, and machetes were being whirled around in a frenzy. Blood geysers intermingled with tiny pieces of bone shrapnel splashed upon the walls, ceiling, and floor with each subsequent blow. The joyfully exhausted group finally ceased their frantic spree and looked around with expressions of satisfaction as the ecstatic LucyFur was rolling around in the thick blood while purring. The ceiling was raining blood as the grotesque droplets succumbed to gravity and splashed upon the saturated floor and festive faces of the party's hosts. The walls had been transformed into scarlet waterfalls. Every inch of every surface of the space was covered in a two-inch thick paste of blood, brain, skin, tendons, and bone as though the entirety of a meat packing plant had exploded within the tight confines.

"This is what we saw as children, brother," Aaron stated followed by Aaron's, "Yes indeed. This was our vision. This is the final game that we saw Josie play. This is her grand finale."

The images of Alexa's beautiful artwork were barely visible behind the thick coat of dripping blood that was being absorbed by the flesh canvass. Every inch of every surface was completely covered in the dark crimson goo. With one exception. At the end of the room, being held up by the dismembered arm of a cowardly demon, was a pair of proud, glowering green eyes that had remained untouched as they overlooked the deliciously vicious events of the evening.

The blood-soaked form of Arima floated above the group.

She exhaled deeply and the trapped dark souls of the dignitaries were released from her soul and into the blessed punchbowl of black liqueur which had been made from the flesh and bile of Vetis. As had been the 'Bacon Surprise.' The group exploded into laughter as Josie let out a satisfied breath and said, "Wow. The owner of this place is gonna be *really* pissed. This is a fuckin' *mess*! Somebody wanna call the clean-up crew? Nice job everyone! I've *never* been so proud of you! Let's go find some pizza! I'm fuckin' starvin'!"

As the cleaned-up and newly clothed group were preparing to depart out the back exit, Lionnel took Josie into his arms and embraced her. Their loving bodies were pressed against one another tightly. Lionnel looked at Josie directly in her sparkling green eyes and chuckled. He wiped a tear from his eye, gazed down at their joined abdomens and said, "Hey. I think that I just felt Erika Ruth kick." The pair began laughing with one another after Josie said, "Yeah. My dad's gonna be *really* pissed about *that*. But he'll get over it. He's going to love being a grandpa."

"Hey! Hey, wake up!" Erick cried out to his screaming wife. Maddy woke up saturated in her own sweat and found herself lying in her bed being gently shaken by her loving husband.

"Whoa, you musta *really* had a bad dream. Are you okay?" a concerned Erick stated softly to his beloved wife.

"Yeah. I was just dreaming about all the shit that has happened. Y'know, all the 'Chads' that I fucked up or killed back when I was a vigilante serial killer. Then, our getting involved with Murder, Inc. and taking out the Underground Autocratic Movement. Then finding out that the demon Vetis was really the one who was trying to conquer the Earth and Enlightenment, led by my real father, the Pastor, and my evil bitch mother. So, then we had to team up with my half-sister Arima and our daughter Josie and a bunch of other people and spirits to rid the cosmos of all the dark souls. Then chasing the twins of the twins and the Twins throughout time. Y'know. Same old, same old. I was just dreaming about all the shit we had to do to save the Earth and Enlightenment. What's for breakfast? I'm fuckin' starvin'!"

"Wow," Erick replied in wonderment. "That really *was* a

helluva dream. But who is Chad? And Arima? And Vetis? *What* twins? And how was your bitch mother involved in this dream exactly? I'm sorry Maddy, but I have *no idea* what you're talking about."

"Wait, what?" the half-asleep Maddy exclaimed as she sat upright in the bed. "Are you telling me that all that shit that I just said was all a *dream*? None of that shit *happened*? That we're just a married couple with a daughter who has never been serial killers or had to battle the forces of true evil to save the cosmos? Is *that* what you're telling me? Don't you dare *Dallas* this shit! Don't you fuckin' *dare* tell me that this was all a dream!"

Erick began chuckling as he hugged his barely awake wife and said mischievously, "Naw. All that shit happened. I just wanted to fuck with ya…grandma."

"You motherfucker!" Were the last words that Erick heard his beloved wife scream as he ran out of the room laughing hysterically while Van Halen's version of "Happy Trails" boomed out of their conjured CD player.

THE END…um…Probably

SONG REFERENCE LIST

The author would like to thank the countless musical artists that have enhanced his entire life. In particular, the author would like to give a heartfelt thank you to the following artists for enhancing the experience of both writing and reading this book.

And thank you, dear reader, for your interest in and support of my work. Whether I have had the privilege of personally meeting you or not, please know that you have my eternal gratitude. I look forward to the time when my work will allow our hearts and minds to meet again. Bless you all.

-Evan

Cracker- "Time Machine"
Screaming Jay Hawkins- "I Put a Spell on You"
The Coasters- "Searchin'"
The Beatles- "Help!"
Jonathan Richman- "Vampire Girl"
Stray Cats- "Stray Cat Strut"
The Cars- "Dangerous Type"

Miranda Lambert- "Kerosene"
The Chordettes- "Lollipop"
Charlie Sexton- "Beat's So Lonely"
The Fifth Dimension- "Aquarius / Let the Sunshine In"
The Modern Lovers- "Roadrunner"
Todd Snider- "Precious Little Miracles"
Urge Overkill- "Positive Bleeding"
Bruce Springsteen- "Crush on You"
Mink DeVille- "Mixed Up, Shook Up Girl"
Peter Gabriel- "In Your Eyes"
Jefferson Starship- "Find Your Way Back"
Sweet- "Wig Wam Bam"
Chuck Berry- "School Days"
Sha-Na-Na- "Born to Hand Jive"
Elton John- "Street Kids"
Nick Lowe- "I Love the Sound of Breaking Glass"
Ethel Merman & Ray Middleton- "Anything You Can Do (I Can Do Better)"
REM – "Walk Unafraid"
Olivia Newton-John & John Travolta- "We Go Together"
David Bowie- "Across the Universe"
The Blasters- "Long White Cadillac"
AC/DC- "If You Want Blood (You've Got It)"
Van Halen- "Happy Trails"